LEAP of FAITH

DL SIGLER

ISBN 978-1-956001-65-5 (paperback)
ISBN 978-1-956001-66-2 (eBook)

Printed in the United States of America

Also by D L SIGLER

CIGALA (Fiction)

The Last Fraction (Historical fiction)

Dancing with Bigfoot (Fantasy fiction)

The Last Voyage of the Ratatouille (Fiction)

Nike Wolf (Historical Fiction)

A leap of Faith (Mystery Fiction)

Dedication

I would like to dedicate this novel to my brother-in-law, Chuck Quiner.

Chuck was my sister's second husband and a big fan of my work. I never really got to know him very well. We live a continent apart. But I always enjoyed his response to my novels.

Thanks Chuck. I will miss you.

I used the word, 'was,' because he died peacefully in his sleep. And it happened on the day I finished writing this book. And now I can't send him a hard copy, and this makes me doubly sad.

But on the adage of, 'Where there is a will, there is a way,' I sent an electronic copy to chuckquiner@heaven.com.

It didn't come back. I'm just say-in…

Chapter 1

"Mom," gasped Dani, "Mom, I think that man is going to jump."

It was a bright sunny afternoon, and Dani and her mother, Sandy, decided to go beach-combing along the coastal waters of Washington State. Dani, who was named after her father, Daniel, lived and worked in Seattle. When her father retired, he built his wife their retirement home. It was on rugged, beach-front property situated on the western edge of the Makah Indian Reservation.

Dani now visits her mother on weekends. She works for Microsoft and mom has taken up painting, mostly seascapes.

A man, in his early fifties, pulled the bus's cord to signal the driver that this was his stop. The bus was just going over a tall bridge. The driver slowed to a stop on the other side. The man had a long unkempt beard and it looked like he had not changed his clothes in weeks. He had a sour odor. He put his pack on the floor under his seat and then slowly got out of the bus. The driver smiled at him and said, "Have a nice day." He closed the door and accelerated down the road.

The scruffy old man slowly walked out onto the bridge's pedestrian walkway. He stopped at the center of the bridge and peered over the rail. He could see the fast-moving river roll under him and as it collided with the sea's tall surf, which caused it to splash high into the air. And then the river relaxed as it emptied into the wide Pacific Ocean.

"Pretty, isn't it?"

"The man turned to the sweet voice and forced a smile, and he nodded at her. The young woman continued on. He gazed at the far horizon where the blue sky melted into the blue ocean and he sighed. He almost felt relieved. He patiently waited until no one was on the tall bridge. He took a deep resigned breath and climbed over the rail. He hesitated…

Dani and her mother were stunned and helpless as they watched in horror when the poor man fell forward. They tried to scream as time itself slowed down. The man rolled forward and he awkwardly spun like a rag doll towards the wild river. He slammed into the water like an inert sack of potatoes.

WHACK!

The sound was loud and heart-wrenching.

Dani screamed and looked at her mother. Her mom dropped the plastic bag of shells that she was holding and quickly ran towards the bridge. When she got there, the man was rolling in the angry water like a log. He was bobbing close to shore. So, she latched on to his shoulders and pulled but the current was strong, stronger than she anticipated. She lost her footing and the cold water started dragging her away from shore.

"**Mom, mom**," screamed Dani as she ran down the beach and waded into the swift water. "For God's sakes, mom, I can't lose you too." Dani reached her mother and hung on to her until other beach-walkers quickly joined in the rescue. They finally managed to pull the man's wet, limp body onto the gravel beach.

When the paramedics finally arrived, they found a hint of life. They told the two rescuers that he probably had internal injuries and a broken back. The driver said, "He most likely will not make it to the hospital alive."

The mother and daughter, with tears in their eyes, hugged each other and left for home. It was a somber and sad walk. In the blink of an eye, life can change drastically or be snuffed out as easily as a candle flame.

Sandy built a fire in her fireplace and poured two glasses of wine and they talked. After the cork was popped on the second bottle, they began feeling a little better.

The following weekend, it was unseasonably hot in Seattle.

Dani quit work early and arrived at her mother's by late afternoon on Friday. The front door was locked and the doorbell never got her mother's attention.

"She must be on the beach painting," mumbled Dani as she worked herself around back. And that is where she found her, but not quite as she expected.

"Mother!" she gasped. "Why are you naked?"

"Jesus, Dani. You gave me a terrible fright."

Dani lowered her eyes and shook her head.

"I am not naked, sweetie." Sandy quickly slipped her yellow blouse back on. She had spilled paint on it earlier. "I am wearing jeans."

"But you were topless, mother! Why?"

"I decided to get a job as a pole dancer."

"Not funny, mom!"

Sandy reached into a cooler and retrieved two beers. She handed one to Dani and opened the other one. "I read somewhere," she went on to explain, "that if you soak in natural vitamin D from the sun, you won't get breast cancer."

Dani opened her beer and took a quick sip. "You know you can buy vitamin D over the counter, mom. That way you don't expose yourself to the neighbors."

"I only have one neighbor and they only come up on the weekends. And besides, I think old Fred could use a cheap thrill now and then."

"Mother…" Dani was at a loss for words. She changed the subject. "That old man on the bridge, did he die?"

"I don't know? There was nothing in the paper. He must have been a vagrant and just out of booze money."

Dani nodded, "Probably." She took another sip of beer, and asked, "Whatcha painting, mom?"

The following week turned wet and cold. Sandy painted inside from behind the large, plate-glass windows that faced the ocean. The surf was tall, and foaming at its mouth, like a huge water dragon. She mixed the blues, and greens, and grays, and splashes of white paint so that her canvas came alive with realistic detail. She was pleased with this piece. She decided to reward herself with a trip to town. And it involved a cold beer and a hot pizza at *Giovanni's*.

As she drove towards the little town of Neah Bay, she passed the hospital and remembered the man and the bridge. Her curiosity got the best of her. So, she pulled into the parking lot. It was more of a small clinic. She went inside and walked up to the front deck realizing she didn't even know the man's name. The nurse in charge was busy writing something. She was tall and bordering on fierce-looking.

She looked up and snapped, "Yes?"

"I am inquiring about a man brought in here last week. He was the one that fell off a bridge."

"Do you have a name, mam?" She kept writing without looking up.

"It's Sandy, miss…?" Sandy was trying to read her name tag. It said, Betty.

Nurse Betty picked up her clipboard and ran a finger down it. "No. We have no Mr. Sanders here."

"I'm sorry. My name is Sandy and I don't know the name of the man I am looking for. He was the one that fell off a bridge."

A light suddenly went on in the nurse Betty's eyes. "Ah, yes. We don't know his name. It seems that he can't remember it. He has amnesia." She then asked, "Are you a relative?"

"No, I was just curious. How is he?"

The nurse softened and smiled. It made her look human. "He was in a coma for a few days. He has a small fracture in his wrist, a few cracked ribs, and bruises. Considering his age and the distance he fell, he is pretty lucky."

Sandy sighed in relief, "Can I see him?"

"I'm sorry. Only the police, and any relatives that may have finally discovered that he has been missing, are allowed in. The police are still trying to find out who he is." She paused, "How do you know him?"

"I pulled the poor man from the water," said Sandy, proudly.

Nurse Betty raised her eyebrows and paused in thought. And she softly whispered, "I think that saving a man's life qualifies you as a very close relative. It's Room 112."

Sandy never got a good look at the man she rescued. All she remembered was his thick, water-soaked beard, long hair, and his dirty clothes. As she worked her way down the hall and around empty gurneys, she developed enough curiosity in her to kill nine cats. When she reached room 112, she quietly tip-toed in.

The old man in the bed was hooked to multiple tubes and wires. His face was shaven and he had thin white hair. He looked frail. He looked in his nineties. He looked dead. The electric charts said differently.

Sandy solemnly walked to the side of his bed and clasped his hand and softly mumbled. "Wow, you must be some tough old bird." She sighed, "What was your hurry, old man. Give or take a year, you could have died in your own bed." She gently laid his hand back on the sheet and whispered, "I am so sorry for you… whatever your name is."

"It's George," sounded a soft voice from behind a light blue curtain.

Apparently, George has a roommate.

Sandy jumped in surprise as the voice slid the curtain back.

"Hi, that's my roommate and his name is George…something. I have been having some memory issues lately."

Sandy recovered her composure and her manors. "Oh, hi, my name is Sandy."

The roommate's bed was in an upright position. He looked comfortable. His lower left arm was in a cast.

He reached out his right hand. "I'm John."

Sandy gently shook his hand. She was pretty sure he smiled but it was hard to tell behind all that tousled hair on his face. He was more what she was expecting to find. This had to be him.

John leaned back against the pillows and asked, "Do I know you?"

Sandy shook her head. "I helped pull you out of the water." She then added, "I thought you didn't remember your name."

"I don't. The police call me John Doe. And so that's the name on my chart. It's okay. Although, I think that I would favor a manlier name, maybe like John Buck, or even John Deere."

Sandy chuckled at his joke. She noticed he had a slight accent; his voice seemed contaminated with a little French. Maybe he's from Quebec? She was beginning to like the guy.

"Would you mind a little company?" She asked as she slid a metal chair beside his bed. She needed to find out more about this strange bearded man. The curiosity-box in her brain was about to burst.

Shortly Nurse Betty came to the room. She peeked inside and told her that the police had arrived and that they had more questions.

Sandy slid her chair back under the window. "John?" she questioned, "Would it be alright if I came and visited you tomorrow?"

"I would like that, Sandy."

His beard moved and Sandy was sure that there was a smile hidden in it.

He added, "And would it be possible to bring real food?"

"How about a pizza?"

The beard didn't hide his affirmative laugh.

Sandy slept with mixed emotions that night. She had no idea why she had asked if it was okay to come back and visit him. And why she suddenly considered him a friend. He was a stranger. And, for all she knew, he could be an ax murderer. And his real last name could be 'Borden.'

'No wonder cats need nine lives.'

Late the next morning, Sandy picked up her pizza, the Hawaiian, and put it in a soft cooler to keep it warm. It was the one she kept by her easel to keep her beer cold, and handy. When she arrived at the nurse's desk, it was empty. So, she discretely slipped into room 112.

The George Something was still plugged into important machines and still looked dead.

John was staring at the soundless TV. The closed-caption was streaming across the picture, but he didn't seem to be reading it.

"Hi, John."

His beard parted into a proper smile. "Hi, Sandy, your purse smells delicious."

Sandy smiled at him as she retrieved the chair. She set the soft cooler on it and started to open it.

"Sandy?"

She paused and looked into his eyes and saw concern.

"What's wrong, John?"

"The police are coming by this afternoon." He paused.

"Why?" she asked. "Are they going to arrest you for something? Are you an ax murderer?"

"No, it's not that. They just want to take my fingerprints and some pictures. They want to see if they can find out who I am."

"Well, that is a good thing, John. Isn't it?" Sandy was a little relieved.

Tears began rolling down John's cheeks and disappearing into his beard. "I am terrified," he said. "I am afraid of finding out who the man was that jumped off that bridge.

"Whatever his name was, he had to be in great pain to do such a thing. I am happy just being John Doe. I don't want to be that other man anymore."

John turned his head and blankly stared out the window. Sandy thought about what he had said. He had a point. She, for the first time in her life, was at a loss for words. For a long time, she listened to the clock on the wall as it irritatingly ticked away. "Why in the hell," screamed Sandy's brain, "is that thing not digital. For Christ's sakes, it's the twenty-first century."

Sandy shook her head. "John, you are not in jail. This is a free country. I say, let's go for a drive. Nobody saw me come in and no one will see us go out."

"But I can't ask you…"

"Shut up!" she said as she helped him to his feet. "God I miss saying that to a man." She quickly found a wheelchair and put John and the pizza on it, and made good their escape out a back door.

Since John left without paying his enormous hospital bill, technically, he was a fugitive.

Sandy hadn't felt this alive since before her husband had died. She drove him to her home trying to stay at the speed limit, which was another first for her. John sat silently in the passenger seat, while the good Sandy cursed the bad Sandy for being such an idiot. When they drove over John's bridge, the good Sandy urged her not to look down.

Dani texted her mother that she was coming.

> I am on my way. And please mom,
> be wearing some clothes!
> ☺

Sandy never acknowledged her text.

When Dani arrived, she didn't bother trying the front door. She went straight to the seaside of the house. And that is where she found her, but not quite as she expected. Mom was standing over a seated man while holding a sharp instrument in her hand.

At least she was dressed.

But what macabre scene was her mother up to now? Was it murder? Was it mayhem? Or perhaps, it just was a haircut? Yes, she was holding a scissors. She now wondered who was going to be the victim of her haircut. Her mother was a marksman with scissors.

"Mother, who is that?"

Sandy, a little startled, turned and pointed the scissors at her daughter, "Oh, hi Dani."

Dani pointed her finger at the sitting man. "Well, who is that?"

Sandy smiled at her daughter and patted John on his shoulder like an old friend. "This is John… Buck…ley, John Buckley. He is my new gardener."

John stood up, reached for Dani's hand, and with a slight bow, he said, "I am pleased to meet you, Dani. Your mother has told me so much about you." John was smiling, but it was hidden in thick whiskers.

Sandy hadn't mentioned anything to him about a daughter. She was impressed with his quick lie. Maybe he was a lawyer?

"Hi," was all Dani could get out. She quickly retrieved her hand. She noticed that the man's hair was mostly gray. He looked old and sinister.

Sandy went back to cutting John's Hair. "Dani, will you please get a bottle of wine and a couple of glasses."

"Sure mom." Dani hesitated. She didn't want to leave her mother alone with that strange man. She decided to hurry.

When she returned, John's hair was combed from front to back in perfect parallel lines. Debonair came to mind; except for his beard, which was still quite unruly, it hid the true age of his face. He could be handsome.

When Sandy took the sheet off John, he stood up. "Well, if you ladies will excuse me, I will freshen up." John smiled at Sandy, which annoyed Dani, and he asked, "May I borrow your scissors?"

"No," silently screamed Dani.

John chuckled when he saw Dani's eyes. "I think it time that we all see exactly what I look like. I sure hope I'm pretty." He turned and walked towards the house.

When John disappeared through the back door, Dani turned to her mother. "Have you gone completely mad? A gardener? You don't even have a garden."

"Well, I decided I needed a garden. That's what old people do. They garden. And they have gardeners…hence John."

"But, but…mother!"

But, before another 'but,' Sandy added, "Oh, by the way, John said that he would like to cook for us tonight."

"He's cooking?"

Sandy reached for the bottle of wine and then poured two glasses. She decided to confess.

She explained what little she knew about her guest and that he was the one that jumped from the bridge. "And that is why I brought the poor wretched soul into my home."

And, she added, "He is a fugitive from the hospital, and he is now hiding out in my spare bedroom."

And that it was no big deal.

"And, I have already gotten rid of your father's old ax."

"Mother, have you gone completely mad?"

Chapter 2

When Dr. Daniel Kaminski saw the oceanfront property on the west coast of the Olympic Peninsula, he bought it on the spot. It was perfect.

"I shall build my retirement home here," he said. And he did. He wasted no time and immediately hired a prestigious architectural firm to design his home on the shores of the largest ocean in the world.

He wanted his design to blend in with the rugged, boulder-filled beach and he wanted it placed as close to the water as was safely possible. And he wanted the design to be contemporary, and yet classical.

"Which is a complete oxymoron," stated the draftsman to his partners after the good doctor had left. But they worked on his design anyway, because the customer had enough money to pay for the many redesigns.

A year later they had finally married the two styles. Daniel Kaminski was satisfied. He applied for permits. And the work began on a home that was neither contemporary nor classic in design. But the client was quite happy with his new structure.

The front of the house was rather conservative in style. It had a modest front porch and tall double doors at the entrance. The rear of the house was a very liberal democrat. Dr. Kaminski could not spend enough money on glass. Across the full width, plus the two stories of the house, were UV-protected, gas-filled, thermo-paned windows.

He was well pleased and quite proud of his new home. He told everyone, "I shall live in this great house by the sea until I am old and then I shall die in it."

And he did. Of cancer. Two years later.

His wife, Sandy, also made the same vow; well just the first half of it.

While they waited for John, who was shaving in the guest bath, Sandy asked, "Dani, will you please run to the garage and get me two bottles of *14 Hands?*"

"Why are you still buying that cheap Costco wine? It's just you. You can afford imported red wine from Italy."

"I like their wine. And at their price, I can afford to drink a lot more of it."

While Dani looked for the wine, Sandy retrieved two wine glasses from her cupboard. After inspecting them for water spots, she took them into the great room. She placed them on the yellow-cedar-burl coffee table in front of the long couch that faced the fireplace.

The great room had a vaulted ceiling, supported with rough-sawed beams that were two-stories above the red-oak floor. The furniture was positioned for maximum view of the pounding surf, or of the stone fireplace that completely covered the north wall.

Sandy rotated two of the easy chairs. They now faced the guest bedroom. She sat on one of them and kicked off her shoes. She put her feet on the coffee table and leaned back on the soft leather recliner. She felt good, a different good.

Dani returned from the garage with a bottle of wine in each hand. She placed them on the counter and rummaged for the corkscrew. "Mom, where did you hide the cork…never mind I found it."

After she opened one, she took a swig out of the bottle. She shrugged. "Not bad." She brought the opened bottle into the great room and poured a little in each glass. She handed one to her mother and then sat on the matching recliner. They both now stared and sipped in anticipation at the guest room door as they waited to see the real face of John Doe. Who was officially renamed, John Buckley.

Dani guessed first. They were playing a game called, 'Guess the guest.'

"A husband who could not go on living after he lost his wife?"

"Romantic!" replied Sandy. It was her turn. "Hmmm, maybe a distraught minister who questioned his faith."

"I like that one mom. How about a minister that knocked up one of his young choir girls?"

"Juicy," chuckled Sandy. She leaned back and sipped. "How about a bank vice-president that got caught embezzling a million dollars and was afraid of what might happen to him in jail?"

Dani chuckled, "He does have a cute butt, for an old guy."

Sandy snickered.

"How about…" Dani paused when she saw the guest bedroom door, slowly open.

Both women leaned forward. Each tensed with anticipation while holding a glass of '14 Hands' in their hands.

John Buckley shyly entered the room. He was wearing dark sweatpants and a gray sweatshirt and an unsure smile. He was not bad-looking. He had a dimple on his chin. And he had shaved off a good fifteen years of age. Possible even twenty.

Dani cocked her head. "Say mister, just how old are you?"

John shrugged his shoulders. "I was hoping you could tell me."

Dani studied him for a minute. "Turn around."

John spun in a circle, as manly as he could.

"Maybe sixty?" She guessed.

"I think you look closer to fifty," countered Sandy.

John rubbed his smooth chin in thought. "I was kind of thinking… maybe forty?"

The woman laughed.

Sandy asked, "Okay, would you settle for a young, fifty?"

John tightened his smile, "How about on old, forty?"

The woman laughed again, as did John.

"Would you care for a glass of wine?" offered Sandy.

John nodded with a pleasing smile. It was his first one as John Buckley.

John took to cooking like a bug to a bed. The late Dr. Daniel Kaminski must have had a little Italian in him. The kitchen he designed was old-world Italy.

The stove was wide and had six, full-size, gas-burners on top. And next to it was a gas-fired pizza and bread oven. The island was as big as a continent. And over it was a stainless-steel ring suspended from the ceiling. On it hung a plethora of pans and pots, and of course, the complaining black kettles. You could almost hear them begging for a fire under their flat bottoms.

The long counter was filled with bowls of grated parmesan cheese, of pressed garlic, of fresh basil, and of chopped white onions. The largest container was full of the main attraction. The dark-red, sliced, Roma tomatoes.

John put a large cast-iron pot on low heat and carefully slid in the romas. Sandy and Dani were sitting on stools at the island across from John. They were quietly watching. The empty wine bottle was between them.

John palmed the full bottle and deftly removed its cork. He topped off the women's glasses. He sniffed the aroma, "Not bad." He looked at the label and read, "Hot to Trot." He raised his eyebrows.

"Horses," blushed Sandy. "They're horses. It's the '14 Hands' Wine Company."

Dani laughed.

"I see," chuckled John.

As he stirred and combined his special ingredients, he explained, "I use cast iron because it spreads the heat evenly. No hot spots. Nothing burns. And the iron seems to release a hint of earthy metal. Kind of like wine in oak barrels.

The two women were mesmerized while they watched Sandy's new gardener as he cooked up a storm. He stirred, he sniffed, he tasted, and then he would pause in thought. And that would be followed by adding a pinch of this, or a shake of that. And it was another sniff followed by another taste. "Perfect," he murmured with a smile. He was a kitchen maestro.

Dani turned to her mother. "He's good. You might have to pay him."

"You might be right." She topped off their glasses and added, "I can hardly wait to see his gardening skills."

They touched glasses.

"You know, mom, he could very well be fattening us up for the kill."

Dinner was to die for. In a good way, not the other one.

After the heavy meal, Sandy built a fire, which involved turning on the gas which makes the fake logs leaped into flame. They sat around the fire and made small talk until John yawned. He was still sore and hurting from his leap from the bridge. He excused himself for the night.

The two women went to the kitchen and tidied up a bit. "You want to sleep with me tonight?" Sandy asked her daughter.

"I would feel safer."

"Me too."

On the way to the master bedroom, Sandy rummaged through a kitchen drawer and found her meat cleaver. She brought it with her.

"Good idea," said Dani as she gathered the sharp knives. "Better safe than sorry."

As Sandy locked the bedroom door and propped a chair against it, she said, "You get the side closest to the door."

It was already too late.

Dani was buried under the blanket on the far side of the bed.

"Aren't you going to undress?"

Chapter 3

When her bedroom window flooded with sunlight, Sandy yawned and stretched, she felt quite alive. She sat on the edge of her bed and glanced at her nightstand, as her feet searched for her slippers. When she saw the meat-cleaver on it, she chuckled and mumbled, "Paranoid people live longer."

She stood up and looked at her daughter who was still sleeping on the other side of her king-size bed. She was clutching her pillow like she was fearful it might escape. And she was snoring. It was that funny little nasally snore that Sandy remembered when she was a child. Sandy smiled at the memory as she quietly slipped into the master bathroom.

The heated tile floor felt good on her feet. A hot shower would do the same for the rest of her body. She reached behind the curtain and spun the handle to hot.

While waiting for warm water, she slipped out of her pajamas and stood in front of the full-length mirror. She inspected her naked body for the betraying signs of age. Wrinkles, blemishes, sagging skin, gray hair. It was her morning ritual.

She had put on a little weight since her husband had died. The sit-ups firmed her belly-muscles and the extra pounds seemed to have gone to the right places. It stretched out wrinkled skin and it enlarged her breasts. She spun slightly. Her bottom was still firm. She was womanly. Even voluptuous. And still sexy. The mirror smiled at her and said, "Fortyish," and then it began steaming up.

She showered.

Dani woke up with a large fur-ball in her mouth. Well, it felt like one. She could hear her mother in the kitchen making coffee. She staggered into the bathroom and put her mouth under the cold faucet. She had a bit too much wine the night before. She turned on the shower and removed her pajamas. She glanced at the mirror before she stepped in. She was built like her father, lean and long. The mirror gave her a thumbs-up.

When she finished, she hurriedly put on her clothes. She could smell the coffee and badly need a cup. As she left the master bedroom, she noticed the cutlery was gone. It made her chuckle to think of how paranoid she and her mother were last night. John really seemed harmless, it was the wine that interfered with their rational thinking, but on the other hand, 'better safe than sorry.'

"Good morning sunshine," said Sandy as she poured her daughter a steaming mug of coffee.

Dani took the cup with both hands and blew on the black liquid. She took a cautious sip. "Where's John?"

"Gone."

"What do you mean, gone?"

Earlier, when the sky blushed behind the Olympic Mountains, John quietly crawled out of bed. He slipped into the guest bathroom and washed from the sink. The shower was too noisy.

Back in the guest bedroom closet, he found some men's clothes. Clothes that Sandy's husband had worn. Clothes that she was not ready to part with yet.

John was looking for jeans and flannel as he flipped through the closet rod. Something comfortable, but only Gabardine, tweed, silk, a thousand ties, and stiff collared shirts were all he could come up with. The slacks were a little long and tight. Her husband was a tall, thin man. He chose a white shirt. It fit okay. He took scissors and cut a couple of inches off the bottom of the trousers. *Beggars and thieves can't be choosy.*

There was a nook off the foyer, designated as an office area. And there was a laptop on a small oak desk. John sat down on the hard chair in front of it and opened the computer's lid. He pressed the on-button. While it was warming up, he rummaged through the desk drawer looking for the computer's password. The drawer was just as cluttered as the desktop. "Hmm, nothing," he whispered. He decided to try a wild guess.

He then typed, DANI; and, *bingo.*

He chuckled and shook his head, "Well that was too easy." He quickly scanned her files out of curiosity. There was nothing important, mostly pictures and a few recipes, and a word document. "A word document, interesting."

He opened the file and began reading it. "Well, I'll be damn. She's writing a mystery novel." He read a little more and he got to the steamy, hot, sex scene. It embarrassed him a little and he quit reading. He chuckled at her writing and had to add a little message. "The Butler did it." It amused him and then he clicked onto the internet.

After five minutes of surfing, he found what he needed. He shut down the computer and went to the garage. He flipped on the light and did a quick tour. The workbench was immaculate and each tool was clean and neatly organized. "Sandy's husband, it seems, was quite anal." After a quick inventory of tools, he left the garage and went back to the great room.

"Ah," he smiled when he saw two purses sitting next to the soft easy chairs. He went through the smallest one first. It was Dani's.

The wallet contained no cash, but it had a lot of credit cards. But in his search for cash, he found a pack of cigarettes hidden at the bottom. "Hmm, so she's still afraid to smoke in front of mother." He placed the cigarettes on top and then picked up Sandy's purse. It was a lot heavier and filled with, 'God knows what.'

She had cash, lots of it. He quickly put a fifty in his pocket and started to set the purse back down. He suddenly decided he needed another fifty. After he replaced the purse, he took one cigarette out of

Dani's purse and her lighter. He put the cigarette behind his ear and left the house just as the sun peaked over the Olympic Mountains.

MapQuest had instructed him to go east on Cape Flattery Road. It was a beautiful morning and a good day for a long walk.

As the sun brightened, John popped Dani's cigarette between his lips and lit it. He took a long satisfying drag.

His lungs immediately objected and he coughed violently. He spit nicotine and threw the cigarette on the pavement and then crushed the foul thing under the sole of his shoe. "Fuck," he coughed again. "I guess I wasn't a smoker in my other life."

He began whistling a lively tune as he walked towards town. He couldn't remember the words but was happy not to have a care in the world.

Sandy poured herself another cup of coffee and then she eased up on the stool next to her daughter. "Yes, he's gone. Vehicles are still here. He must have gone on foot."

"Wow," said Dani. "I was just starting to like him." She faced her mother. "Did he take anything?"

Dani suddenly remembered leaving her purse by the leather recliner. She quickly jumped off her stool and looked for it. It was not where she had left it. It was on the sofa. She quickly opened it and noticed the cigarette pack was unhidden and on top. She slid it to the bottom of her purse and retrieved her wallet.

Her credit cards were still there. She sighed in relief and then noticed that her mother's wallet was on the island's counter.

Again she asked, "Did he take anything?"

"I think I'm missing some cash."

"Oh, mom…how much?"

"I don't know. Not much. Maybe a few of twenties, maybe more."

"You don't know?" asked Dani.

"Do you know exactly how much cash is in yours?"

"Yes," scoffed Dani.

"Really? Well then, how much is in your purse right now?"

"Nothing; I don't carry cash. That's what criminals are always looking for."

"Oh," scoffed Sandy, "So, by not having cash, that keeps your credit cards safe; and that way thieves don't bother themselves with stealing your purse."

Dani detected a little sarcasm. "Maybe."

And while she had Dani on the defensive, "When did you start smoking?"

"Mom, were you in my purse?"

"Maybe," same sarcasm. "I guess not having cash in it doesn't stop criminals or mothers from going through it. Doesn't it?"

"Sorry, mom. So, which are you?"

Sandy shook her head and sighed, "God, I need a cigarette."

"Yea, me too. Do you have a lighter? I think mine was stolen."

After a light breakfast, they decided that a walk on the beach would be nice. They walked south, away from the bridge. They chatted and looked for agates. They spotted a lot of seals and a lone gray whale. It was late in the season for a gray. They had a good walk even though they avoided the subject that was most on their mind, John.

Dani spotted a large driftwood log that a storm had washed up on the beach. It was time for a break. They sat and stared quietly at the agitated surf as it pounded the beach sand and gravel.

"Would you like another cigarette, Mom?"

"I thought you were never going to ask."

As they smoked, the lazy old sun rolled west. They relaxed and enjoyed each other's company while sitting on their driftwood perch.

"I'm hungry," said Sandy as the sun sunk to eye level. "There is still a lot of baked spaghetti in the fridge."

"I am starving! And I'm, *Hot to Trot*," snickered Dani. "I saw another bottle in the garage."

And like an old mare and a filly, the two women trotted back to Sandy's contemporary, plate-glass, barn.

Sandy slid the pan of leftovers in the oven and beside it, she nestled Italian bread that was slightly basted in butter.

Dani retrieved the wine, brought it to the kitchen, uncorked it, and poured the wine into long-stem glasses. With one glass in her left hand and the bottle in the other, Dani went into the great room and sat on the long couch. She snuggled into it and leaned back, and put her feet on the thick coffee table.

Sandy joined her. It was time to play their guessing game.

Dani went first. "John suddenly remembered who he was and went back to the bridge."

"A bit morbid," said mom.

"I didn't say he jumped."

"True."

"Okay, why didn't he jump this time?"

"I didn't say he didn't jump, either."

Sandy scoffed. "Now you're starting to remind me of your father."

"Okay fine; he jumped."

Sandy waited for her to add something…anything. "So, he's dead?"

"I'm not finished mom." She added, "He survived the fall. And now he has to do it over and over again, just like Groundhog Day."

"You mean like the Bill Murray movie?"

"Yes, he has to do it every day until he gets it right."

"What's that… to die?"

"No mom, until he falls in love."

"With who?"

Dani snickered. "With you, I guess."

Sandy shook her head and chuckled. "I've been there and done that. Maybe it's you he is supposed to fall in love with."

Dani gasped at the thought, and added, "But unfortunately, this time the poor man died on the way to the hospital."

Soon, the old-world aroma of baked spaghetti drifted into the great room and got the game-playing women's attention as they remembered the man that cooked it. They toasted. "Here's to John the chef, wherever you are."

As the sun began its slow descent on the far horizon, it seemed in no hurry and neither were they. The couch was facing the endless sea and the setting sun shined brightly through the tinted glass. They sat silently and watched. The baked spaghetti would be done soon.

"Mom, do you think we will ever see John again?"

"I don't know.

"Maybe; I feel that someday, he will turn back up into our lives again."

"It was too bad we didn't take his picture. Google has a database of missing persons. We could have researched that, and maybe have found out who he really was. Now we will never know."

"Probably not," said Sandy. "He once told me that he was terrified of remembering who he was before he jumped. I guess, for his sake, it is better this way."

"You're probably right," said Dani, even though she was dying to find out anything about this mystery man.

They silently watched old Sol as he touched the sea. Each of them was lost in deep profound thought, and in sipping the wine.

Suddenly, their serene moment was rudely interrupted by a man pushing a small wheelbarrow across the back yard. He was wearing nice slacks, a white collared shirt, and a baseball cap with a Seahawks emblem on it. It was pulled low over his eyes.

"Mom, is that man stealing your wheelbarrow?"

"No, I don't own one. Maybe it's Fred's."

They quietly watched with interest as to who this strange man was. The odd man looked up and waved. It was John.

With mixed emotions they scrambled to their feet and slid open the sliding glass door and went out onto the back patio.

John took his one-wheel-dump-truck and parked it behind the garage. It was fire-engine red and it hauled a shovel, a hoe, and a few miscellaneous small garden tools.

"Hi John," Dani was still holding her wine glass. "I thought you ran away from home. Where did you go?"

"To town," he flashed an innocent grin.

"And who did you steal the wheelbarrow from?" asked Sandy.

"It's yours. I bought it for you. Do you like it? You want to go for a ride in it?"

Dani laughed and almost spilled her wine.

"No thank you. Where did you get the money for my new wheelbarrow?"

"Oh, here," John reached into his pocket and pulled out a receipt. He put it in her empty hand and then he pulled out a couple of one-dollar bills, a nickel, and three pennies. "And here is your change." He said with a proud smile. "I didn't think that you would mind." He shrugged his shoulders and explained, "Well, I need these tools to garden your garden, properly."

"Were you in my purse, too?" asked Dani.

"Oh here," said John as he retrieved the lighter from his pocket. "And I might have taken one of your cigarettes."

He turned back to Sandy, "I'm starving. I could eat a horse," which made Dani choke on her glass of *14 Hands*.

Sandy sighed. "I put last night's leftovers in the oven. It should be ready."

Sandy ushered the wayward guest inside. She and John went to the couch while Dani retrieved another wine glass for John. When Dani returned, she filled John's glass and added some more wine to the other two glasses. She then sat on the coffee table and faced her mother and the cigarette thief. "Nice hat, John."

"You like it?"

"Okay, John," sternly interrupted Sandy. "Why didn't you ask me for the money? I would have gladly given it to you. I simply will not tolerate anyone going through my purse."

"I am very sorry, Sandy. I just didn't want to wake you."

"I had the door locked. How did you know I was sleeping?"

"I could hear you snoring."

Dani snickered.

"I was not snoring. That was Dani."

"I was not, mom. I don't snore."

"Yes you do," said John. "And so does your mother."

"I do not," scoffed Sandy.

"I see," said John as he piously folded his hands, "I heard two people snoring, so who was that other person sleeping with you two?"

Sandy changed the direction. "Oh, by the way, is that my husband's shirt?"

"Maybe," said John. "I found it in my closet."

"Your closet!"

"Yes, the one in my bedroom. I just borrowed it." John decided it was his turn to change the subject. "I think our dinner is ready. We don't want to burn anything, do we?"

John stood up. "Let's eat. I had a long walk today. And I'm starving." John looked at Sandy, "We can discuss my wages over dinner."

Sandy glanced at her daughter and shook her head. "You're enjoying this, aren't you?"

Dani shrugged her shoulders and burst out laughing.

Chapter 4

Carlos left his small village in Central America when he was a small boy. His younger brother followed him. They made their way to Tijuana, Mexico, where they grew into adults in the back alleys of this notorious border town. They made good money in these narrow alleys selling drugs and panhandling gringos from America. Eventually, they made enough to move north. Carlos is now a Canadian citizen and has a nice little home in Victoria. He still continues to run drugs back and forth between Mexico and Victoria where there is an excellent market for his contraband.

His vehicle of choice is a sixty-foot *Pacemaker Motor Yacht,* powered with twin, Caterpillar turbo-diesel engines. He had extra fuel tanks installed, so he doesn't have to refuel his yacht along the way. He runs in the international waters off the coast of American. And never, if he can help it, whenever foul weather is predicted.

His brother, Miguel, is his partner and he always travels with him.

Carlos checked his weather fax before he left Tijuana and it told him it would be smooth sailing, it said mild weather all the way to Alaska.

He had also installed a secret side door on the yacht's hull. It was in the forward cabin's V-berth where he kept his contraband. If he was approached by the coast guard, he would face his starboard side to them and Miguel could secretly dump his weighted bags of Marijuana, and of heroin, and of cocaine, into the sea from the port side without being seen.

So far, he only had to do it once.

On this trip he was carrying added contraband, which would double his profits. It was not something he had to market himself. He just had to deliver them to a secret location near Victoria where someone would pick them up. He tried to refuse. Drugs are one thing, but humans made him very uncomfortable.

The cartel made him a comfortable offer that he could not refuse.

When a very high-pressure system collides with a dense low-pressure system, it can create very confused seas, at best. *Sailor take warning!*

The trip from Tijuana was pleasant and relaxing and continued that way until they were off the coast of Washington State.

Carlos was at the wheel when he heard the weather channel on his marine radio suddenly gave three long wails, "High seas and with winds gusting to forty knots." And then it issued a small craft warning.

Carlos looked out his windshield and could see the distant dark cloud that he was headed into and he cursed at his weather fax. But he wasn't worried all that much. It would just be an uncomfortable ride; he had been through worse. It would just take a little longer, and then he would be home.

"The Straits of Juan De Fuca should have better weather," he said to his brother as he throttled up for more control in the high seas. He began crowding the shoreline to shorten the distance to the Straits of Juan de Fuca and its calmer water.

The large, heavy yacht seemed to tame the wild incoming rollers, and the ride became almost fun. Carlos turned his wheel towards each wave and the sharp bow would split each one like a knife, as it sliced through it. The sea would splash clear over the bow as the boat charged towards the next wave. Carlos really loved his little ship.

Suddenly!

"**Dios Mio**," cursed Carlos when he saw it coming. A large rogue wave rose up towards his port side. It was coming at him fast. He spun the wheel, turning his bow towards the wave just as it picked him up. He was trying to ride over it. But it was too steep for his long, heavy yacht and he began sliding sideways down the wave. At the bottom of the trough, the wave broke over the yacht and it disappeared under the churning foam. After a few seconds, it bobbed to the surface and the yacht righted itself. The boat's deck was flooded with seawater and the engine hatch-cover was gone. The engine compartment was drenched in saltwater and both engines died. The half-million-dollar yacht was now at the mercy of Mother Nature and she was pushing the helpless boat towards the rugged coast off of the Olympic Peninsula of this northern state.

"**Mayday, mayday, mayday**," hysterically called Carlos on the VHF, marine radio's emergency channel.

Miguel, who soiled himself, started praying while his white knuckles gripped the console.

"**Mayday, mayday, mayday**," screamed Carlos again. "Where in the fuck are they?"

"**Mayday, mayday, mayday**," he kept calling. And then he heard static. He adjusted the radio's squelch knob.

Finally, "This is the United States Coast Guard. Please state your emergency?"

Carlos went on and explained what had happened, and he gave them his GPS coordinates. The coastguard said they were patrolling the Straits of Juan De Fuca and would be there shortly. And that they would tow them to the nearest safe harbor, which would be at Neah Bay, in Washington State.

Carlos and Miguel now had another emergency. They both quickly made their way to the bow cabin and quickly disposed of their illegal cargo. Miguel refused to throw the girls into the water. Carlos had to do it himself. He was the one that agreed to bring them.

They had now lost their cargo but at least saved the yacht. "We will make it up on our next trip," said Carlos. Miguel still had a very bad feeling lodged in his stomach.

It seems not all of the contraband had sunk. Some of it washed up on the western shore of Washington's pristine rugged coast.

Chapter 5

John woke up with the sun. He stretched and hopped out of bed. He knew that it was going to be a good day. He covered his small arm cast with a plastic garbage bag and sealed it with a little scotch tape, and then quietly slipped into the shower. The hot water running down his back made him feel like a new man. In fact, he really was a new man, and this was the first shower he could remember. Although, he probably had showers before he was John Buckley.

The new John found the hot water not unpleasant. In fact, he wanted to spend the rest of the day under the soothing, hot water. But he didn't. After the shower, he looked for some underwear in the chest of drawers in his bedroom. Hankies, doilies, candles, flashlights, vases, he stopped looking.

He had started a list of additional garden supplies that he needed Sandy to get. He added to it: *T-shirts and briefs, preferably, boxers*

He went to his closet and found another nice pair of light-colored slacks. He cut a foot off the legs and put them on. They were now a few inches above his ankles and comfortable. He smiled.

He pulled a soft, light-blue shirt off its hanger. It felt smooth, like silk. He cut the sleeves in half and then slipped it on. "Much better," he sighed. He put on his old leather shoes and went into the kitchen for coffee.

On the countertop was the new coffee maker. It was one of those that you feed a small cartridge to, push a button, listen to it go clickety-click several times, and then watch it drain into your mug. If you want a full cup, you have to do it again. But it's fast.

The sky was blue and the sun was up and the day was warm. Last night's storm was somewhere east. It had the makings of a perfect day. John's project for today was the unruly shrubs and weeds around the house. They needed disciplined and a severe pruning. And so, with a cup in hand and a smile on his eager face, it was time to earn his keep.

As he walked across the back patio to fetch Sandy's new pruning shears and red wheelbarrow, he couldn't help but hear the squabbling of birds circling the beach at the water's edge. He studied the flock convention for a minute. There were Seagulls and crows and they were circling something close to the water. He decided to investigate.

The fat gulls seemed to be in charge or at least had the upper hand. The crows cursed and cawed at the dirty-gray sea birds.

As John approached, they took to the air. The crows landed in nearby tall spruce trees and the seagulls landed on the water. Both species watched from a close, but safe, distance. John cautiously approached and gasped when he saw what had their attention. There was a body on the beach. When he got closer, he could see that it was a young girl. He began walking a circle around her. He could that she was badly bruised and battered. She probably washed up in last night's pounding surf.

John stooped down to get a good look at her face. It was pretty much gone.

"**Oh, John**!" shouted Sandy. She was walking his way. "What you looking at?"

John stood up and yelled, "**Wait**. I need a broom and a cell phone."

"You need what?" Sandy was sure she heard him wrong. By this time Dani had joined her.

"I need a broom and a cell phone," yelled John again.

"He needs a broom and a cell phone, mom."

"That's what I thought he said. What do you suppose he's doing?"

"One way to find out. You grab a broom; I will get both phones."

John had walked towards the house so that he could meet Sandy just out of sight of the body. She came back holding her broom. Dani was right behind her.

"What's going on?" Sandy asked.

"Some poor girl has had a terrible accident and I need you to call 911. We are going to need the police and an ambulance."

"Oh my God," exclaimed Dani. "How bad is she? Who is she? And what's the broom for?"

John paused and looked for the right words. There weren't any.

"She's dead."

Both women gasped and looked towards the beach in shock.

"Sandy," John stepped between her and the ocean. "You call 911 and tell them that there is a dead woman on the beach, okay? And then you give them your address, okay? And then you should wait for them by the road, okay?"

Sandy quickly nodded at each command, as she stared blankly at John.

"Sandy, what did I just say?"

"Um, umm, 911, and, and, wait."

"That's good. Now go."

As Sandy turned to run, John stopped her. "Broom please."

She tossed him the broom and she began dialing her cell phone as she ran towards the house.

"What do you want me to do?" asked Dani. She sounded a little more in control.

He handed her the broom. "Here, I need you to keep the birds off the poor girl's body. She looks bad enough as it is, without having her eyes pecked out too." He then held out his hand, "Give me your cell phone?"

"Okay, here." She said as she looked away from the body and back at John. When she glanced back at the body, the birds were already on the beach. "Oh, shit," she gasped. She raised her broom and charged the scavengers with a blood-curdling yell. Both species took to the heavens.

Dani watched carefully as John inspected the body. He used her phone's camera and took a lot of pictures and at all different angles. When he heard the distant sirens, he handed her back her phone. They waited and guarded the remains in reverend silence.

The first to arrive was the reservation police.

Sandy's home was on the Makah Reservation. These wise American Indians took a strip of land, between the ocean and the road, and divided it into building lots. They then leased these lots for ninety-nine years to rich white men. This gave the tribe a tidy monthly income and they got the property back in less than a hundred years. At which time they could take the land back or renegotiate a new lease.

This was all done before casinos or it probably never would have happened. Sandy still owned the house that was on the leased land and would so, until long after she died. And then Dani would inherit and probably own it till she died, as well.

When Sandy flagged down Officer Leaning Bear, he pulled into her driveway. He had another officer with him. Sandy quickly led them to the scene of the accident.

Leaning Bear was tall and thin. He wore a black Stetson hat and high-heeled cowboy boots, which made him look even taller. Today's Indians have given up their feathers and moccasins for the more functional cowboy hats and boots.

He had a single, black braid that hung down from the back of his head. His tan uniform was impeccable. He was packing a stainless-steel Ruger revolver around his waist. It had a long barrel and was of a high caliber, probably a 44 Mag.

Behind Officer Leaning Bear was Officer White Owl. She was young and was built quite sturdy. She was packing a black leather bag that contained, crime scene tape, a camera, and other important police stuff. She also wore a black cowboy hat.

Leaning Bear glanced at the dead girl and then went straight to John. "I'm Officer Leaning Bear and this is Officer White Owl." He rested his right hand on his stainless-steel piece instead of trying to shake John's hand. This was his first possible murder. He was used to reservation drunks, speeders, fishing and hunting violations, and domestic disputes. The body made him nervous but he did a good job of concealing it.

"Who are you? asked Leaning Bear.

"I'm John Buckley."

"Are you related to the victim?"

John shook his head, "No."

Leaning Bear turned to Dani. "Who are you?"

"I'm Daniela Kaminski."

He then turned to Sandy. "What is your name?"

"She's my mom."

"That's nice. Does your mom have a name?"

"Sandy Kaminski."

"Do any of you recognize the victim?"

He heard "No," in triplicate. He pointed to the neighbor's house. "Who lives there?"

"Fred and Doris," answered Sandy, "They only come on weekends."

"I will need their full names and a phone number."

Meanwhile Office White Owl had put up the yellow, crime-scene tape, and she started taking pictures and measurements. After that, she combed the area for anything unusual. It looked like a case of accidental drowning. Possibly the victim fell off a pleasure boat. The autopsy would reveal any alcohol, but with the beating that she took in the surf, it would be hard to find any evidence of foul play unless she was shot or stabbed.

By the time the paramedics arrived, the Reservation police were done. The body was covered and reverently loaded in the white ambulance. It left without sirens. The two officers had no more questions. They gave Sandy their cards and told her if anything else suspicious washed up, to give them a call. They then left.

Later that somber day, the women had to make an emergency run to town. They were out of wine. They also had John's list of needs. As Sandy backed her Volvo out of the driveway, she heard John holler, "Oh wait, I need some socks." Sandy nodded and flashed an *okay* symbol with her left hand and she continued to back out and on to Cape Flattery Road. And she and Dani were off.

John stayed at the house to get back to his important pruning job, which was interrupted because of the unfortunate beach incident. He put the shears in his back pocket and pushed the wheelbarrow to the garage side of the house. It was the side that was the most in need of his attention.

About the time that he filled his wheelbarrow with clippings, a white Honda car pulled into the neighbor's driveway. Fred and Doris had finally made it for the weekend.

Fred got out and gazed at the backyard hoping to see Sandy. But all he saw was the wide yellow tape. He then saw a strange man standing beside a red wheelbarrow. So, while Doris unloaded the car, Fred decided to investigate the strange man in Sandy's bushes.

"Hi," said Fred from a distance. He didn't want to startle the stranger in the light-blue short-sleeve shirt.

John ignored him, hoping he would go away.

He didn't.

Fred walked closer and cleared his throat.

John couldn't stall any longer. He turned and pretended surprise. "Oh, hi! I'm sorry, I didn't hear you coming."

"Hi, I'm Fred. I am the neighbor." He pointed towards his house. It was the only choice.

John laid the shears on the clippings in the wheelbarrow. "I'm John and I work for Sandy. I'm her new gardener. What can I do for you?"

Fred smiled and they shook hands. He seemed harmless enough.

Fred was short and a little overweight and was wearing blue-denim bib-overalls. He had cut them off at the knees. He was bald and wearing

Carhartt hiking boots. He looked more like a gardener than the blue-collared stranger, wearing nice slacks, that he was talking to.

"How much do you charge," Fred asked as he surveyed his own yard.

"I'm sorry Fred; I am pretty much booked up for the season. Here let me give you my card." John quickly patted all his pockets. "I seem to be out of cards. I will bring you one and slip it under your doormat when I'm finished here."

"Thanks," said Fred. But he seemed a little disappointed. He was actually really hoping to catch Sandy painting. "It was nice meeting you. I have to help Doris unload the car." After he left, John decided to work on the other side of the house.

As he wheeled his load, he noticed that Fred got back just in time to help his wife carry in the last load of groceries, the beer.

John was just about to get into the shower when he heard the rumble of the garage door opener. His roommates were home. He quickly hopped into the tub-shower and closed the plastic curtain. This was his second shower of the day. As the hot water ran down the sore muscles in his back, he felt good, he felt like a king.

He soaked for a while longer and then smelled the pizza. His need to eat overpowered his need to shower. He turned off the water and toweled off. He wrapped the towel around his waist and headed to his bedroom. It was at the other end of the hall. He scurried down the narrow passageway and at its center-opening, he glanced towards the kitchen.

Both Dani and Sandy were sitting at the island already drinking wine. They raised their glasses to him as he streaked by. They shamelessly chuckled.

Once safely inside his room, John headed for the closet and clean clothes. And there, neatly stacked on his bed, was Christmas. There were T-shirts, boxers, sweatpants, matching sweatshirts, western-fit jeans, and the remembered socks. Sandy also surprised him with a pair of Nike shoes. She was a keeper.

Clothed with underwear and sweats, he left the room a new man… again.

On the counter, there were two kinds of pizza. A goat cheese thin-crusted one sprinkled with green leaves of different eatable plants and then there was the cowboy pizza. The manly pizza. It was chuck-full of meat. He chose wisely, but the cheese on it was very hot and it burned his mouth.

"Wine?" offered Sandy.

"Do you have cold beer?" mumbled John.

Sandy nodded.

"Please,"

They took the pizza and beverages, and placed them on the great room coffee table. It was more comfortable in there. They sat around and ate and drank with the enthusiasm of boys raiding a watermelon patch on a sweltering day. And then it became time to play the guessing game. This was a new one for John.

Sandy announced the topic. "Just how did that dead girl wind up on our beach, and who was she?"

Dani guessed first. "She was swimming with her boyfriend and got a leg-cramp, and when he tried to save her, they both drown. His body will wash up tomorrow morning."

Sandy shuddered. "Hmmm, romantic. So it's Romeo and Juliette. And Juliette washed up on our beach. But I don't know if I can take another body."

"I kind of like this game. It's intriguing," said John as he leaned back on the leather couch and made a tent with his fingers.

"Well, she wasn't wearing a bathing suit." Sandy pointed out. "She must have fallen off a boat."

"I like that," agreed Dani. "Yes, she was fishing with her boyfriend, Romeo, when she fell in. And then Romeo… well you know the rest of the story."

"Well, I'm thinking it was murder," said Sandy to make it more interesting. "She got into an argument with Romeo while they were walking on the beach, and he picked a rock up and caved in her skull."

"Or maybe," Dani added, "She was married to Romeo and they were out on an afternoon sail and he dumped her overboard for the insurance money."

"I like that one. At least no more bodies will end up on my beach."

Dani turned to John, "What do you think?"

John's eyes were on his beer can, it was empty. But his thoughts were far away. He looked at Sandy. "I wouldn't be surprised if more bodies do wash up along the shoreline. What was left of her dress was exotic and expensive. She was small and her eyes looked oriental, probable Chinese. Her hair was dyed blond and her wrists had red marks around them. That means she was restrained. Probably with those plastic ties that police now use. Her abductor must have cut them off before he threw her overboard, or they would have still been on her. I am not sure why he dumped her.

"I'm guessing she was being trafficked and that there are other victims out there. Perhaps the boat she was on was spotted by the coastguard and gave chase, and he had to dump them in a hurry."

John looked up and smiled. "I need another beer." He stood up and started for the kitchen.

Sandy stared at John, speechlessly.

"Wow!" uttered Dani. "You sure are good at this game."

Chapter 6

Tap, tap, tap."

John woke up with a start. He faced his bedroom door. "Yes, is that you Sandy?"

No answer.

He quickly leaped out of bed and opened the door a crack, and peaked out. Nothing.

"Tap, tap, tap."

It came from his window. He quickly covered his manhood with a pillow as he looked at the pervert in the window.

It was Monday morning. Dani clocked in early at Microsoft. She was at her desk staring at her personal computer. She had discretely taken pictures of the girl on the beach and of John's face. She googled missing persons and she experimented with the picture of the girl's face first. There wasn't much of a face. So she wasn't expecting it to find anything. The computer's little wheel spun in a circle, computing, computing, and finally, it found two possibilities. Pleasantly surprised, she clicked on the first one.

Quasimodo - last known location, Notre Dame Cathedral

Dani chuckled as she hit the second choice.

John Merrick – alias, Elephant Man - last known location, London, England

Dani giggled out loud as she put in John's image. The computer could not find a match in the US. She then included English-speaking countries and the computer still could not find anything.

"Apparently, John has not been reported as missing yet." She said to herself.

Detective Dani decided she needed to somehow get a DNA sample from John. She googled DNA and found it to be a pretty technical process to go through. She would have to stick with pictures.

"I will solve the mystery of the mystery man, if it was the last thing that I ever do."

"Pardon me?" said coworker Kathy.

"Oh, nothing."

"Tap, tap, tap," went the pervert.

John chuckled when he saw who it was. It was a fat robin violently pecking at his image. And with no uncertain terms, he was telling the little pecker-head that this was his territory. John shooed him away and began to get dressed.

The new jeans felt right and the T-shirt made him look manlier. The only thing missing was a pack of cigarettes rolled up his left sleeve. The new hiking shoes completed his ensemble, perfectly.

Weeds and unruly bushes, beware!

He took his mug of coffee and strolled to the beach before his ole landlady got up, just in case.

There were no new bodies, *thank God*. He inspected the tide's high watermark for clues. It was another beautiful day. Nothing really caught his eye except for a couple of nice seashells. He pocketed them. He noticed a seagull on the beach pecking at a clear sandwich bag with what looked like pieces of white bread in it. The scavenger took flight without taking the bag.

"Hmm, what can be in that bag that's too disgusting for a Seagull," wondered John. He considered them gray rats with feathers. He carefully retrieved the bag. The bread crumbs turned out to be wet clumps of white power. John nodded his head and smiled. *The plot had thickened.*

John stashed the bag on the top shelf of his closet in his Nike shoe box. He then joined Sandy in the kitchen for another cup of coffee. She had just gotten up.

"Good morning, Sandy."

Sandy sipped her coffee. "Any more newly-dead people today? I saw you on the beach."

"Nope, everything was alive and well. Well, except for these." John pulled the shells from his pocket and placed them on the counter.

"Pretty." She picked them up. "Mother of pearl and this one is a dentalium shell. They're pretty rare. Good find."

Sandy focused on John's new work clothes. "Well, you look more like a gardener today."

"That reminds me. I am going to need a load of topsoil dumped on the south side of your house for a proper garden."

"Oh flowers, good. What kind?"

"Just herbs and vegetables," scoffed John. "I can't possibly cook without fresh herbs."

"And maybe a few flowers?" pleaded the garden owner.

John tightened his lips, "Maybe."

Sandy had a small TV in the kitchen to keep her company. Since John was there, she didn't really need the TV. He was much better company. But out of habit, she turned it on. She muted it so that they could talk. She had it on the news and the weather. John kept glancing up at the streaming news running across the bottom.

"By the way, I have a lunch appointment with my writing group. You will be on your own today. And please don't buy anything."

"Okay, fine." John sipped his coffee. "I will just cut the grass."

"I will be back later this afternoon. Will you be cooking?" She knew he was, and her mouth smiled in anticipation.

John glanced back at her. "Yes. What would you like?"

"Surprise me. I can stop at the store and get anything you need."

"Do you like chicken marsala?"

"Almost as much as sex," said Sandy without thinking. This was followed by an embarrassed blush.

John restrained his laugh and pretended not to notice her bright color. He reached for a pen and the grocery list. He started writing down what he needed.

Sandy went to the fancy coffee machine and slid her cup under the spout and pushed the button.

She turned. "Would you like a cup?" she pointed to John's empty mug.

"Please," said John, without looking up. When he finished writing, he handed her the list and with a wink, said "You're going to love my Marsala sauce. I promise it will make you climax." He couldn't help himself.

Sandy ignored his joke.

John glanced back at the streaming news. And the first item on local news, he found what he was looking for.

The US Coast Guard rescued a Canadian vessel last Friday night. The ship had floundered during the storm off the Washington coast and lost its engines. The captain and his brother were fishing when a rogue waved flooded their engine compartment. Boat and brothers survived fine. Towed to Neah Bay…

When Sandy had finished her coffee, she excused herself to shower and put on her face. She was excited to meet with her writing group. She took her writing very seriously; well, that and her paintings.

Before John loaded his wheelbarrow with tools, he went into the garage. He remembered seeing two bikes hanging from the ceiling. One was a single-speed three-wheeler and the other one had several chain sprockets that would give him many gears. It had two thin wheels and it was very lightweight.

"Perfect," he said as he squeezed the tires for proper air pressure.

The gardener then went mowing.

After Sandy had left, John put the lawnmower back into the garage. He gently lowered the bike. He straddled it and pedaled around the driveway and checked out the gears. It felt good. He went in and packed a sandwich, a white shirt and tie, and a clipboard, for his trip north. He really wanted to inspect the yacht moored in Neah Bay.

He put on his Seahawks' cap and peddled his ass north. He had no idea how far or even where the marina was. He was going to Google map-quest it but Sandy took her laptop with her. She needed it for her writing group. He had bought Sandy's new wheelbarrow in the town of Neah Bay. The marina had to be somewhere around there.

After inquiring and getting directions a few times, and given a helpful shortcut, he finally found the marina. And there it was, and the suspected large yacht was tied up to a dock. It was the only large yacht in the marina.

He had arrived there shortly after the noon hour. He parked his bike and then found a bench overlooking the marina. While he ate his sandwich, he studied the huge, white yacht. He could see two men and they looked like mechanics, working on it.

After his quick lunch, he put on the white shirt and a paisley tie. With clipboard in hand, he strolled on up to the yacht. He climbed on board and stared down the open hatch at two men working on the diesel engines.

"Excuse me," said John to one of the grease-covered mechanics. "I am with the Marine Insurance Company. I am here to take a couple of pictures and inspect for any other damages that may have been incurred during the storm."

The two looked at him blankly and said, "Okay?" followed by a shoulder shrug.

"Good," said John firmly. "I shan't be but a minute."

John first went into the lower cabin and down into the bowls of the boat. He started searching lockers, cubby holes, the bilge, the galley, the staterooms, and any place where contraband would be stashed. In a large storage locker on the port side, he found the secret detachable door through the yacht's hull. On the floor were three plastic wrist restraints. They had been cinched but now were severed.

"God damn bastards," cursed John. "There **are** more bodies out there." He had the right boat. From there, he went up to the pilothouse and rummaged through the clutter on the chart table. He finally found a name. He wrote it on his clipboard along with the name of the boat, *Casa de Mar*, and its Canadian registration numbers.

When he went back out on deck, one of the mechanics had crawled up on deck and was waiting for him.

John had the clipboard under his arm. "I have all I need. Sorry to have disturbed you. I will now be on my way."

The mechanic blocked his exit. "You said you were going to take pictures. Where's your camera?"

"I used my phone." John patted his back pants' pocket. They could not see that it was empty.

The mechanic held his ground. "Do you have a business card?"

"Sure," said John with confidence. "Here," he reached into his empty shirt pocket and then gasped. "I left them in my car. I will get you one, immediately." He squeezed his way around the man. "Pardon me. I will be right back."

At the top of the dock's ramp, John walked into the parking lot and kept going until he was out of sight. He then crawled back to his bike. He took off the shirt and tie, donned his Seahawks Football baseball cap, and made his getaway. On a bicycle.

After dodging dogs, pedestrians, teenagers on cell phones, vehicles, and other stationery objects, he finally made his way back to Cape

Flattery road, which would cut across the peninsula to the Pacific Ocean and Sandy's side of the peninsula. Once there, he would turn left at the Makah Passage Road and peddle until he reached his new home, and place of recent employment.

At least that was the plan.

His legs were pumping pedals as fast as his heart was pumping blood. At this rate, he would be home in no time or dead of a heart attack. He slowed to catch his breath. He would still beat Sandy home and be back in plenty of time to replace his borrowed bike. He was beginning to like his new, two-wheeled vehicle. And, because he had no driver's license, he decided to purchase it from Sandy. Since it was used, he should get it at a good price. And she could just take the money out of his wages. He began whistling as he crested a hill and started down it. His windblown hair was now streaming behind him as he picked up speed.

It was a long, steep, downhill run and he was making particularly good time when he heard the unexpected pop of a blowout. The tire on his front wheel failed, miserably. He held tightly on the wobbling handlebars while easing on the brakes, and he almost made it. The bike hit the berm's soft shoulder and it was instantly cart-wheeled, causing its passenger an ungainly landing.

A pickup truck, an older green ford, just happened to be coming up the road. In it were a Makah woman and her twenty-year-old son. And they had witnessed the whole thing. The son, who was driving, quickly came to a stop, and then they both ran to the poor's man's aid. They knelt down by the unfortunate soul that was lying motionlessly in the roadside ditch.

"Do you think he is dead?" signed the mute son to his mother.

Chapter 7

John, ungracefully landed on his back a little startled and quite stunned. He looked up into the vast blue sky and it was empty except for one small cloud. As his eyes focused on the cloud, he could see a comforting face in it. It was the face of Jesus. And Jesus was smiling at him. He became very disconcerted.

He closed his eyes and tried to regain his wits. He felt no pain, at least not yet. The cast on his left arm seemed to have protected it against further damage. He became distracted by the sound of a vehicle stopping. Then he heard the slam of two car doors.

He looked back up at Jesus. He was afraid that if he even blinked, he might lose Him, forever.

Soon, two faces were peering down at him; one was a middle-aged woman and the other a young man.

"Is he dead?" asked the female.

The young male shrugged his shoulders and decided to find out by poking a stick firmly on the male victim's chest.

"**Ouch**," John gasped as he took his eyes off Jesus. He looked at the boy and tried to sit up before he could poke him again.

But that effort brought tears of pain to his eyes. "Ohhhh," he gasped and he settled back down with his chest pounding in pain. He had cracked a rib.

He began looking for Jesus again. But the shape in the cloud had changed. It looked more like a polar bear. Jesus must have gone back to heaven.

"Do you want me to call an ambulance?" asked the woman.

John shook his head. He was still catching his breath. He could not afford to go back to the hospital for a couple of reasons. "No, I am okay," he whispered hoarsely. "How's my bike?"

The concerned woman looked towards the bike. "I don't know." She turned to the boy, "Henry, will you please fetch the poor man's bike." He nodded.

"Hi, my name is John," whispered John hoarsely. "Will you please help me sit up?"

The woman carefully helped John to a sitting position.

"My name is Abey. It means 'Leaf,' in our old language. I was named after my grandmother. Not many speak our language anymore. My grandmother taught it to me. But she is old and doesn't get around much now. She now lives with us."

John nodded but he wasn't really listening.

Abey was a big girl. She was tall, with big hips that filled out the long flowered dress that she was wearing. She had a handsome face that softened when she smiled.

John watched as Henry carried the bike his way. Both wheels wobbled and the frame was bent at an odd angle. The bike had not faired the accident as well as its passenger.

"This is my son, Henry. He doesn't speak. For some reason, he is unable to produce any sound from his throat or wherever it comes from, no matter how hard he tries, but he hears just fine."

"Hi, Henry." John forced a smile.

Henry nodded; then he loaded the bike into the back of the pickup.

"Where do you live, John? I can take you home."

"Umm, I don't remember the address. I just moved here. I am a gardener and I work for Sandy Kaminski. She is putting me up until I get my own place. Do you know her?"

"Kaminski? Sorry, I don't know any Sandy Kaminski. I can take you to my house until Hector gets home. He works for the Res. He knows everyone. He will take you home."

Carefully they loaded John into the cab of the pickup. Henry rode in back while his mother drove. A short way down the highway, they turned on to a narrow gravel road. It appeared to be an old logging road, and as Abey made her way up it, it felt like that she went out of her way to hit every pothole on it. The road wound through thick, second-growth timber until it finally reached her home.

Her residence was a double-wide trailer complete with chickens and a lot of noisy dogs. The metal home had a covered area that extended across the front side of it, and it had a porch swing on one end. The added structure had never been painted, so its weathered wood blended in nicely with its surroundings.

Abey parked up close to the porch. She and Henry helped John onto the porch and into the wide swing. They were accompanied by the dogs. Each dog seemed to object to the stranger until he could personally sniff and growl his opinion of him. Once satisfied, they quieted and curled up contentedly under the porch swing.

"You look like you need a beer," said Abey.

"Oh, you must read minds. That would be great."

Abey disappeared inside and Henry unloaded the old Ford pickup. He dropped the tailgate and slid out a white cooler. He latched on to both its handles and hoisted it up. It was heavy and full of something. He brought it to the front porch and slid it on the decking. He returned to the truck and unloaded Sandy's crippled bike.

John studied the bike from the porch swing. "Maybe with some leverage, a long bar, and a big hammer, it looks like it can be salvaged. Maybe?"

Henry leaned it against a tree stump and came back to the porch. He smiled at John as if saying hi before he went inside.

Abey soon appeared with two beers, they were long-neck Budweiser's. She twisted the cap off one effortlessly.

"Thanks," said John as he took the bottle from her. He took a drink and sighed. The cool liquid made him feel a little better.

Abey sat on a metal chair that was close to the porch swing. "I called Hector. He said he knows exactly where your 'Sandy Kaminski' lives. He said he was just at her house a couple of days ago. It was for some kind of accident on the beach behind her house."

"Oh, Officer Leaning Bear; he is your husband?"

Abey nodded.

"Nice man. I liked him. He carries a big gun."

"It's a 44 magnum," she said proudly.

"Is he any good with it?"

"He can hit rabbits with it."

"A bit overkill, isn't it?"

"He shoots them for practice and I cook the meat for the dogs."

John had noticed an abundance of dogs to feed. "That's nice." He took another satisfying sip of his medicinal Bud.

As did Abbey.

Shortly, Henry came out of the house wearing a backpack and carrying a blue cooler of ice. He stopped and smiled at his mother.

"You be careful," she said.

He nodded and added a tap to his chest with his fist.

"I love you too. Bring me some more fish."

He grinned as he turned and walked to the Ford truck. He loaded the cooler and the backpack into the pickup's rusty, metal bed. When he opened the passenger door, he slapped a side panel and one of the dogs quickly leaped onto the seat. Henry adjusted his weathered, baseball hat and crawled behind the wheel. As he headed down the bumpy road, he stuck out his arm and waved.

Abey waved back even though her son couldn't see her.

"You know, he doesn't have a driver's license."

"Really? How does he get away with that?

"His father's a cop." She laughed. "Anyway, when I called Hector, he told me that he had a prisoner to take to Seattle and that he might not be back till morning." Abey stood up and opened the white cooler, the one from the pickup. "Do you like salmon?" she tipped the cooler so that John could see in it. There were several nice silver-gray fish that were packed in ice. She picked one up so John could get a better look. "These are an early run of silver salmon. Henry caught them this morning. "He and his father built a cabin on the coast. That is where he is headed now. The boy lives to fish. His father taught him and used to fish with him a lot."

John looked at the fish and his mouth watered, as he pictured them frying in butter. He couldn't remember if he ever had eaten one, but apparently, his tongue did. "How do you cook them?"

"I usually broil them with some seasoning and lemon slices. And you're welcome to join us for dinner."

"Oh, that sounds very nice. I would be delighted, thank you."

"Good," she replied. "She picked out two of the fish. "I'll be right back."

Abey went inside with the salmon. She filleted them and put them on low heat. When she was done, she grabbed two more beers and rejoined John. She handed him one.

John took a sip of it. "Will your son be back, tonight?"

Abey shook her head. "He pretty much lives at the fishing cabin in the summer. He likes to get an early start in the mornings. He brings me his catch in the late afternoon. He catches a lot, so I usually end up just freezing them."

"So, he spends the night in the cabin? Sounds to me like he might have a girlfriend."

Abbey sighed. "I wish. Since he can't speak, he had a tough time around girls. I worry a lot about this, but he says he is okay with it."

"I see that he signs."

Abey nodded. "I learned to read sign, but his father never bothered. And now Hector doesn't seem to have time to fish with him anymore. It is sad.

"My husband thought Henry was brain-damaged, and the kids at his school picked on him. Kids can be so cruel sometimes. So, Hector pulled him out of school. And since he taught him to fish, Henry now wants to get his own commercial fishing boat. Hector thinks it is a good idea and said he would help him buy it. Which is good, but I still wish he would have finished school first."

John leaned back on the swing and gave it a little kick. The rusty chains creaked and complained a little. "He should. He seems like a bright boy."

"He is. I have been buying him books, and he really likes to read. I don't think it would take much for him to get his GED."

Abey opened another Bud. "So, what's your story? What brought you here? Was it love? Are you sleeping with your landlady?"

"No," chuckled John. "She's been very good to me. And hasn't offered. She's a nice lady."

"A lady? Oh, I suppose she's a proper wine drinker. A red, right?"

John laughed and the beer relaxed him and he started to feel comfortable around Abey. He had had enough of a buzz to tell her the truth, and he did. He told her about his loss of memory and of how he ended up in a hospital. And of how Sandy adopted him like a puppy.

"She feeds me; well, actually I do the cooking. She has a daughter that comes on the weekends. The daughter is very protective of her mother and is watching me like a hawk. They are sweet together."

John then added, "I would appreciate you not telling your husband about my memory loss and of ditching the hospital without paying."

Abey smiled. "I like you, John. I see no harm in you, or in telling anyone about what you have told me. Your secret is safe with me."

She took a sip of her beer and added, "Hector told me where you live. I can take you home if you like? But you must stay for dinner."

"I would like that and if it's all right with you, I wouldn't mind sleeping right here on your porch with your fine dogs. I have pretty well stiffened up and the thought of moving, and of the trip down your rough driveway, makes me hurt just thinking about it."

"I'll get you a blanket. I've had many a good nap on the porch swing myself."

When the salmon was done, Abey brought out two plates and ate with John. They ended the meal with a couple more beers and John now felt no pain. He fell asleep in mid-conversation. It had been a long day for him. Between peddling his ass up and down the reservation, and the bike accident, he had quite exhausted himself.

Abey carefully lifted John's feet and rotated him to a sleeping position. She slipped a pillow under his head and covered him with a thick quilt. "Poor little man," she said with a warm smile, and then she quietly went inside and had a beer with her mother who just got up from a late afternoon nap.

Grandmother Leaf ate leftovers while watching a little TV.

Abey retired for the night.

And John had a very strange dream that night.

Chapter 8

Sandy's cell phone lit up at 7:42 AM, as it vibrated across her nightstand.

She blinked her eyes into focus and reached for the phone. She glanced at the tiny picture tube. Dani was calling.

"Hello," she said as she muffled a slight yawn.

"Hi mom, did I wake you?"

She sounded way too perky. "No," lied her mother. "I was just drinking coffee and thinking about you."

"I came to work early and thought I would check in on you."

"I'm fine, honey. John hasn't chopped me up with an ax yet." Hmm, she suddenly got to thinking about her mystery novel. 'The gardener, with an ax, in the bedroom.' It had possibilities.

"How was your writing group, yesterday?"

Sandy knew that Dani didn't really care about her woman's writing group. She was making small talk waiting for her to bring the subject of, 'what's John up to now?'

"It was good, Dani. We met at *Giovanni's*. I learned a lot of new approaches to mystery writing, yesterday. It lasted all afternoon."

Dani knew that that meant, 'we drank a lot of wine.' She then casually asked, "So, how is your garden coming."

"Oh, it's fine, but my gardener didn't come home last night."

"Oh, really?" Now, this is what she was waiting for. "Did he go on another walk-about? Did he take any more money?"

By this time Sandy was in the kitchen. She put a clean coffee cup in the machine and pushed the button. "No, he's not on foot. This time he took your father's bike."

"**I knew it**! I could see it in his eyes that he could not be trusted. Have you called the police yet?"

"Not yet. I think he'll be back. I kind of trust him."

"Mom, you should call the cops.

"Oh," Dani was interrupted. "I gotta go. My boss just walked in."

"Okay, bye honey."

Sandy picked up her coffee cup and walked to her front door and looked for the morning paper. It was on the driveway. She retrieved it and looked as far as she could see down both ends of the road. The only signs of life were a doe and a fawn in Fred's front yard. No bicycle, no John.

"Oh well," she sighed. She wandered back inside. She was missing the strange man. She thought she was used to living by herself. She cursed her husband for dying and then started crying. She hated herself for being so emotional.

"Maybe I will paint today. Maybe I will paint naked. Fuck 'em all."

***

"Good morning, John."

Abey had such a sweet soft voice for such a big girl. Kind of like a meow from a lion. She was holding two cups of coffee. She slid the metal chair closer to the porch swing and sat on it.

John had previously been staring at the porch ceiling counting all the knots in its plywood covering. He tried to sit up earlier but his rib objected and his leg muscles seconded it.

He took a breath for his second try, gritted his teeth and swung his feet to the floor.

Abey could see his eyes watering in pain. She ignored it and handed him one of the cups.

"Thanks."

"You want some cream, or maybe a little painkiller in that?" she asked.

"Like aspirin? Or maybe even morphine?"

She chuckled and held up a bottle of Jack Daniels. "I was thinking this might work."

John smiled and nodded. "You and Jack are now my new best friends."

She poured a little in both cups and asked, "How did you sleep last night?"

John took a long sip of the spiked coffee and it warmed his tender chest all the way to his toes. "I slept good, thank you. But I did have a very strange dream."

She added a little more medicine to John's cup. She corked the bottle without putting any more in hers. "So, what did you dream?"

"Last night, while I was lying here contently watching the stars in a cloudless sky…"

"It was a nice night last night, wasn't it?" interrupted Abey, as one of the dogs walked up and put his head on her lap.

"Well, last night a strange thing happened, or I was dreaming. I heard someone come up on the porch, and since the dogs didn't bark, I thought it was your husband. It was fairly dark and all I could see was his form. But he looked almost too big to be Hector. And he moved very quietly like he was barefoot.

"I watched him pet one of your dogs and it licked his big hand. After that, he helped himself to one of the beers in the cooler. Well then, I figured he must be one of your neighbors. So, I said, 'Hi.'

"He was startled and grunted something. He perked up and looked right at me. That's when I saw his face. I kid you not, it had to be Bigfoot!"

Abey stroked the mutt on her lap between his ears and looked back at John, "Go on."

"Well then he walked over to me and studied me for a second. I said 'Hi' again. He grunted again. I was speechless and, I swear, he smiled at me. He pulled the quilt up close to my neck like he was tucking me in. He patted me on my head, took another beer, and left.

"Crazy dream, right? How come you're not laughing?"

Abey smiled warmly. "You weren't dreaming, John. That was Gary. I haven't seen him in quite a spell. But I always leave a couple of beers for him just in case he happens by."

"Who's Gary?"

Abey chuckled. "You were right; he's a Bigfoot and a big secret around here. He lives up in the mountains. Rumor has it that he found a small child that survived a plane crash and raised her in the woods as his own."

"Your shit-en me?"

Abey chuckled and shook her head. "Say, how about some breakfast?"

For breakfast, Sandy had a bagel with cream cheese on it. And a glass of wine. And then another. It helped. She began feeling a lot less melancholy.

She put on her long, cream-colored robe and cinched it. As she put her easel under her left arm, she picked up her basket of watercolors in the other hand. She planned to spend most of the day on her private beach while she painted the comforting blue colors of the sea.

She set her easel up at the high tide mark. She quickly glanced towards her neighbor's house for any signs of life. There was no vehicle in the drive. The house was empty. She took off her robe and laid it neatly on her stool. She sat on it and took a deep breath of salt air and sighed. It felt good being totally uninhibited.

And then she painted like the free spirit that she always wanted to be.

John was feeling much better and was able to walk into Abey's humble metal-home on his own. It didn't have a dining room, but the kitchen was large. In the center was a Formica table with chrome legs. The cabinets were white press-board, and the window over the porcelain kitchen sink was louvered. The table's matching chairs had padded, plastic seat-covers on them. John felt like he just walked into a 60's diner.

Abey was busy frying fresh salmon fillets in bacon grease on the electric stove. John slowly eased into one of the chairs at the table.

Abbey turned and shook her head. "Not that one. That's grandma's chair."

"Sorry." John slid over one. "Where is your grandmother?"

"Gathering eggs."

Abey poured John a cup of coffee and went back to her stove.

Grandma pushed open the screen door and walked in carrying a basket with several brown eggs in it. She was scrawny and bent over. She was wearing a long green dress and was barefoot. Her face was quite weathered. It looked like she had earned a wrinkle for each year of her life. Her dull gray hair was long and down her back.

Once the screen door slammed shut behind her, she walked to the kitchen sink and set the basket on the adjacent counter. She took the coffee pot from the stove and poured herself a cup. She took a sip and then went to the kitchen table and sat in *her* chair.

She took another sip and ask, "*Who is this?*" in her language.

"John," answered Abey.

She set down her cup and sniffed suspiciously towards John. "*Who is John and why is he here?*"

Abey answered her in the Makah language while John sat quietly and listened. He knew that they were talking about him. Finally, the old woman seemed satisfied and went back to drinking her coffee. Abey started frying the fresh eggs in the bacon grease.

"Well, what did she say?"

"Oh, she just asked who you were, and I told her about your accident. She then wanted to know if you were all right."

"That's nice."

"And if you were married."

John became curious. "Why?"

"She said if you're not married that she would share her bed with you."

"Really!" gasped John. "And, so what did you tell her?"

"I told her that you are already sleeping with your old landlady."

"Good," said John with mixed emotions.

"But, she tell me she's not jealous type and she said she would share you."

"You tell her that I am flattered and that I would love nothing more than to climb into her bed, but my ole lady **is** the jealous type."

"That is too bad," said grandma Leaf.

John looked at Abey who shrugged her shoulders. "I told you she taught me to speak the Makah language. I never said that she couldn't speak or understand English. She just prefers the old ways."

Abey turned off her stove. Breakfast was ready. And after the three of them had feasted, it became time for Abey to take John home.

When John pointed out Sandy's home, Abey commented what a nice house it was. She pulled into the driveway and parked.

John got out of the car. "Thank you for bringing me here."

Abey nodded, "You're very welcome."

"And thanks for the bed and breakfast."

Again she nodded, but didn't put the car in reverse.

"And thank you for saving my life."

"It was the least I could do, as a good Christian woman.

"I really enjoyed meeting your grandma."

"Thank you. I think she liked you."

John sighed. "You really want to meet my ole landlady, don't you?"

Abey shut off the car engine. "Well if you insist." She got out and followed John to the front door. The door was locked, so he rang the doorbell several times. No answer.

"Maybe she went to the store. I will check around back."

Abey followed.

John checked the back door. It was unlocked. He opened it and started to go in.

"Hey, is that her?" Abey was pointing to a woman with a small paintbrush in her hand near the surf. She seemed to be painting in the nude. She seemed intently focused on her canvas. Abey began laughing.

"Hey Sandy," called John while obverting his eyes towards his shoes. "Are you decent?"

"Fuck!" cursed Sandy as she scrambled off her stool. She quickly put her robe on. When she saw who it was, she threw her hands in the air and started to scold him for not announcing that he was coming. "And where have you been?"

Sandy suddenly noticed that John was not alone. She felt quite embarrassed and maybe a little jealous seeing her gardener with another woman.

"Oh, Sandy, I am so sorry. I had an accident yesterday and this nice lady came to my assistance." John pointed towards Abey. "And this is Abey. She is a Makah Indian. And she just lives down the road. On the reservation." The look on Sandy's face made John a little nervous.

Sandy, by this time, had walked back to the house and had regained her composure. She became curious.

"Hi Abey, my name is Sandy." She shook her hand. Sandy noticed how big and firm they were. She turned back to John. "So, tell me about this accident. Were you in a vehicle?"

John nodded.

"Was it a two-wheeled vehicle?"

John nodded again. "I can explain."

Sandy cut him off. "So, you fell off my husband's bike and this nice lady brought you to her home, and then you slept there."

John nodded again. "You make it sound…bad"

"Oh, you have a husband?" said Abey, and then she turned to John. "You didn't tell me that she had a husband?"

John shrugged. "Yes, she has, or had. Anyway, he's dead." Been that way for a while now. So, it's no big deal." He looked at Sandy and realized he might have been a little harsh. He saw the same look on Abey's face.

"So, did you sleep with her?" asked Sandy.

"Oh, hell no. She's married to Officer Leaning Bear. You did see the size of his gun, right?"

Sandy nodded.

"And he shoots rabbits with it, right Abey?"

Abey nodded shyly. "Well okay, I guess that I should leave now."

Sandy regained her senses and relaxed. "I'm sorry. I think we should start over. My *old* tenant can be a little trying at times.

"I know it's a bit early but would you care for a glass of wine?"

"That would be nice, Sandy. I don't suppose you would have beer instead?"

"Beer it is." Sandy pointed to the patio furniture. "Make yourself comfortable." She scowled at John and disappeared inside.

Abey sat at the round cedar table while John turned the crank that opened its wide, green umbrella. Once fully opened, he sat across from Abey. Sandy returned with two cold bottles of IPA and two glasses. She set them on the table.

"Please excuse me." Sandy was feeling very unsexy in her bathrobe. "I will be right back." She smiled and scurried to her bedroom to put on something more appropriate. After quickly slipping on her blue jeans, and a nice fitting top, she took a quick glance at her mirror.

"Fuck!" She stopped in her tracks. She had blue paint on her face and her hair was a mess. It was bad, Chernobyl bad.

Abey and John each took a long draw from the beer bottle. They both ignored the chilled glasses.

"Your house-mate is not bad looking, for an *old* landlady. And the way she yells at you, it sounds pretty intimate. Are you sure you're not sleeping with her?"

"Heaven's no. And I said 'ole, landlady, not old.' She's a good Christian lady that is just trying to help me get back on my feet. I am not even sure she likes me."

Abey snickered. "You know she just ran back inside to smarten herself up, and I'm sure not for me."

"Five bucks says she comes back wearing tight pants with a matching low-cut blouse."

John took another drink of his beer and ignored the bet. But he became curious.

When Sandy finally returned, she was carrying a tray that held two more beers, a full bottle of wine, and a long stem wine glass. She slowly bent over as she set the tray in front of John.

John looked up and couldn't help but notice that her blouse was unbuttoned at the top, and she was not wearing a bra. He took one of the beers. "Thanks." He then looked at Abey.

"I told you so," she whispered.

Abbey had a good visit and sized up both Sandy and John. After finishing her beer, she stood up. "I must be going. My son will be coming home soon and I have to clean and freeze his catch." She shook Sandy's hand, "It was very nice meeting you."

Sandy stood up and walked Abey to her car.

When Abey left, she turned to John. "Do you care to explain yourself? And where in the hell is my husband's bike?"

"I know who killed the girl on the beach," said John with a huge grin on his innocent face.

The best defense is a good offense.

Chapter 9

It was Thursday afternoon when Dani found out who killed the girl on the beach. Well, not actually the name of the villain. Her mother informed her that John had figured who did the dastardly deed and the name of the boat that it happened on.

"What's his name, mom?" asked Dani through her cell phone. She was on her afternoon coffee break.

"John has it written down on a clipboard. He left it at Abey's."

"Who is Abey?"

"She was the woman that helped John, when he broke a rib."

"Oh my God. How did John break his rib?"

"He broke it while riding your father's bike. He claimed he was being chased by the bad guys. And after he gave them the slip, he crashed the bike."

"There were killers chasing him?"

"Yep and when Abey found John lying along the road, she took him home and he spent the night with her. And he also said something about a Bigfoot too."

"He slept with Abey, the bastard."

No." Sandy clarified, "Abey is Officer Leaning Bear's wife."

"His wife. What is he crazy? Did you see the size of Leaning Bear's gun?"

"I know. And he shoots rabbits with it."

"Mom…Oh shit I gotta go, See you tonight."

Dani was beside herself. Her question box was about to explode. She left the break-room and went to the lady's room. She splashed soapy water on her eyes and then went looking for her boss.

"I am sorry," she informed her supervisor with a raspy voice. "I think that I might be coming down with something. I don't think I will make it to work tomorrow."

Her boss took three quick steps back. It was almost a leap. "You look terrible! You should go home now. I don't want you back here until you feel better."

"Okay, I will leave, if you insist." Dani lowered her head and tried to sound sincere.

She insisted and quite emphatically.

Dani went home to pack a few things. While she was filling her overnight bag, she got a text from her mom.

Need a book on sign language. Please buy one. XXX

Dani texted back.

Why??? ☺

Sandy never returned her text.

Dani arrived at her mother's house at exactly 8:47. She would have been there an hour and fifteen minutes sooner; except she missed the 5: 20 ferry to Kingston, by five minutes.

This came about because the bookstore she had stopped at was sold out of books on 'signing.' But there was another bookstore that was six and a half minutes away and they had two different kinds of books on signing. When she got there, she bought both of them. She had a little time left and would have made the ferry if she hadn't stopped at Safeway and bought wine. "Oh well," she sighed. "I guess I will have something to drink while I'm on the ferry."

Between the digital clock in her car, and her phone, and her job at Microsoft, she lived in a digital world. That was how she knew the exact time of her arrival at her mother's, even though it made no difference. To her it was 8:47; to her mother, it was a quarter to nine. *Much simpler.*

Dani parked in the driveway. She put the books in with the wine and strapped her purse over her shoulder. She grabbed her overnight bag with her free hand, got out of her car, and then kicked the door shut. She made it to the front door in one trip. She was in a hurry.

Sandy was sitting in the great room watching TV. She had a glass of wine in one hand and the remote in the other. She heard her daughter come in.

"Hi, mom."

"Hi, Dani." Sandy pushed the off-button and got up to give her daughter a hug. She paused when she noticed her daughter's eyes. They were a little swollen and red. "What is wrong with your eyes?"

"Nothing," she said as she looked around the great room. "Where's John?"

"In bed. You want a glass of wine?"

"Sure. Why is he in bed?"

"His rib was bothering him. Well, that and the six beers he drank as a painkiller." Sandy poured her daughter a glass of wine. "Did you bring the book on *signing*?"

"I brought two of them. I wasn't sure which one you wanted… since you never answered your text," which was spoken with a little disdain.

Dani retrieved the books and put them on the coffee table in front of her mother. She picked up her wine glass and took a sip. One of the books was hardbound and the other had a thin softcover. They both said, 'SIGNS FOR DUMMIES.' One was an actual book of sign language and the other was a 'Far Side' comic book.

Dani picked up the comic book. "This one is actually quite funny. I read it on the ferry. I am guessing you wanted the other one. Why do you want to learn sign language, anyway?"

"It's for John."

After they finished the bottle, and after Sandy explained what had happened to John, as far as she understood it, she told Dani the name of the Yacht, and the name of its registered owner. Dani became impressed with her mother's new detective-gardener's abilities at crime-solving, but with bike riding, not so much.

When they retired for the night, Dani felt comfortable enough to sleep in the other guest bedroom.

***

"Miguel, my brother, is my little ship ready?" asked Carlos from his home in Victoria over his cell phone.

"*No Carlos, lo siento*! The starboard engine, it refuses to start. The mechanics are replacing its injectors now. They think they are bad. There was some seawater in the fuel, my brother."

Miguel stayed in Neah Bay Marina with the boat to make sure it got up and running as fast as possible. Carlos had a business and a wife and a daughter in Victoria. Miguel only had a lover in Tijuana.

Carlos Hurtado and his younger brother, Miguel, were born in Central America, in a very poor village. When Carlos turned ten, he left home and worked his way north. He worked dirty, backbreaking jobs for pennies and had to steal to survive. Miguel followed. The brothers were very close.

By the time they reached Tijuana Mexico, ten years later, they became hardened and very streetwise. They had stolen a small fishing boat as they worked their way up the Pacific Coast of Central America and Mexico. Once in Tijuana, they hired out their boat to gringos to fish for marlin. The money wasn't bad. But for Carlos, it was never enough.

Carlos loved drinking beer and watching pole dancers while being served by topless waitresses. His brother preferred male waitresses.

It was at a gay bar that Miguel was propositioned. His name was Ramos and he was sitting on a barstool drinking Patron Silver tequila. He motioned for Miguel to join him.

Miguel nodded, and as he sat on the stool next to Ramos, the bartender poured another glass and slid it in front of Miguel. They touched their shot glasses and filled their mouths with the smooth tequila. Miguel had never tasted such fine liquor.

Ramos asked for a refill and then turned to Miguel. "You and your brother own a small charter-fishing boat in the harbor."

Miguel studied the man beside him. He was wearing dark shorts and a white embroidered silk shirt. His black hair was combed straight back. He was quite handsome. "Who are you? And how do you know this?"

He smiled which made him even more handsome. "I have eyes."

The bartender refilled their glasses and winked at Ramos. Ramos tipped him, handsomely, and turned back to Miguel. "I need a mule." He lifted his glass, "*Salud.*"

Miguel thought the second glass tasted even better than the first. His chest became very warm…and very happy. But then it is always warm in Tijuana.

"What kind of a mule," asked Miguel? "I would be very happy to get you any color that you want." His brain was a little fuzzy.

Ramos laughed. "I am in need of your services. And I will pay handsomely."

Miguel looked into his big brown eyes. "And, I am in the need of money. But I must warn you, I cannot guarantee that you will catch a mule from our boat. But any other fish, no problemo, *Señor.*"

Ramos studied Miguel hoping he really wasn't that ignorant.

Miguel burst out laughing. "*Lo siento.* My brother sometimes finds my humor…not to his taste. Please tell me, what do you need to be transported, and to where would you like the package delivered."

Ramos slapped Miguel on the back and shouted, "*Señor* bartender, more tequila." He then turned to his new business associate, "Shall we talk money?"

Another ten years and several boats later, each of which progressively got larger and faster, the Hurtado brothers had become a very important asset to the Mexican cartel.

"Miguel, we must leave this weekend. Ramos has texted me; our next package is ready."

Miguel, from the yacht's pilothouse, looked down at the mechanics. He watched as one gave the signal to try and start it again. He turned the key for the starboard engine and it roared to life. Miguel put the cell phone to his ear. "The engines are running. I will leave out of here in the morning, my brother, and I will pick you up in Victoria's inner harbor." He shut off the phone, and in a cabinet under the chart table, he pulled out a bottle of Patron Silver. He filled a round, thick-bottomed, whisky-glass with the clear liquid. He kicked back on the captain's chair and sipped the smooth tequila.

He had found, as he wandered earlier through this one-horse Indian-town when he was bored and looking for watering holes, that they only had cheap tequila, and that they had were no gay bars. He hoped that he would never have to come back here ever again. Although, it did have a nice Italian restaurant.

He took solitude in that soon, he would be in Tijuana drinking with his lover.

***

"Ding…dong," said the chimes.

Dani set down her coffee cup. "Are you expecting someone this morning, mom?"

"No," said Sandy as she slid off her stool and went to the front door.

When she opened it, the UPS truck was just backing down her driveway. On the welcome-mat was a small brown box and it was smiling at her…an Amazon smile. She picked it up, quite puzzled. It was lightweight. She shook it. She closed the door and went back into the kitchen while studying the coded ticket.

"What did you order, mom?"

"I didn't order this," said Sandy as she studied the label, "But it does have my name and address on it."

John, who was drinking coffee with the girls, suddenly perked up. "Oh good, that's for me." He quickly retrieved the package from her and began opening it, like a child at Christmas.

Sandy was becoming suspicious. "Where did you get the money for this?" She knew John had no money or credit cards.

"Oh, you bought this for us." He flashed a grin and added "Thanks. I will pay you back."

"With what?"

"With my gardener earnings, of course."

"We have never discussed wages; and, and, how did I buy this?"

"On your computer. You know you really need a stronger password. And did you know you can buy anything on Amazon?"

"How did you get my credit card number?"

"Your computer remembered it. And it wasn't that much extra money for overnight delivery."

Dani laughed. She was enjoying this.

"By the way, since you brought it up, how much are you paying me for my gardening services?"

"Minimum wage. And, by the way, when was the last time you gardened? And, I am subtracting your meals and your lodging."

Sandy shook the small parcel. "And, by the way, how much did our new toy cost?"

"And what is it," asked Dani?

John opened it and pulled out a small brightly covered package from the bubble wrap. It was an electronic device, of some sort. He handed it to Dani.

"It's a tracking device," said Dani as she read its label. "Cool! Who are you and mom going to be tracking?"

"The killer."

"Cool!"

Sandy pulled out a paper tablet and a pencil. She had other concerns. "How much exactly did our tracking device cost us?"

"I got it for a big discount. It is a rebuilt one." John smiled. He was stalling.

"I need a number, John. A total number, including shipping and handling and taxes. Bottom line, John."

John gritted his teeth and whispered, "Five hundred and eighty-five dollars…and change."

"**What!**" gasped Sandy, and then she vigorously wrote down the numbers.

Dani laughed again and turned to John. "How does it work?"

"It sends a signal. We just download an app on a cell phone and it finds the signal. Just like the phone company always know where your cell phone is. Only this is in reverse.

"Cool! How do we get the killer to wear our little tracker?"

"We just put it on his boat when he's not looking."

"Cool! And how do we do that?"

"Ah, I am glad you asked that. This is where you and your mother come in."

Dani was bursting with excitement, "When?"

Sandy looked up from her ciphering. "As best as I can tell, and even with a slight salary increase, you are going to be working for me, for a long, long, time."

She looked at Dani, "What?"

Chapter 10

"Put on something sexy," said John as he slipped the batteries in the tracking device. "Hurry, we don't have much time." John had seen that the boat's port of registration was from Canada. He was pretty sure that was where it was headed as soon as it was up and running again. Canada isn't that far as the seagull flies, but it is a different country. Once the boat left, it would be very hard to find. And to discretely hide a tracking device on it would be impossible, at best.

"And, I need your cell phones."

While John was pairing up the device to the phones, the women went to putting on sexy outfits and with great emotions. One was very excited, but the mother was having doubts about the proposed upcoming caper.

Dani was the first to emerge from her bedroom, and she was looking quite sexy. She was wearing tight, dark-green shorts and a pale green sleeveless, low-cut, revealing top. "How's this?" she beamed.

"Perfect," John said, but secretly wishing that she had a little more to reveal. "What's taking your mother so long?"

Dani shrugged her shoulders. But she suspected.

When Dani entered her mother's bedroom, she found her frozen in front of the full-length mirror. She was just dressed in panties and a bra.

"Wow, mom; that might be a little too sexy."

Sandy scoffed. "I don't know what to wear. I haven't done sexy in years, and I damn sure am not wearing what you are."

Dani ushered her mother into the walk-in closet. She picked out a pair of blue jeans. "Here put these on." Dani perused the long closet-rod of tops. She stopped at a long-sleeve denim shirt. It was tastefully embroidered in a western pattern. A cowgirl; this could work. "Here put this on."

Sandy got one arm in.

"Stop. Take your bra off."

With great hesitation, she did. She decided to trust her daughter. As she buttoned it up, Dani stopped her on the top two buttons.

Dani was pleased. A sexy cowgirl. She proudly ushered her mother to the kitchen and presented her to John.

John nodded with a pleasing smile. He then walked up to Sandy and unhitched another button. "Perfect." And secretly, he meant it."

Dani drove with excited anticipation and her speed matched her excitement. John was sitting beside her with a death grip on his seat. Her driving was a bit out of his comfort zone. Sandy was sitting behind them and was worried that one of her breasts might fall out. No one talked. They all knew their duties.

"There, that's the boat," said John as he pointed towards the floating docks in Neah Bay's marina. You couldn't miss the large, white yacht. The other boats were small commercial fishing vessels or small pleasure boats. And there was one houseboat and three small sailing crafts. The yacht was definitely a sore thumb.

Sandy parked in view of the marina. They watched the yacht for a few minutes. No one seemed to be working on it. The hatches were battened down and everything looked shipshape. Apparently, the mechanics had finished. The yacht looked empty, but John assumed that the owner was still on it and getting it ready to leave.

It was time.

The tide was out, so they had a good view of the marina. Sandy and Dani quietly got out and adjusted their tops, and then they walked towards the steep ramp. John also got out and painfully made his way to a bench overlooking the marina. He was still very sore from his accident. It was decided that, if he saw anything suspicious, he would signal with his baseball cap.

So far, so good.

Salmon season was in full swing and the crab season had just opened. There were a lot of sport boats, commercial fishing boats, and crabbing vessels leaving the harbor. Everyone was very busy getting underway. No one seemed to notice the two sexy women meandering down the dock. They had more important things on their minds as the fishermen hurried down the docks with their tackle boxes, fishing rods, crab traps, and coolers of beer.

So far, so good.

The two self-employed detectives soon arrived at the target. Dani went towards the stern and Sandy inspected the bow for a place to plant their secret device. The bow was way too high for Sandy to stash anything. The stern wasn't much better. There was a crane on the upper deck for lifting the boat's tender in and out of the water. Somewhere up there would be perfect, but someone would have to get on the boat. Sandy gave the tracking device to Dani.

So far, so good.

There was a boarding ladder near the stern, so Dani decided to chance it.

Sandy vigorously shook her head, no.

Dani ignored her mother's signal and tip-toed up the ladder anyway.

"*Señorita*," a handsome face suddenly appeared over the side. "How may I be of service?"

Crap!

"Sorry, sir," gasped Dani. "I didn't see you. I was just admiring your pretty boat."

Sandy threw her mothering instincts to the wind and quietly disappeared.

"Would it be possible for you to show me the inside of your boat?" Dani put on her sexiest smile. "I just broke up with my boyfriend. His boat was a lot smaller." That line usually gets most men's attention.

Miguel looked closely at Dani from head to toe, and then shook his head. "I am sorry, but I must leave here, very shortly. I have an appointment in Victoria."

Apparently, she wasn't his type. Dani was speechless as she backed down the boarding ladder. Usually, it was her that had the appointment excuse. She began walking down the dock trying to decide what to do. It was time for her to come up with a plan B, whatever that was.

When John saw someone come out on the deck, he quickly headed for the dock ramp. If he didn't breathe, it was less painful. Knowing that that wasn't going to work, he resorted to short breaths and a painfully fast-walked down the dock.

When Dani saw John coming her way, she discretely pulled the tracking device from her purse and slipped to John as he walked by. "I think he's gay," She whispered to him, and then she went looking for her cowardly mother.

"*Señor*," called John when he reached the yacht. "I love the name of your boat, *Casa de Mar*, your *Home on the Sea*." John looked up at Miguel and gave him his sexiest smile. He smiled back. Unfortunately, Dani might be right.

But, so far, so good.

"I work on that crab boat." John just picked a large boat on the other side of the marina. "I could not resist looking at your fine little ship. It is *exquisito*; it is beautiful, unlike the one I work on."

"*Gracias Señor*. What happened to your arm?"

"Oh, this?" John pointed to his cast, "Rogue wave."

Miguel nodded. He understood completely.

"My name is John, and I am our boat's cook.

"I make the very good *enchiladas*. And with my special *mole* sauce, they are the best this side of Mexico. It makes my captain fat and happy. He give me a raise."

"My name is Miguel." He gave a slight bow. "But *Señor* John, I must differ. My mother, she makes the best *mole* sauce in all of Mexico. Please, my friend, come aboard and we can compare recipes."

"*Gracias.*"

So far so good.

After they talked recipes, John had a short tour of the decks. John managed to discretely fasten the tracking device's magnetic plate to the underside of the metal boom on the upper deck. He then thanked Miguel for the lovely tour and casually left. As John made his way back to the dock, Sandy and her daughter caught up to him.

They walked in silence until they reached the car.

"I need a glass of wine," exclaimed Sandy as she climbed into the back of Dani's car.

Dani hopped in behind the wheel. "Make that a cold beer for me."

John breathlessly slid in the passenger side. Literally, he was holding his breath to keep his ribs from moving. "Make mine a short glass of morphine or a tall single-malt scotch."

"Giovanni's?"

"Good call mom."

Giovanni's Restaurant was on the edge of town. At the most, two minutes away.

***

Giovanni was a bank accountant and worked his whole life in a high rise in Seattle. He worked in a cubicle and he hated it. He was by nature a social man. He loved meeting new people, but his tall cubical and job description forbade it.

His son, Mateo, finished college as an accountant, just like his father. Mateo got a job at a casino on the Makah reservation. It was there that he met and married a Makah Indian woman.

When Giovanni retired, he and his wife, Anna, decided to move somewhere near their son. His new daughter-in-law found her new in-laws a nice little two-story home on the south side of Neah Bay. Giovanni was happy and his wife was round. She loved to cook. So, they decided to convert the first floor of their rustic home into a restaurant. Anna would cook pizzas and pastas, and her social husband would wait tables. He now could happily mingle until his heart was content.

Anna liked cooking Italian, but most of her customers preferred burgers and fries with a cold beer. After all, her customers were meat-eaters. But her rendition of buffalo wings became very popular with her special Italian sauce.

The restaurant was an immediate success. Giovanni and his wife were very happy and became even happier the following year when a beautiful granddaughter joined their family.

***

Giovanni's eyes lit up when he saw Sandy walk through the door. "Sandy, it is so good to see you. I have a table by the window that I save, just for you."

Dani was the next through his door. "Ah, Dani, it is good to see you too." Giovanni paused and cocked his head slightly as he noticed how sexy these two women looked this morning.

As he seated them, he mentioned, "You both look quite lovely today."

Sandy blushed and buttoned her blouse. Dani flashed him a perky smile.

"Shall I bring a bottle of red wine?"

"Yes, please," said Sandy.

"Make it a cold beer for me," said Dani.

Giovanni nodded. "Would you like a menu? Or do you already know what you want?"

"We'll take a menu." They were patiently waiting on slow-moving John.

As Giovanni turned to leave for the kitchen, John had finally made it through the door.

Giovanni smiled at his new customer. It was one he had never met. "Good morning, sir." The place was almost empty. "You may sit at whatever table pleases you. I will be right with you."

John smiled. "Thank you. The table with the sexy woman pleases me."

Giovanni was taken aback. And he stepped between the new customer and his good friends, the sexy women.

"It's okay Giovanni, he's with us," replied Sandy as she gave John a dirty look. She then mouthed to John, 'Not funny.'

John walked up to Giovanni and shook his hand. "I am John. I am new here. I am Sandy's new gardener. Sandy has told me so much about you, and I am honored to meet you. She says that your buffalo wings are the best this side of Buffalo, New York."

Giovanni relaxed and smiled. "It is my wife's recipe."

"I too cook," said John. "You must give me her recipe."

"Ah, but I cannot. I am sworn to secrecy. It is a matter of Italy's reputational policy, and my wife would kill me." He then asked his new customer, "Would you care for something to drink?"

"A glass of scotch, please. And very little ice."

As Giovanni went to the small bar area of his quaint restaurant, John joined the sexy women.

When Giovanni returned with the scotch, John asked, "I don't suppose another stranger came in for a meal? His name is Miguel and he has a boat in the marina."

"Is he a friend of yours?" Giovanni placed to glass on the table in front of John.

"No. I just met him. He seemed nice and he showed me his boat.

"Yes, I remember him. He came in here yesterday. He drinks tequila and he has a brother, Carlos. He says he fishes with him sometimes."

"Right, and he lives in Canada." Which John knew from the boat's registration.

"Victoria," Giovanni said, "They both now live there. He said that they were born in Guatemala. But it was too poor to stay and try to make a decent living there."

"What do they do for a living now?"

"He said that he and his brother are in the import-export business. Whatever that is?" Giovanni looked at Sandy. "Are you ready to order?"

"Yes."

After Giovanni left with their order, Dani turned to John, "Wow, you sure are good at this detective business."

John flashed a devious smile. He raised his glass. "Here's to Neah Bay's newest private detective service."

Then the odd clink of, a long stem glass, a beer bottle, and a scotch glass, touching, sounded; as they toasted to a new partnership in the best restaurant in town.

Chapter 11

Dani blinked the sleep from her eyes while she fumbled for her cell phone. It lit up and showed her the time, 9:06, which was all Dani needed. She slid out of bed and put on a robe and went into the kitchen. It was past coffee time.

"Good morning, mom."

Sandy glanced up from her morning paper and nodded.

Dani replaced the used coffee pod with a fresh one and pushed the start button. She then searched for a doughnut, but alas, there were none. "Mom, I wish they would add a button to this coffee maker that said, *hot cinnamon roll.*"

"Mom?"

Sandy looked up again. "What?"

"What are you reading that is more important than me?"

Sandy chuckled. "Sorry.

"It says here that there is a missing priest from a parish near Toronto." She looked up. "That's in Canada."

"I know where Toronto is. So what?"

"It says that he has been missing for three weeks now. His name is Father Hartman and there was no sign of foul play. They give a toll-free number and they're asking that if anyone has seen or heard from him, to give them a call."

"Wow, mom; is there a picture? Do you think that it could be John?"

"No picture."

"Where is John? Is he still in bed?"

"He was gone when I got up. All the vehicles are accounted for. He must be on a walk-about."

"My God, mom, He's walking around with a broken rib and a cast on his arm. What is he, the Energizer-bunny? Maybe a higher force is watching over him." Dani gasped, "Maybe he is a priest."

John liked getting up early, even before the worms do. It was his time to think. There were no distractions. He now was sure of who had murdered the girl on their beach. Now he just needed to prove it. He walked the shoreline looking for more clues or at least something, to tie the girl to the yacht.

He also brought with him, the signing book so he could practice sign language as he walked. He knew the cop's son, Henry, had a cabin along the beach somewhere between here and Cape Flattery. He was hoping to run into him. Since Henry fishes this coast every day, John thought he might have seen something. Plus, he felt that the boy was hiding something from his mother.

As John walked, he found the erythematic pounding of the surf on the beach comforting. It wasn't aggressive or threatening, just steady as it ran up the beach and then retreated like a duckling following its mother.

A lone raven appeared to be following John. He circled high and seemed to be just as curious as the man watching him. John enjoyed the company. He was pretty sure it was a good omen.

John was only making about a mile an hour with his slow inspection of the beach. He began wishing he had packed a lunch. Shortly, he got a whiff of smoke. He was guessing it came from a wood stove; and hopefully, it was in Leaning Bear's cabin. As he rounded a point, he saw someone fishing. Since not many people live along this coast, the odds were pretty good that it was Henry.

John stopped to watch. When he got a glimpse of his face, he could tell it was Henry. John stayed out of sight and observed the young fisherman. He watched the boy take his long rod and tip it way back over his shoulder, and then with a quick thrust of his right arm, he tossed a shiny lure a goodly-ways into the sea. Henry lifted the rod slightly and slowly began reeling in the lure. His face studied the water and his fingers were poised for any kind of vibration on the pole.

Nothing.

He cast again.

Suddenly the rod bent in half and even John could hear the drag on his reel scream, as the fish started running for the cover of deep water. Henry followed his catch into the surf as he put resistance on the spinning reel. He needed to slow the fish down before he ran out of line. Slowly, ever so slowly, Henry put more and more pressure on the nylon line that connected man with fish. The fish tired and Henry slowly and carefully reeled him in. As he got closer to shore, the fish got his second wind, or in this case, water, and he ran for the safety of the sea. But once again, Henry played the fish and finally brought him back into shallow water.

The exhausted fish lay in the surf's edge. It was drained of energy and just laid there waiting for a quick death. Henry raised a hardwood club to put the fish out of its misery. He hesitated and admired his red salmon. It was huge. It was the size of a king salmon. He was proud of this fish. He could hardly wait to show it to his mother.

The salmon flopped in desperation and somehow, it threw the hook. And with a gurgling laugh, the trophy fish flopped back into the water and swam away only to become a great fish story. Henry made wild gestures towards the sea and shook his fist at the sky. John did not have to consult his signing book to know that he was swearing loudly in sign language.

"**Henry**," shouted John. "That was a beautiful fish. And I am a witness who can back up your fish story."

Henry spun and stared at John who was walking his way.

"Henry Leaning Bear, it's me, John. Do you remember me? The bicycle accident?"

Henry's eyes brightened and he nodded.

"Hi," he signed.

John mimicked the hand signal.

"I am sorry you lost that fish. Red salmon, right?"

Henry nodded and he opened the cooler beside him. He already had other nice fish in it.

John whistled, "Nice fish. Your mother is going to be very happy with those."

Henry nodded proudly.

"I have a question for you. Since you spend so much time on this beach, have you noticed anything strange wash up on shore lately?"

Henry motioned for John to follow. He set his rod on the cooler and walked towards an old, wind-blown, gnarly spruce tree. It was one of the few that refused to die in the cruel high winds and salt spray of this desolate shore. Behind it laid a large, black plastic, garbage bag. It was half full.

Henry handed it to John and signed him something.

"Okay, thanks. You go back to fishing," said John as he dumped the contents on the ground. He inspected each item before he stuffed them back in the bag. Most of it contained plastic water bottles and beer cans. There were a few broken glass jars, a couple of bottle caps, a lot of shredded plastic bags, a condom, cigarette filters, and a shoe. A woman's shoe. John kept the shoe.

John looked back in the trees and got a glimpse of the cabin. It was small with a green-metal roof. He could smell the smoke coming from its narrow metal chimney.

John began to wonder, "It's summer; why the fire?" He suspected Henry was not alone.

John picked some pink, fireweed blossoms and walked back to Henry. He was sitting on his cooler changing lures. John smiled at Henry and handed him the flowers. "Here give these to your girlfriend."

Henry jumped to his feet and emphatically signed, "I don't have a girlfriend."

"Okay then, give them to your boyfriend."

"I, I, I ..." he was stuttering in sign, "I don't have a boyfriend!"

"Okay, Henry, sorry." John calmly asked, "Which is it, boy or girl?"

"Girl," sign Henry.

"Good for you, Henry. I promise I won't tell your mother."

That made him smile. He opened the cooler and handed John a fish.

That made John smile. "And I promise I won't say anything to your father, either."

Henry reached down and handed John another fish. "Thanks, Henry. You are a good man and I am really going to enjoy these fishing trips with you."

And so, with an old shoe and two nice red salmon, John headed home. "I bet Sandy and Dani would love some fresh blackened Salmon, tonight."

That evening, John grilled the salmon and served it with wild rice and asparagus. He recommended a cold beer to finish the culinary experience. And it did nicely.

The sun was setting, so they sat in the back patio on wood Adirondack chairs and watched ole sol as he officially brought an end to the day. They toasted as he disappeared.

"Tomorrow's Sunday," commented Dani. She paused and turned to John. "Mom and I are going to church. Would you care to join us?"

Sandy choked on her beer. "Sorry, wrong pipe," and she looked at Dani and figured out where she was going with the question. "Yes, we would love for you to come with us. We are trying out different churches. Do you have a favorite?"

Dani added, "That is, if you want to join us."

"I would be delighted to worship with you two. Which God have you chosen for tomorrow?"

"We haven't decided yet," said Sandy. She looked over at her daughter who was frantically scrolling through her phone's internet trying to find a list of churches in the area. "Do you have a preference, John?"

Dani looked up. She and her mother waited for the right answer.

"You know I can't even remember the last time I went to church."

Dani looked at her mom and shrugged her shoulders. It was not the answer they were looking for.

"It was a joke. I have amnesia." He chuckled and added, "But, a catholic church does sound nice."

Sandy lightly laughed and Dani forced a snigger. The joke wasn't that funny, but he did give them the answer they were looking for.

"Yes, I was thinking that I wanted to try that church too, mom," Dani quickly searched for the nearest one. "There is a St. Anne's in Forks."

"What time is mass?" asked John. This showed that he was familiar with this denomination. He may well have been a priest.

"It says here, they have an 8'clock mass and a second one at eleven. And there is a brunch after the 11 o'clock one."

"A brunch," grinned John. "Well, eleven it is." He paused for a second and added, "I have wanted the talk to the good people of Forks, anyway. I am curious about something suspicious that I heard that is going on there."

This got the women's attention. "What?"

"Oh it's something big."

Chapter 12

Each morning Sandy gets into an argument with her mirror about what to wear. It's Sunday and she is getting ready for church, and she hasn't been in one for a while.

"Your church clothes seemed to have shrunk," said the mirror.

"Let's see, something tasteful, something conservative and yet hinting of sexy, and something that makes me look thinner." The mirror settled for two out of three. She dug through the closet's top self looking for a small matching hat. She wasn't sure if it was the right one, but the mirror, "Okayed" it. Now it was time to leave.

Dani looked stunning. Of course, being young and thin, she would look good in sweats and Helly Hansen's. "Wow mom," she said when she saw her mother, "You look good." She then asked, "Do I need to wear a hat?"

"I don't know. When I was in grade school, the nun told me I would go to hell if I didn't wear a hat in church. But I think that it was just her law and not the Pope's."

John smiled at Sandy. "You do look quite fetching in that bonnet."

John was wearing the dead man's ensemble again. He had borrowed another one of her husband's white shirts. He split opened the left sleeve; so that he could slip his cast through it. He put on a blue-striped tie and casual slacks. He was clean-shaven except under his nose. A mustache was sprouting. He wore his own Nikes. He was presentable and looked comfortable.

Dani drove, conservatively this time.

The town with the Catholic Church was south and to the east of Neah Bay. After about a thirty-minute drive, they came to the logging town of Forks. It was a lot bigger than the quaint little town of Neah Bay. It had a truck stop and a café that advertised, 'Breakfast all-day,' and it had tire shops, and chainsaw shops, and shoe shops that specialized in Calk, spiked-soled, logging boots. There was a grocery store, an Ace hardware, and a few motels. At the edge of town was a graveyard that had a lot of fresh flowers leaning on granite headstones. The logging industry has an accident rate, only second to commercial fishing in Alaska.

St. Anne's Church was just off Highway 101 at about midtown. The church was a simple, but functional, wood-framed building. It was light-blue in color and had vertical siding. The parking lot was filled with pickups. Most had big knobby-tires on them, especially the older ones. In front of the church was a tall post and on that, was a white cross that reached high into God's sky.

Dani parked her little car beside a monster truck.

Sandy entered the church, first. She found an empty pew near the back. She slid in. Dani made sure John was seated between them, just in case the Mass triggered any bad memories. Sandy was catholic as a child and remembered the old Latin Masses. But this church now had modernized, and it had become more personal. The altar was moved forward and the priest now faced his audience, and he says mass in English.

Well, sort of.

Father Mahajan, the pastor at St. Anne's had an accent. He was Indian. Not local, but foreign. There were other changes too. Like the hymns sung at Mass. Sandy remembered, as a child, the organ and the old organist. She was a frail little thing wearing a frock and wire-rim glasses. But she had a voice that was ten times her size. The songs did not have much of a beat. But they were solemnly sung with enthusiasm.

On the left side of the main altar, she remembered as being reserved for Mary, the mother of Jesus. But in its place, there was a percussion band made up of a small group of Makah Indians. They had authentic

Indian drums decorated with faux eagle feathers, probably turkey. There were six of them in all, five were women. Three of them had drums and three had microphones. And their music was actually quite heavenly. They melted the old world sounds with a new beat.

Sandy became very impressed with this new warm religious experience as she loudly sang along. She was now seriously considering rejoining her church.

After Mass, Sandy and Dani took the pastor aside. They needed to find out about the missing priest from Canada. They were hoping that he might know something. Dani was sure all the parishes had received a BOLO for the missing Toronto priest, Father Hartman.

"Father," said Sandy, "That was a beautiful sermon today. And the music was very good and inspiring."

"Thank you," replied Father Mahajan. "This is the first time I have seen your faces in here. I take it this is your daughter."

"Yes. I am Dani." Dani shook his hand, not exactly sure what the protocol was. She was sure Catholics only kissed the Pope's ring.

Father Mahajan looked towards John. "Well, I sure hope to see you and your husband in here more often."

"Oh, he's not my husband. He's my gardener."

"I see. Do you want to go to confession?"

Dani laughed. "No, she's not sleeping with him. Well, I don't think so."

"Nooo," scoffed Sandy. "I am not."

Dani continued. "But this is why we are here. He has amnesia. Have you heard about the missing priest in Toronto?"

Father Mahajan nodded.

Then Sandy asked, "What can you tell us about him? Do you know what he looks like? Do you think it could be my gardener?"

Father Mahajan looked over at John and studied his face. John was following the parishioners towards the parish kitchen. "He is similar looking from what I can tell. The picture they sent wasn't very clear."

He looked back at Sandy, "Have you approached him on this matter?"

"No Father. He said that he does not want to know his past. He said that if it was horrible enough to make him leap off a bridge, he does not want to know where he came from," explained Sandy.

"He tried to commit suicide?" The priest made the sign of the cross. "The poor soul."

"What can you tell us about the missing priest?" asked Dani.

Father Mahajan lowered his voice. "This is kind of delicate. Father Hartman worked at a Parish school for boys. There was a younger priest that was assigned there from another parish. And it turns out he was molesting some of the boys. This young priest hated himself for this sin against God and confessed to Father Hartman his sin, and he promised never to do it again. But he was weak and Father Hartman could do nothing about it, because of his vow of secrecy in the confessional." Father Mahajan shook his head. "I think I would have left too."

"How do you know this?" asked Sandy.

"A couple of the boy's parents went to the authorities. He is now in jail."

After an awkward silence, Father Mahajan changed the subject, "I'm hungry. Let's get some flapjacks. These lumberjacks cook them the size of truck tires, and they're so thick and firm, you darn near need a chainsaw to cut them." The good father then ushered his newest members in for a feeding.

The church hall was behind the church itself and it was connected with a breezeway. Inside there were two rows of tables and chairs. People and pancakes were parked at these tables, chewing and chatting away. Above the serving area was a sign, 'the JESUS DINER.'

"Where's John?" Sandy asked. "I know I saw him come in here."

Dani was distracted by all the young, male loggers. They were wearing tight T-shirts and clean blue jeans and were busy forking down huge stacks of pancakes. She finally spotted John and pointed. "There he is."

"What's he doing in the kitchen?"

Dani shrugged her shoulders. "Swapping recipes?"

"Shall we get in the line?"

When they got their trays up to the serving window, John spotted them. He quickly went to the window. He seemed to be enjoying it back there. He looked right at home. They both began to suspect that he just might be a man of God.

Sandy put a cup of coffee on her tray and then slid it up to John. "I see you found another job."

"Ah, it's just for today. But don't worry, I will continue to be your gardener. Pancake?"

"Just coffee for me, thanks."

John put three pancakes on a platter and added a hardy slab of butter and then he slid it on Sandy's tray. "The maple syrup is on the table. Enjoy." He ignored Sandy's objection and grabbed another empty plate.

Dani was next in line. She looked John in the eye, "Don't even think about it!"

"Oh, come on. It's for Jesus."

Dani shook her head, "No thanks." And then she slid her tray back out of his reach.

John grinned and put five pancakes on a plate. "Men like women with a little meat on their bones." He leaned far out of the window and slipped the stack on her tray. "You better eat them all. God's watching."

"Fine," scoffed Dani.

And as her tray slid down the line, John shoveled on an obscene amount of butter. "Enjoy."

John decided he was done in the kitchen and hung up his apron. He put one pancake on a plate and joined Sandy and Dani. He set his unguarded plate on the table and as he pulled up one of their hardwood folding chairs, both women promptly filled his plate.

John laughed and picked up his fork. After a little maple syrup, he stuffed his mouth and drank hot coffee like a starving logger. "These are actually really good. Are you sure you don't want some back?"

"No thanks, we're good."

When he finally washed down the last bite with coffee, John asked, "Well, what did you find out? I saw you talking to the priest."

Sandy shrugged her shoulders, "Nothing."

Dani was sure that they were not talking about the same thing. "Find out what about what?"

"Anything about the Bigfoot rumor. These people seem to be hiding something."

Dani laughed. "That's just a legend started by people selling souvenirs. He's not real." Dani saw the serious look on John's face. "Why? Do you really believe in him?"

"Didn't your mom tell you that when I spent the night at Officer Lean-Bear's, that I actually saw a Bigfoot. And he drinks beer."

"Really?" Dani burst out laughing. "That's crazy. You're kidding, right?"

"His name is Gary and Abey told me this was not the first time he has helped himself to a beer."

"Are you sure it's not a man in a tall hairy suit? When I was in college, a lot of the guys pulled stunts like that."

John sighed and realized that it did sound a little farfetched. "You're probably right. But he looked pretty real."

Dani shook her head. "*Really*? As compared to what? I mean, how many Bigfoot have you seen?"

She had him there.

John looked at the pancake on Dani's plate, "Are you going to eat that?"

Dani shook her head. "You keep eating like that, and pretty soon people will be mistaking you for a Bigfoot."

Sandy choked when she laughed.

Chapter 13

Carlos Hurtado was short and built like a bull, and just as mean. His hair was gray and thinning. His brother, Miguel on the other hand, was tall and handsome and he still had thick, black hair. He had a personal stylist that dyed it regularly.

Carlos was married and had a daughter. When he moved to Canada, he had bought his family a rundown Victorian-style house in an older part of town overlooking the water. He paid more than it was worth, but since he was making a lot of money running drugs, he could remodel it. And he did. After that, he bought a small restaurant near the harbor. It was the perfect place to clean his drug money. He named it, 'Carlos's Cantina.' He turned it into a Mexican restaurant and bar. His wife ran the place. And when they were in town, Miguel tended the bar while Carlos distributed his contraband to his customers.

Carlos told his wife that she was the prettiest businesswoman this side of Mexico. And she prayed to Jesus that her restaurant would succeed. And her prayers, along with Carlos's laundered money, were answered tenfold.

"Miguel, *Dios Mio*!" Carlos had just walked into his Cantina. It was early and the place was empty. "I got a call from Tijuana. The cartel is very upset we did not deliver those girls. They now have three more girls to replace the ones we lost. And they said that we better not fuck up this time."

"Did you tell him it was not our fault? It was the storm. We had no choice." Miguel poured himself a Patron.

"They don't care," said Carlos as he took his brother's glass of Patron. "They threatened to find different mules." He drank Miguel's shot of tequila.

Miguel refilled the glass and then he filled another one for himself. "When do we leave?"

"Now, pronto."

But *pronto* is Mexican for, 'First we finish the bottle' and, of course, that is always followed by a *siesta.*

Carlos told his wife that he and Miguel were going fishing for a few days and that he would catch fresh fish for the restaurant. But he always bought the fish in Tijuana.

Carlos's wife was beginning to suspect that they were doing something more than fishing. Some of the fresh fish that he claimed to catch only swam in southern waters. But she was a good wife and never said anything. She just prayed for his soul and put a little extra in the collection basket.

Carlos and Miguel left early the following morning.

***

John woke up early Monday morning to the sound of something tapping at his window. His annoying red-breasted friend had returned. John opened the window and shooed it away. He dressed and went to the kitchen. It was time for coffee anyway. It was Monday morning. Dani had left for Seattle the night before because she had to be at work early. Sandy was still sleeping.

John took his coffee and went into the great room and began pacing in front of the tall windows that faced the ocean. All he could think about was the poor dead girl that had washed up on Sandy's beach, and that she needed justice. He decided that he needed to talk to the tribal police. It was time to borrow another vehicle.

He set down his coffee and went to the garage and pushed the little button that opens the overhead door. He took Sandy's three-wheeled bike out to the driveway. After he inspected the tires for proper air pressure, he closed the garage door. He picked up a white plastic cooler and went back into the kitchen, and he packed a small lunch. He threw in bottled water and a couple of beers. After he retrieved his shoebox of evidence from his closet, he left Sandy a short note. He quietly went out the front door and loaded his cooler into the large basket behind the seat. If a regular bicycle was a car, this was a pickup truck. So, his new vehicle should be manlier. At least that was what he kept telling himself. Fortunately, it was red and not pink.

Soon he was wheeling his ass up the highway towards Neah Bay and the tribal police station. He soon found that he had to share the road with huge logging trucks and they took up a lot of room. They were courteous and slowed down when they passed. Most would tap their horn as they went by and give him a thumbs-up sign. They admired his courage at riding a girl's bike in logging-country.

John parked his vehicle between a police cruiser and an old jeep with wide off-road tires on it. He picked up his shoebox and headed towards the front door and went inside.

He walked up to the front desk and asked to see Officer Leaning Bear.

"I'm sorry he is not in now," said the stout female receptionist wearing a uniform and a revolver. "Is he expecting you?"

"No. Do you know when he will return?"

"Not really. He has gun practice this morning."

"I see. So, he's rabbit hunting."

She smiled. "How did you know?"

"Lucky guess." John smiled at her. She seemed nice. "He has a partner. Umm, Officer…White…something?"

"Yes, Officer White Owl."

"Is she in?"

"Yes," she said as she picked up her phone. "Who shall I say is calling?"

"John, John Buckley."

"There is a John Buckley to see you." She paused, "Okay."

"She will be right out."

"Thanks. Nice gun. Do you shoot rabbits with it?" She shook her head.

Officer White Owl took John back to her desk. She shared a large room with other tribal police. "Sit." She said as she pointed to a chair across from her desk. "What can I do for you?"

Officer White Owl was newly hired. After high school, she worked as a waitress for a couple of years while still living at home. She bored and decided that she wanted to become a detective and solve murder mysteries. She idolized Louise Penny's stories of Inspector Gamache. What he was in eastern Canada, she wanted to be in western Washington. So, she joined the police academy.

John sat down on the chair that she pointed to and placed his Nike shoebox on his lap. He gave her an unsure smile.

"Do you remember me?"

"Yes, you are Mrs. Kaminski's Gardener." She was reading from her notes. She was quite efficient. She looked up and smiled, it was a warm and friendly one, even with the Glock 40 pistol strapped to her sturdy hips.

"What can I help you with?"

"Well…Officer White Owl…"

"Please call me Mary."

"Well Mary, this is about the dead girl that washed up on Sandy Kaminski's beach."

"Yes, our Jane Doe in the morgue." Which was the official name for an unknown female victim.

"Yes Jane Doe." John paused in thought. It had just occurred to him that, that was his last name a couple of weeks ago. 'I wonder if we are related.' He then chuckled at the irony of it.

"Go on." She said.

"So, have you found any reports of missing girls that match her description?"

Mary shook her head and added, "We have her death listed as an accident. The autopsy did not reveal any foul play."

"I see." John said, and then asked, "Did the autopsy reveal any red rashes around her wrists?"

Mary got up and went to a filing cabinet and pulled out the Jane Doe file. It was thin.

She sat back down and quietly read it. "It says here that there were rashes around her wrists that were probably caused by bracelets that were torn off in the surf along the rocky beach." She looked up. "Are you going somewhere with this?"

"Yes. I am pretty sure she was killed, and I know who killed her." John opened his shoe-box of evidence.

Mary leaned back on her chair and studied John's face. It looked deadly serious. "So you know who killed her. Interesting. Go on."

John reached in his box and carefully retrieved three plastic jip-ties. "You need to check for DNA on these restraints and I bet one of them will match your Jane Doe. The others mean there are more dead girls out there."

Officcr Mary put on thin plastic gloves and carefully bagged the zip-ties. "Where did you find these?"

"I found them on the boat that the poor girl was tossed off of."

Mary leaned forward, skeptical. She picked up her pen. "Okay, please tell me who the killer is."

"His name is Carlos Hurtado. He is the yacht's registered owner. Or it could be his brother, Miguel. He rides with him. Or even maybe he has a Mexican crew."

Mary looked up from her pen. "So, you're pretty sure that it was these Mexicans that offed the girls."

John nodded.

"Well, that narrows it down." She then asked, "Are you some kind of a cop? Did you get a search warrant?"

"No, I'm just a gardener trying to do the right thing. And by the time I figured it out, there was no time to get a search warrant."

"You know that if the DNA matches, we can't use it as evidence."

"I know. The boat is registered in Canada and it has already left. If I waited, the evidence would have been gone. Either way, the evidence wasn't going to be used. But at least we know who the criminals are. We will just have to watch them closely."

"And how do you propose we do that?"

"Ah, I am glad you asked. I have planted a tracking device on the yacht." John pulled out the instructions and the code that came with the device. "Hand me your phone."

Mary was pretty sure that this was illegal, but the Gamache in her, let John put the app on her phone. She was kind of impressed with this Detective Gardener.

When he finished installing the app, she offered to buy him lunch. "I need to know what other secrets you may have hidden in your little shoebox."

John grinned, "Giovanni's?"

When they walked out to the parking lot, Mary asked, "Where's your vehicle?"

"I think it would be better if you drove. It's this cast, and with the steering and the shifting, it can be a little thrilling for my passengers."

"I understand. You better not let me catch you driving then."

"Don't worry, you won't."

Chapter 14

Sandy poured her second cup of coffee and then went into the great room. She sat on the long leather couch facing the fireplace and put her feet up on the coffee table. She placed her cell phone beside her and slowly sipped her coffee. She could feel Dani thinking about her and knew that she would call before she finished her coffee.

Her feeling never proved her wrong. While she waited, she got an erg for a cigarette.

Dani Kaminski was right on schedule.

Sandy's phone buzzed and vibrated with excitement as its little picture tube flashed, 'Dani.'

"Good morning, Dani. Hiding from your boss?"

"Not this morning. She already went home. She came in with a slight sniffle, and by the time she made her rounds, we all told her how bad she looked. She became convinced that she had caught the flu. She decided that she didn't want to infect us and went home to a bowl of chicken soup.

"It will probably take her all week before she figures out it was just a pollen allergy. She gets it every year at this time."

"Well that wasn't very nice," scolded Sandy

"I know. It just kind of caught on with everyone in the office as a joke. We didn't realize that she was so gullible."

"Well, people believe what they want to believe, Dani."

"I guess you're right, mom.

"Anyway, I emailed that parish in Toronto and asked for a recent picture of the missing priest. I told them I knew of a man that had amnesia, and that it might be him."

"Did you get the picture?"

"Not yet. I will forward it to you when it comes in." Dani then asked, "So how is John's sore rib this morning?"

"It must be okay. He left on a bike before I got up."

"I thought the bike was broken."

"Your father's is. He's on my bike."

Dani broke out laughing. "You're kidding me! He's riding around town in your little, red, three-wheeler?"

"Yep." Even Sandy had to laugh at the mental image. "For him, I think it might be safer."

"He needs a driver's license, mom."

"I offered to buy him an old used pickup. This way he could find more landscape work and then pay me back with the extra work. The problem is that he can't get a driver's license without an ID and, since he doesn't want to find out who he was, he may never get one."

"So, where is he off to this morning?" asked Dani.

"Fishing, I think. He left a note."

"And…"

Sandy picked up the note. "It says,

> Borrowed your bike and some fishing gear that I found in garage.
>
> With luck, we will be eating salmon for dinner tonight.
>
> Love, John"

"**Love?** John. What does that even mean, mom? Are you sleeping with him?"

"Oh hell no! For Christ's sake, he might be a priest. I'm pretty sure it would be a mortal sin.

"And stop laughing! To tell you the truth, it feels like I have adopted him. And he's starting to feel like an errant son."

"Sorry mom, so how **is** the garden coming?"

***

Giovanni motioned with his hands. "Mateo, *por favor*, come meet my friends."

Mateo was taller and thinner than Giovanni. He had darker hair and a short, trimmed mustache. He was wearing jeans and a loose polo shirt and a porkpie hat. He was sitting at a small table. He stood up, smiled professionally, and walked towards the table that John and Mary White Owl were seated at.

"John, I would like you to meet my son, Mateo. And Mateo this is John, and you already know Mary."

John stood up and shook his hand. "I am very pleased to meet you." Mateo had a very firm grip.

"Pleased to meet you too, John. I see you had the Pappardelle pasta with the meat sauce." He looked up at Giovanni. "It is elk today, right?"

Giovanni nodded.

"The meat comes from the reservation and the pasta from Italy. It is one of my mom's specialties and my favorite." He then turned to Mary. "I see you have your regular, the buffalo wings."

"You want one?" offered Mary.

Mateo shook his head, "But, thanks. My papa and I have an appointment at the marina."

"Yes, today, the tribe is launching a new whaling canoe. The State Fishing Department opened a whale hunt for the tribe. It is for one whale or for two weeks of hunt, whichever comes first. And since Mateo is married to a Makah, he has been invited in on the hunt as a paddler."

Giovanni motioned with hands towards the kitchen. "Fawn, please come and meet my friends." He then explained. "She is Mateo's wife and she is helping Anna cook today while we are gone."

Mateo's wife, Fawn, was a pretty little thing wearing a blue-flowered apron. She was shy and wouldn't make eye contact unless spoken to. She quickly joined her husband and relaxed a little when he put his hand on her shoulder.

John stood back up from his chair and shook her hand with a light squeeze. "I am honored, Fawn."

Anna came out of the kitchen with a pot of coffee. "You two are going to be late," she scolded as she ushered her men out the door. "Giovanni, he just talk, talk, talk. Would you two like some dessert?"

Mary nodded.

John raised his empty mug, "Just coffee for me."

Anna filled John's cup and left for the kitchen.

"**A whale hunt**?" exclaimed John, "I thought whales were protected."

"It is a cultural thing," said Mary. "Our ancestors lived off whales until the English came and killed off most of them. Then the English give us cows to eat. Now our young won't eat whale. They say it taste's bad."

"Really! What does it taste like?"

"Chicken," she said with a straight face. And then she laughed. "I'm kidding."

John just shook his head.

"It actually tastes more like bald eagle."

"**What**!"

"You white men are so gullible." She snickered.

Shortly, Fawn came out with a large slice of chocolate cake and two forks. "I baked this myself this morning," she proudly said as she set the plate between them. She nodded with her shy smile and went back into the kitchen.

John was the first to fill his fork and got most of it in his mouth. He washed it down with coffee. "Check your phone." He filled his fork. "Has our target left yet?"

Mary took the first bite, while she chewed, she scrolled through her phone for the new app. A chart popped up on its tiny screen and a flashing red dot showed exactly where the yacht was. They were on the Canadian side of the Juan de Fuca Straits, and just across from Neah Bay. They were headed towards international waters.

Mary swallowed. "They are on the move, John." She looked up. "So, what is our next move?"

"We have to track them. We need to see where they pick up the drugs and the abducted girls. If it is in Mexico, there is not much we can do. We just have to wait for them. I am sure they will stay in international waters and when they get close, they will come on the Canadian side of the border. This means that we will need both the United States and the Canadian coastguard to pull this off.

"And without hard evidence, both countries might balk. And if the yacht comes through at night, which seems to be their plan, they can dump their cargo without being seen, if anything goes wrong. In that case, it would be better not to risk it."

"What should we do?" asked Mary.

"We really need to find a way to connect our Jane Doe to the yacht. Or, catch them in the act. Since we have no hard evidence, we will have to watch them close and wait for them to make a mistake."

John forked down the last piece of cake. "I think we might need a boat."

Mary paid and John left a generous tip. John made a mental note to ask for another advance on his salary.

Before John headed south on his three-wheeled truck-bike, he wrote down Mary's phone number.

"I will keep in touch." He said.

"How? You don't even own a phone." she said.

"I will keep my landlady's phone close by."

"Are you sleeping with her?" she asked.

"No," he said."

"Liar," she said.

John worked up a sweat peddling south. On the map, it looks like it's downhill. But it's not. And this bike was heavier than the one he wrecked. John was looking for Leaning Bear's cabin. He wanted to try out fishing and was hoping that Henry Leaning Bear would show him a few tricks. There were not that many long gravel driveways that meandered towards the beach. He found it on his third try.

When John got to the cabin, he parked his bike. He didn't see Henry on the beach, so he quietly went up to the metal-covered awning over the front door. It was quiet inside. There was a small window by the wood-planked door. He peeked in.

Henry and his girlfriend were sitting across from each other carrying on a conversation…in sign language. Her back was towards John. She had blond hair and it was tied into a ponytail. She was wearing a flannel shirt and blue jeans. He could see enough of her face to tell that she was petit and definitely not Indian, and most likely deaf. This was probably why Henry had kept her a secret. John saw a small rifle leaning against the back wall and decided it would be safer not to surprise them.

John crept back to his rig. Once safely there, he hollered, **"Hey, Henry! Let's go fishing. Are you in there?"**

John waited by the bike.

Shortly, Henry opened the door and walked out. John pick up his borrowed rod and with an excited grin, he waved it at him and said, "Look I have my own fishing gear."

Henry lowered his exasperated head and smiled. He couldn't help it. It was the enthusiasm that he could see in a fellow fisherman. He motioned for John to go on to the beach.

Henry inspected John's pole and nodded approval and then he opened John's meager tackle box and roared in laughter, silently. He shook his head and closed John's tackle box. He went to his own box and found what he needed, a silver flasher. He attached it to a long steel leader. Next was a large hook wrapped in purple streamers. It looked like a baby squid.

He handed John the pole and pointed to the sea. "Let's go fishing," he signed. John flashed him an understanding grin.

John rolled up his pant legs and went knee-deep in the water. He put his thumb on the real, wound up, and tossed the setup into the surf. He quickly started reeling in the fake squid. He caught nothing on his first attempt. The sport is called *fishing*, not *catching*. An hour later, John was still fishing.

He decided to sit on his empty cooler to rest his complaining rib, and he was a bit disappointed. He watched Henry cast and then slowly reel in his line. Henry could feel the action of his lure, as it flowed through the water. He was an artist with a rod and reel. No wonder his cooler was almost full.

"What am I doing wrong, Henry?"

Henry grinned and signed, '*Patience.*' He set his rod on the rocky shore and joined John. "*The - fish – are – there.*" *He* said with his hands. "*You – must – tempt – them - or – annoy - them. If - hungry, - they – bite. If – angered, - they - bite.*"

"I see," said John. His rib was feeling a little better. He picked up his pole and waded back into the surf. John took a breath and tossed the lure into the foaming breakers. He visualized the rubber squid behind the flasher and reeled it in slowly as he took the tip of his rod and gave it small jerks.

It took another half an hour but finally, he got the attention of a feisty Coho salmon. It felt like he angered the fish because it latched on to the lure and shot to the surface. The whole fish came out of the water and was shaking the lure so hard, that it looked like he was trying to throw it back to the shore. John cackled in delight and his ribs stopped hurting. The adrenalin overrode the pain.

Henry was also pleased. He quickly retrieved the net and helped John land his fine fish. John proudly put it in his cooler. He was now hooked. "Are we fishing tomorrow?"

Henry nodded, yes. And then he suddenly remembered. "*No,*" he signed. "*I – am – going – whaling.*"

Chapter 15

The Motor Vessel *Casa de Mar* charged along the invisible line between Canada and United States. Her twin Cat diesel engines were purring like tigers. The yacht's hull was slicing the Pacific rollers like a surgeon's scalpel. Carlos was at the wheel. Miguel was below heating up some *enchiladas* for their lunch.

The yacht was Carlos's baby. He studied the gauges carefully and was constantly listening to, and feeling for, sounds and vibrations coming from the engine room. He still had concerns after being swamped by the rogue wave a little over a week ago. He was beginning to relax. So far, everything looked and sounded good.

Shortly Miguel came up into the pilothouse with a tray of hot enchiladas and two cold Coronas. He set the food on the chart table and handed his brother a beer.

"Gracious," said Carlos. "You are going to make some man a good wife someday."

Miguel ignored the comment and sat on the first mate's swivel chair; he took a long draw from his beer. "It is good to be on the water again, Carlos."

Carlos nodded with a grin and switched on the autopilot as they both ate.

While the brothers ate, the hungry twins were eating up diesel. Good clean diesel fuel. The mechanics installed new fuel filters and water separators. And they got most of the water out of the fuel tanks. They left important instructions that the filters should be monitored closely. They had no idea how much seawater the tanks had actually taken in. They had hung a clipboard on the engine-room wall, explaining that the engines would be fine if they drained the water in the filters, twice a day, or until no more water collected in the bottom of the glass-covered filters.

But neither brother read the memo.

The noon-day sun warmed this part of the world to a comfortable seventy degrees. The seas were calm and soon the yacht would be in international waters, and then they would turn south and follow the continental shelf until they reached Mexican waters.

They were both leaning back on their captain's chairs sipping their second Corona, when Carlos's sensitive ear heard a slight hiccup. Miguel missed it. Carlos jumped to his feet and studied the gauges. Everything looked normal. Oil presser, good. Engine temperature, good. Gear-box temperature, good. These were the critical life support systems of a boat engine.

Another hiccup. Miguel heard it this time. And the starboard engine died. Its twin was still running fine. Carlos made sure the autopilot was on before he sprinted towards the engine room. Miguel followed.

The small engine room was spotless. The walls and ceiling were insulated for sound and were painted white for visibility. There was enough room to check the engine for loss of fluids of any kind, and it had room to replace oil, or to add reverse-gear fluid, or check the coolant level. Barely.

Carlos switched on the light and crawled towards the silent engine. He was not a mechanic. But he knew that diesel engines, if properly maintained, would run a very long time. These engines were still young. He searched for something obvious. Miguel was no help. His knowledge of diesel motors was less than Carlos's.

Suddenly the port engine began coughing and sputtering, like a chain smoker. And then it died. The engine room went black and became deathly quiet.

Miguel fumbled for the battery-powered light switch. When he flipped it on, he hit the clipboard with the important memo on it. It hit the deck with a loud clank.

The mighty yacht was dead in the water.

***

Before John left with his freshly caught salmon, he had a serious talk with young Henry about his secret girlfriend.

"What is your lady friend's name?"

Henry began spelling out her name with his hands. John had not gotten this far in his studies of this silent language. All he saw was a short name. Probably three letters.

"Sue?" he guessed.

Henry nodded. It was wrong, but it was simpler and it kept it a secret.

"You need to speak to your father."

A stern negative headshake was Henry's response.

"What, do you plan to keep her a secret forever?"

Henry nodded with a slight shrug of his shoulders.

"Do you love her?"

Henry sighed with an obvious fond feeling.

"Your parents are going to find out sooner or later, Henry. You should tell your dad first. Fathers understand these feelings and he will help sway your mother. Mothers, on the other hand, are very protective of their babies. There will be no woman good enough for her son. You really need your father on your side."

Henry stood there, thinking about what John had just said. He never had a close friend and this white man was quite genuine. Henry was beginning to feel fond of him.

John hopped on his three-wheeler. It was time to leave. He turned and studied Henry's face. He could see that he made a slight impression. "See you later kid, I got fish to fry."

Henry gave John a warm smile and signed, "If – I – talk – to – dad, - you – will – need – fishing - license."

Touché!" John laughed. He shook his head and waved as he peddled his excited ass home.

***

Buzz went Sandy's phone. "Hi, Dani, what's up?"

"Mom did you get my email?"

"No, I'm painting."

"Are you outside, painting?"

"Yes. What's in the email, Dani?"

"Are you topless?"

"Maybe. Why, what's in the email?"

"It's the picture of the missing priest. Oh my God, it looks just like John. The priest has a short beard and mustache. Do you remember what John looked before he shaved?"

"Yes. A bum with a shaggy, gray beard."

"I think it is him!" said Dani. "Is he there now?"

"No…oh wait, here he comes."

"Quick, put your top on, mom. For God's sakes, he's a priest."

Sandy laughed. "Gotta go, bye." She pushed the red disconnect button. Sandy was fully dressed. It was the only time that she took her blouse off that Dani had caught her. It amused her to let Dani think that she did it all the time. Call it pay-back for all the times that her daughter exasperated her.

John was pushing Sandy's bike from the side of the garage and heading towards the back patio. He planned to clean his catch there. He didn't see Sandy painting by the surf.

"**Nice bike**," shouted Sandy.

John looked towards the shout and waved. He ignored the sarcasm. "Oh! Hi, Sandy." He began walking her way. "What are you painting?"

"Nothing, really." She started to gather up her things. "I got bored and came out here, but nothing inspired me. I have just been sitting here and enjoying the view." She then folded her easel. And that's when she noticed John's left arm. "Where's your cast?"

John laughed. "I had it removed."

"Who removed it?"

"Henry. He's Officer Leaning Bear's son."

"The cop?"

John nodded.

"I didn't know that Leaning Bear's son was a doctor."

"He's not. He's a fisherman. And he's pretty good with a hatchet and a fillet knife."

Sandy handed John the easel. "Please don't tell me anymore."

John laughed as he tucked the easel under his cast-free arm and picked up the canvas. They began walking back towards the house.

Sandy was carrying her basket of watercolors. "Did you catch anything?

"I thought you would never ask." John went on and on as he described his fish tale with animated enthusiasm.

He finished with, "And did you know that you need a license to go fishing?"

"I suspected," said Sandy.

"Do you have a fishing license?"

Sandy shook her head.

"Well, you must get one. And I will teach you to fish. It takes much skill and a lot of cleverness. Fish are smart. I know they don't look it. But it takes a lot of finesse with a rod to convince Mr. Salmon to strike your lure. And then there is the art of landing him, which is a whole new skill. They are also stronger than they look. And yes, to your question, we will be eating salmon tonight because I have acquired such a skill." When they got to the patio, John opened the cooler and proudly displayed his catch.

"Wow, John, nice fish. I will get us a bottle of wine, so we can celebrate your new *skills and cleverness* as a fisherman."

"Excellent idea, Sandy." As she left for the kitchen, John rolled out the water hose, put his catch on the patio table, and then cleaned his fish. He happily hummed as he filleted the fresh feast and made quite a mess of Sandy's pristine patio.

While John was busy, Sandy quickly checked her email. She opened the attachment from Dani. She double-clicked on the attachment and the photograph of the missing priest filled her screen. Sandy gasped at the resemblance. But she still wasn't convinced. Or possibly, she didn't want to be convinced. The past couple of weeks she had developed a fondness for the feisty man. Suddenly a fantasy had bloomed behind her eyes, as she thought of John being a priest, and of the mortal sin to have him.

She quickly hid the computer picture in with old recipe files. Priest or no priest, he couldn't be trusted. She thought about changing her password. But she decided not to.

By the time she returned with the wine, John had the fish on the barbeque. John was sitting on an Adirondack chair facing the sunset. She set the bottle on the small table between the chairs and sat at the other one. John poured the wine and they both sat silently sipping in the setting sun.

"May I see your phone?"

Sandy handed it to John. He went to the tracking app. He knew that the yacht had left Victoria earlier when he and Officer Mary White Owl had last checked it.

When the chart popped up, it showed the yacht out of the Straits of Juan de Fuca and it was a short ways into the Pacific Ocean.

"They're on their way Sandy, see." John handed the phone back to Sandy.

Sandy studied the screen and the red dot. "So, what do we do now?"

"We watch. We wait. And somehow we intercept them when they come back."

"So, what's your plan?"

"I am still working on that. I can tell you this; it involves a small, fast boat."

"A fast boat. I like it. Where are we going to get a fast boat? Are you planning on stealing one?"

"Maybe." John had a wicked grin on his face, it was bordering on sin. "But first, let us eat. The salmon is ready"

Chapter 16

Carlos paced the upper deck of his yacht. He was trying to get a signal on his cell phone. "I am going to kill him, Miguel. I paid a lot of money to the mechanics to work on my boat." He cursed in Spanish and then calmed, just slightly. "Miguel, get me the satellite phone, *por favor.*"

"*Sí,* Carlos." Miguel quickly went to the pilothouse to fetch his brother the satellite phone.

Without propulsion, the yacht was at the mercy of the sea. The large pacific rollers and the prevailing westerly's, turned the yacht sideways to the waves. The boat now rocked from side to side. It was very uncomfortable and it made walking the deck very difficult and unsafe. One had to hang on for dear life.

Carlos went back down to the engine room. Since it was below the water-line, the rolling was less severe. He picked up the clipboard and read the memo and cursed again. When he finished reading Miguel showed up with the phone. He snatched the phone out of his brother's hand and he handed the memo to Miguel. "Read that." Carlos then dialed his mechanic, Roberto.

"Roberto, I am going to kill you. I paid you good money to fix my little yacht. Both engines, they stopped running. I need you to come get my engines working again, mucho pronto."

"*Sí,* Carlos. Tell me your coordinates."

Carlos looked down at his phone and read off his position. Roberto confirmed it and recommended they clean the fuel filter and try and start the engine on their own. "If that works, call me back."

Carlos and his brother found a toolbox. Miguel read the instructions on the memo while Carlos got his hands dirty.

The satellite phone rang.

Miguel answered. "*Hola.*"

It was Roberto. "Oh good, it is you. *Por favor*, tell Carlos that I cannot come today. The coastguard restricts your area to emergency and commercial vessels only."

Miguel relayed the message.

Carlos snatched the phone with his greasy hands. "Roberto… idiot, this is an emergency."

"They said the Makah Indians are going to hunt whales in your area and they are not letting any boats interfere with the native cultural hunt. They said unless you are drifting into shallow reefs, you can wait. And to call them on channel 16 if it becomes a real emergency. And then they will tow to a port."

Carlos handed the phone back to Miguel. "You tell him to stay close to the phone." Carlos began putting the port engine filter back on. He cleaned the filter to the other engine and turned the fuel valves back on. The fuel flowed back into the filters. They looked clean and free of water.

So far, so good.

The engine-room had its own starter button. Carlos made the sign of the cross and pushed the button for the starboard engine. The huge bank of batteries sent 24 volts of DC current to the starter motor and the engine spun. And spun. And spun.

And nothing.

He tried the port engine and it wouldn't start either. Carlos cursed. "Get that damn Roberto on the phone."

"*Hola,*" answered Roberto.

"It still won't start," replied Miguel.

"Have you tried both engines?"

"*Sí*," said Miguel.

"That's okay," Roberto sounded calm and reassuring. "It means that you have air in the lines. No problem. This means that you must bleed the injectors."

Miguel turned to Carlos. "He says that we must bleed the injectors."

"You tell that son of a bitch that if this doesn't work, the next engine I bleed will be his heart."

"Carlos says…"

"I heard," groaned Roberto the mechanic.

***

"Tap, tap, tap."

John sat up in bed. He blinked a few times. "That damn robin!" He climbed out of bed and went to his window. And with a loud growl, he whipped the curtain back and scared the bejesus out of the little feathered feign.

The robin screamed and jumped back landing in a large bush. It was Dani and her feathers were quite ruffled. And she was now tangled in the broad-leafed rhododendron bush.

John, likewise, almost leaped out of his boxers. He quickly opened the window. "Are you all right?"

"Why would you do that? And no I'm not all right. I'm stuck."

"I will be right out." John threw on a sweatshirt and his sweatpants. He quickly went out the front door and found Dani quite helplessly held by the mean, gnarly bush under his window. He chuckled as he reached for her hands and pulled her free. "I am so sorry. I thought you were the robin."

"Who's Robin?"

"I really scared you, didn't I? He stopped snickering and asked, "Why were trying to get in my window?"

"I forgot my key. Stop laughing. Is mom up?"

"Not usually this early. And, why are you here this early? And why aren't you at work?"

"I called in sick." As they worked their way to the front door, she pulled out her cell phone. "Did you see this?" Dani handed John her phone. The tracking monitor was up on her screen. "The boat has not moved all night."

Once inside, John studied the screen and Dani made two cups of coffee. She handed one to John and then went to the refrigerator for the *Half & Half* for her coffee. "What are they waiting for, John?"

"I don't know. Maybe they pick up their cargo at sea from another boat. Or a foreign ship." John took a sip of his coffee while he studied the screen. "Maybe they are broken down. But I doubt it. They would have called for help by now. They are not that far from Canada."

"Dani, what are you doing here?" said Sandy as she came out of the master bedroom. She was wearing a soft yellow robe and her hair was quite unruly. Even without makeup and with wild hair, she was still an attractive woman.

"Good morning mom." Dani retrieved another cup and slid it under the coffee maker. "Have you checked out the picture I sent you in your email?"

Sandy nodded and asked, "Why aren't you at work?"

"I called in sick. Have you told him yet?"

John perked up since he was the only 'him' around. "Told me what?"

"Nothing," said Sandy.

But Dani couldn't help herself. "I found out who you are…or who you were." She pulled from her purse a print-out of the missing priest from Montreal and handed it to him, "Look!"

Sandy just lowered her head and sighed.

John took the picture from her and quietly studied it.

Dani pulled a silver cross out of her purse. And with a beaming smile, she said, "I bought this for you." She then reverently hung it around his neck.

"Wow, I don't know what to say."

Sandy could see the disbelief and the apprehension in John's eyes. She wanted to give him a comforting hug. And she wanted to kill her daughter. She did neither.

Dani saw the look on her mother's face and started to feel that she might have ripped the Band-Aid off too fast. She went on the offense. "I'm starving. You two get dressed, and I will buy you breakfast at Giovanni's." It worked. Food is a great distraction, that, and naked.

The drive to the restaurant was quiet except for Dani's nervous babble. She could see that she had overstepped a little, and she was trying to make John feel better. And to lighten the situation, she babbled on even harder.

John ignored the noise and studied the picture. He, like older men, only used the bathroom mirror to shave by, splash on some Old Spice, and then a quick comb of hair. In fact, in a police lineup, most men could not even identify themselves. But women, on the other hand, carefully look for gray hair, or wrinkles, discolored teeth, a mole, or just about everything on anyone's face. So, John trusted Dani's female eye. 'Perhaps,' he thought to himself, 'maybe I am that lost priest.' But, it still did not feel right. His memory stayed locked somewhere in a dark corner of his brain. 'Oh well, maybe after a hardy breakfast.'

Giovanni's was packed. Most of the vehicles were pickup trucks that filled the small parking lot. The excess vehicles spilled out, and onto, both sides of the street.

"I wonder what's going on," said Dani as she stopped in front of a spot that was too small for a truck, but just right for her small car. She carefully parked and the three of them worked their way to the front entrance.

Once inside the door, there were three couples in front of them. Giovanni was busy taking orders and seating quests. On the far corner booth, a patron suddenly stood up and waved at John. It was Officer

Mary White Owl and she was sitting with Officer Hector Leaning Bear. They each had a half-eaten doughnut in front of them.

John waved back.

Mary motioned for him to join them. What the heck. "Follow me, girls," said John as he threaded his way through the busy dining area.

Mary slid in next to her partner when she saw John approaching. Sandy and Dani slid into the booth facing the officers. John found an empty chair and slid it on the end of the table. He sat down.

"You remember Sandy and her daughter Dani," he said to Mary and Hector.

Mary nodded.

"Yes," said Hector, "Mrs. and Miss Kaminski."

The Kaminski's smiled and said, "Good Morning."

John looked for Giovanni. He was busier than a queen bee during mating time. "I will get us some coffee." John walked to the countertop in front of the kitchen. He hooked three coffee cups in the fingers of his left hand and grabbed a full pot of coffee in the other. He filled empty cups on his way back to his table. When he arrived, he filled the three he had brought and then topped off Mary's and Hector's cup. The pot was now empty.

Giovanni finally made it to their table. "Welcome, my friends. I am very glad to see you here today. We are running a little behind, but I assure you, your breakfast will be superb. Do you wish to see a menu?"

"Sure," said John.

Hector and Mary shook their heads. "We just had a doughnut."

"But I must insist that you have a decent breakfast," replied John. "You have criminals to catch. And besides, Dani's buying." John opened the menu with a huge payback grin.

Giovanni had a towel draped over his left arm. "May I suggest the eggs-benedict with a side of sourdough pancakes?"

John looked up at the smiling Italian and said, "That sounds good. Make it the benedict and pancakes for five, Giovanni. And, could we have a plate of warm English muffins with some fresh blackberry jam while we wait?"

"Excellent choice, John." He picked up the empty pot and went to the kitchen, dropped off the order, grabbed a fresh pot of coffee, and continued his rounds.

Dani gave John the look. John ignored it. She deserved it.

"What's going on? Why are there so many people in town?" asked Sandy.

"A whale hunt!" replied Mary White Owl. "Our tribe has been granted a permit to take a whale. This whale hunt was what describes our tribe and its culture before the white man took control of our country. My grandfather has many, many stories of these traditional hunts and of our old ways."

"I thought the whales were protected," said Sandy.

"They are," answered Mary. "Or they were. But, so is our way of life. The whales are making a comeback, but the Makah are still slowly going extinct. We should be on the endangered list."

Sandy leaned back on her chair. "I never thought of like that. I will be cheering for your people today." Sandy lowered her head thinking, *your people! How racist.*

John quickly came to Sandy's rescue. "Hector, I understand that your son is on one of the canoes today."

"Yes, he is," Hector smiled proudly. "He is a strong boy and very good at finding and catching fish. I expect he will have a whale of a story tonight."

Everyone chuckled at his joke, even Sandy who couldn't get the *'your people'* comment out of her head laughed.

"Yes, your son is a good fisherman. He has taught me a few tricks," said John.

"You have fished with my son?"

John nodded. "Your fishing cabin is close to where we live."

Hector looked over at Sandy. "Your gardener lives with you?"

"No," she said. "I mean, I rent out a room to him. He is currently working off his room and board with his services."

Dani rolled her eyes.

"I mean I am trying to help the poor man get back on his feet." Sandy decided to shut up before it got any worse.

Hector looked back a John. "Do you understand Henry's hand-language?"

"A little. It's not that hard, especially since he can hear, I don't have to sign back."

"That is true," said Hector softly. "I watch him and his mother sign and I am beginning to understand most of what he says."

"So, why don't you go fishing with him? I think he would like that."

Hector leaned back in his chair and sipped his coffee while he thought about it.

John added, "He has a girlfriend that stays with him in your fishing cabin. He seems pretty serious about her."

Hector leaned forward. "I suspected that. What do you know about her?"

"Not much. He won't talk about her. I am pretty sure that she's not Indian and I think that she's deaf. I saw them sign to each other."

"When did you meet my son?"

"Oh, it was last week. I had an accident and your son and your wife helped me. They took me to your home, patched me up, and then in the morning Abey brought me and my mangled bike home."

"Accident?" Officer Hector sounded concerned. "Was it a hit and run?"

John shook his head. "Nope, the tree is still there."

Hector shook his head and laughed.

"Although, I do have a question, Hector. "Do you have a neighbor that's tall, wears a hairy jacket, and likes your beer?"

"Was he barefoot?"

John nodded.

"Oh, that's Gary. He doesn't come around often. Abey usually leaves a beer out for him. He's pretty shy."

Detective John, or Father John or Vagrant John then asked, "Is he a Makah Indian?"

Hector shook his head. "He is from a much older tribe."

John knew that Hector was skirting something, so he went for the kill. "Is Gary a bigfoot?"

But before Hector could answer, breakfast showed up. Giovanni proudly filled their table with his culinary delights. The smell alone was heavenly and thus the mouth watered in anticipation of its first bite.

When all of Giovanni's customers were seated, he stopped to make an important announcement. He then proudly informed his patrons that his son was one of the paddlers on the great whaling canoe.

"Mateo will be paddling beside Hector's son, Henry. Ah, the leviathan, it does not have a chance." He proudly patted Hector on the back. "King 5 News is already here. They will record the hunt and we will be able to watch the whole thing on the news tonight. I am sure it will go nationally."

He turned to Hector. "It is a proud day for our sons, Hector. A very proud day."

"I will be cheering for *your people*!" said Sandy without thinking, again.

Chapter 17

Carlos was standing between two Cats and up to his elbows in grease and diesel fuel. "Hit it again." Miguel pushed the starter button. The big electric starter engaged the flywheel and began spinning the drive shaft in the Caterpillar's port-side marine engine. And still, the stubborn engine would not start. Carlos's throat was raw from cursing and he had to resort to exasperated sighs. He loosened another fuel line trying to bleed the air out of it.

The injector pump pushes fuel at high pressure down a steel line to the injectors at each cylinder. It will only pump liquid, and with air in the line, the fuel doesn't move, the air in the line just compresses. So the injector tips have nothing to spray into the piston's cylinder. Without fuel in the cylinder, the engine simply won't run. '*Comprender?*'

"Hit it again." Miguel hit the starter button. And once again, nothing could be heard but the mechanical spinning of a rotating motor. And it was beginning to sound like the starter motor was slowing and tiring a bit. But motors do not tire. It was the batteries that were weakening.

Carlos loosened another fitting. "Hit it."

The engine spun and Carlos saw a little fuel ooze from one of the lines. Pretty soon air bubbles were mixed with fuel. He quickly tightened that line.

"I think we are getting close," he said hoarsely. "Again."

Again, Miguel pushed the starter button. Another line started squirting fuel. Carlos quickly tightened it and that cylinder came to life and sputtered like a newborn. Carlos then tightened all the lines.

"Miguel, I think it will start this time."

They both made the sign of the cross and Miguel put his thumb on the starter button.

"Hit it, Miguel!"

The engine turned over and one piston began firing. But the starter was sluggish and diesel engines need to compress fuel and oxygen to ignite. Another piston fired. With one more piston, they wouldn't need the starter. They were so close. Miguel pushed harder on the button trying to give the starter motor more…more start.

The starter motor suddenly up and quit. It became silent. The batteries were dead. The engine room darkened. Both brothers cursed and then they walked up on deck.

Carlos cleaned his hands from a roll of paper towels. "Hand me the phone, Miguel." He punched the send button.

Roberto looked at the incoming call and saw that it was Carlos. He hesitated, took a breath, and answered. "Carlos, my friend, please tell me your Cats are purring."

"**Nada**!" Carlos yelled at the phone. "Okay Roberto, now it is an emergency. You must come. You either give me a jump or tow me to Tijuana."

"*No hay problema*, Carlos. You have a generator on board. It is in a locker on your stern. It is a Honda. You pull-start it, and then you have lights. And in a couple of hours, your batteries should be charged."

Carlos stared at his phone and squeezed it hard. He hoped hard enough to choke the annoying mechanic on the other end.

"Hello? Carlos, are you there?"

Carlos turned off the phone and looked at Miguel who just got back with a bottle of Patron. He took the satellite phone and handed his brother the bottle.

Carlos took a long drink and then he handed the bottle back to his brother. Miguel put the bottle to his lips, but then stopped. He pointed, "Look Carlos, a whale!"

***

Officer Mary White Owl was an impressive eater. She was probably the smallest at the table and the only one to clean her enormous breakfast. All through breakfast, she kept glancing up a John. It became obvious she had a personal question. Officer Hector Leaning Bear kept glancing at Sandy and Dani, and then at John. He obviously had a personal question. Dani glanced at her phone, and then at John.

It was quite apparent that there was an elephant sitting on the table that was being ignored. Finally, Hector excused himself to go to the restroom.

"**What**!" said John to Officer Mary?

She looked at Sandy and Dani, paused, and then pulled out her cell phone.

"It's okay," John told her. "They know."

Mary gave a relieved sigh. "Then you know that the yacht was parked just off the coast of Washington all night. What are they waiting for?"

"We think that they are waiting for their supplier." said Dani.

Sandy added, "Or maybe they have an engine problem."

"Let me see your phone," said John to Sandy. She slid it to him. John studied it for a few seconds. "They have moved south a little during the night. It looks like they are drifting. I am guessing engine problems."

"Oh, here comes Hector," warned Sandy."

"That's okay," replied Mary. "He knows."

"He knows about the tracker and the plastic cuffs, and that I was on the boat?"

Mary nodded.

"And he's okay with it?"

"Not really. He was quite pissed. But he seems more concerned about stopping these men." Mary reached into her purse and pulled out a couple of photos. "I searched the internet for the name you gave to me and I found a Carlos Hurtado that owns a Mexican restaurant in Vitoria.

And, he has a brother, Miguel Hurtado, who works for him." Mary slid the pictures across the table. "Do you recognize them?"

"That's Miguel," said Dani and John at the same time. John added, "I have never seen the brother."

Hector, by this time, arrived. "I see you showed them the pictures."

"Yes, and they have identified Miguel."

"Good." Hector sat back down. "Now all we need is the proof." He took a sip of his coffee. It was cold. "It would be nice to connect them to Jane Doe before they kill any more girls. But right now, we can't touch them."

Since the elephant had been exposed, John asked. "Have you told your wife about Henry's girlfriend?"

Mary perked up, "You never told me that Henry had a girlfriend. Who is she? When can we meet her?"

John gritted his teeth. "Sorry. I thought you told your partner."

"You told the Kaminski's about her?" Hector snapped. "Are there any other secretes your people haven't told me about?"

Sandy smiled at the 'your people' remark.

Dani couldn't help herself. "Yes, **John's a priest!**"

***

Meanwhile, the yacht, *Casa de Mar*, has finally gotten its port engine up and running. Carlos, with a wrench in one hand a rag in the other, is elbow deep in grease. He is bleeding the fuel lines on the starboard engine. It proves to be a bit more stubborn.

With one engine running, the batteries are charging, and if the other engine doesn't start, they can motor back to Victoria without a problem. But Carlos needs to get to Tijuana and pick up his cargo of drugs and three more girls. The cartel does not tolerate delays.

***

"Who in here knows what a coxswain is?" The shout came from Mateo, Giovanni's son. He was standing just inside the entrance door.

The restaurant quieted at the unexpected question. Well, except a couple of teenage boys who were snickering.

John stood up. He recognized the young man. **"I know what a coxswain is."**

Mateo looked puzzled at John, and then he remembered. "Ah, John. You will do nicely. Please come with me."

John was a little bewildered himself, mostly because Mateo didn't wait to explain. John turned to his breakfast friends, "I will be right back." He followed Mateo out the entrance door.

When John got outside Mateo was already halfway across the parking lot. Mateo motioned to John, "Hurry!"

John began jogging towards Mateo who finally stopped by a car on the road with its engine running.

"Mateo, what's going on?" asked John when he caught up to him.

"Get in. I will explain on the way."

Chapter 18

Two years ago, a mighty red-cedar tree was felled and then sixty-foot of it was drug to a level spot near Neah Bay. A temporary plastic tent was erected over it, as a dry workshop. Makah wood carvers set to work with hand tools. But they used steel tools rather than the stone ones that their great ancestors used. They began whittling, and chopping, and chiseling, and carving, away on this thick log in their spare time. They were building a Makah whaling canoe. Once they had the inside hollowed out, they filled it with water. They then built a large fire and heated basalt and granite rocks. They used these small hot boulders, just like their ancestors, to bring the water to a boil, so that the cedar would soften and bend.

It took a week of constantly reheating the stones. Once they had the water bubbling and the wood pliable, they put spreaders across its beam to widen the canoe into a seaworthy craft. Now it had room for two rows of paddlers, yards of rope, and plastic floats. Originally, they used seal bladders as floats. It would be powered by twenty strong Makah paddlers.

Once the canoe was shaped, intricate designs were carved and painted on both sides of the canoe. A long forward angled bow was then added that was tapered like a huge wooden knife. This tall thin bow would slice through the wild Pacific waves as the boat charged forward. Behind this bowsprit, was a platform for the barrel-chested Indian to throw his eighteen-foot-long yew-wood harpoon.

The stern was notched in order to slip in a long, wide paddle in it that was used to steer the boat. It had a low platform so that a man could stand while steering the canoe with his rudder-paddle. He was the second most important man in this traditional whaling canoe.

It is now two years later and the only thing missing is a fleeing whale.

The canoe was tied up to a dock in Neah Bay Marina. The eighteen men, that were chosen to hunt the whale, had been practicing on weekends all spring on their whaling canoe. They were now beating drums and chanting a prayer to God in excitement, as they waited for the scheduled starting time. The news media was there. It was an exhilarating and emotional time. And that's when it happened.

"**Mateo, Mateo**," shouted Raymond Little-Wolf as he came running down the dock.

"What is the matter, Ray?"

Ray took a breath. "It is my wife; she is going into labor. And I have to do something."

Mateo understood that even if someone else took his wife to the hospital, Raymond would be distracted and should not be on today's hunt, especially since he was the one steering the canoe, he was the coxswain. "You go, Ray. Take your wife to the hospital. We will be fine."

"Are you sure?"

"Yes, you go, and tonight we will smoke a big fat cigar in honor of your new son."

"You want me to do what?" John was incredulous at Mateo's offer. He was surrounded by anxious Makah would-be whalers in dire need of a coxswain. It wasn't a hard job, but it was a very important one.

The more John thought about it, the more it sounded like it might be fun.

"What the hell!" he said. "What's the worst that can happen?"

Mateo slapped him on the back. "That's the spirit. Thank you, John. I know you won't regret this. And chances are, we won't see anything anyway. And besides, it's a nice day to go fishing." Mateo handed John his steering paddle. "Let's go find us a whale, shall we." They scurried down the dock to the waiting canoe. And with mixed emotions, they boarded.

John quickly took his position on the stern. He slipped his steering paddle in its slot and gave Mateo a thumbs up. They shoved off. The crowd cheered and the news cameras filmed. Today John was making history. John, with his white collared shirt and cut-off slacks, looked quite professional as he steered his paddlers out of the calm waters of Neah Bay.

Once they cleared the breakwater, the swift canoe shot out into the vast, blue, hills and valleys of the largest ocean in the world. John's stomach muscles suddenly tightened. It looked a lot different out on the water and the vessel under him felt pretty small. He put a death-grip on his steering paddle and a grin on his face, and joined in on the Makah whaling chant.

And not very far from the exciting whale hunt, Carlos and Miguel were having an important philosophical discussion.

"*Dios mío, Miguel,* you fucking idiot. Do not press that fucking button until I say I am ready."

Miguel replied with his Corona beer can, by just missing his brother's head with it.

And also, not very far away, Sandy had just returned to the table from her third trip to the restroom. Hector and Mary had left thirty minutes ago. "What the hell do you supposed happened to John?" she asked Dani. "He said he would be right back."

Giovanni heard. He went to their table. He was still holding a coffee pot.

"No more coffee for me," said Sandy. Dani just covered her cup with her hand.

"I am so sorry, ladies," sighed Giovanni. "I thought you knew about John. It is Ray Little-Wolf and he is having a baby."

"Really?" questioned Dani while wondering who Ray Little-Wolf was and where Giovanni was going with this.

Giovanni laughed. "No, no. It is Ray's sweet wife that is having the baby. This is their second child. They asked me and Anna to be the child's godparents. Anna, she is so…"

"Focus, Giovanni, focus" said Sandy. "Where is John?"

Giovanni chuckled. "Oh, right. John is on the whaling canoe. He is their new coxswain."

Both Sandy and Dani gasped. "**Really**!"

"I know, isn't that great news?"

John intently watched the harpooner who was intently searching the sea for the blow of a whale. He would point in the direction that he wanted to canoe to go. John just followed his finger. At the top of each tall wave, the harpooner would scan the rolling blue surface for the tell-tale exhaust of the water and fog-filled air of a gray whale. These thirty-ton mammals feed near the shore on shrimp all during their spring migration north. By now they are working their way back to the Mexican coast and to their wintering waters.

The day was clear and the sky was the color of a sapphire. The Makah were chanting in rhythm with each stroke of their wide wood paddles. The moist salt air was clean and warm. John never felt more alive.

They were followed by a support boat that would assist the canoe if anything happened. And if the canoe did harpoon a whale, there was a Makah on the support boat with a large caliber rifle to quickly kill the whale, so it wouldn't suffer.

An hour later the coastline's details disappeared and it just became the edge of a continent. The seas calmed a bit and the rolling swells became softer. And it was on the top of one of these swells, that John saw a white Yacht. It was still a long way off. But, John was sure that it was Carlos and Miguel's boat. It distracted him for a second while he thought about the brothers and what they could be waiting for.

"**Devil Fish**!" roared the harpooner.

Devil Fish is what the coastal Indians called the gray whale and for a very good reason.

The harpooner had found their whale. He was pointing towards a mist of water vapor that drifted over the surface. John quickly steered the canoe towards the vapor and when saw the whale's wide-back as it took a breath and rolled under, he gasped. "We are going to need a bigger boat!"

The crew of paddlers stopped chanting and quickened their strokes. The chase was on. Each time the whale surfaced he was a little closer. John watched the water ahead and adjusted his course. The whale didn't seem to be concerned.

Finally, they closed in on it. He brought the canoe up on the left side of the whale because the harpooner was right-handed. He cocked his thick arm and waited for the whale to submerge about three feet so that his tail would not slap the water and swamp their canoe. When the timing was right, he leaped into the air and drove the harpoon's barb deep into the whale's back. The steel barb was attached to a long rope, and fastened to the rope were several large, round-floats. As the whale dove, the coiled rope and the floats were quickly yanked out of the canoe.

The Makah had done it. They have gotten their whale. They all stood up and cheered. John grinned and cheered the loudest. They then knelt back down and started chasing their whale. The old gray whale turned tale and began swimming towards the safety of the deep blue sea.

But the whale could not stay underwater very long. He was panicking and dragging eight floats that kept pulling him back to the surface. It didn't take long before the excited crew on the canoe started to catch up to their whale.

Just as they passed the rear float the whale dove for deep water. He took down all eight of the floats. They stopped paddling. They knew he would not be down very long. They waited to see where he would surface. The support boat eased in close and then stopped their engines. The Makah with the elephant gun flicked the safety off and wearyingly, stood on the bow, and waited.

One may wonder why a 30-ton animal will run from a 180-pound man. I can answer that with a question. 'Why does a 180-pound man run from a bumblebee weighing less than an ounce?' Getting stung from either beast is unpleasant, which kicks in our primal instinct of flight. But some men anger, and want to fight and swat the offending stinger. And, so do some whales when they are stung by a steel barb. Hence the term, Devil Fish.

The gray whale looked up at the surface and saw three boat hulls. The offending hull was the dark narrow one in the middle. He swam towards it, and with the momentum of a freight train, he plowed his head into the floating hull.

The giant red cedar hull split in two, as it exploded skyward. Twenty-two men were launched into the air and were scattered like blown dandelion seeds.

When the whale surfaced for the second time, the hunter in the support boat took quick-aim and shot the whale in the head. The recoil from the elephant gun knocked the shooter on his ass. The whale died instantly.

Carlos looked up from the engine and Miguel took his thumb off the starter button and then spun towards his brother.

"What was that?"

"It sounded like a gunshot!"

Chapter 19

Carlos and Miguel scrambled up on deck to see what was going on. They gazed in disbelief at the incredible chaos that was unfolding around their boat. The first thing that got their attention was the rolling red water and a floating dead whale, and they saw a white Bayliner support boat that was rescuing men that were floating in the water. And, in the middle of all this, they saw the two halves of an Indian whaling-canoe. And there were still a lot of frantic people waving and shouting from the water. Nothing looked right. Then a small plane began circling close to the water. It had KING 5 TRAFFIC written on its wings.

"What just happened, Miguel?"

Miguel shrugged his shoulders and pointed to an approaching Coast Guard boat. "I think we better leave, Carlos. And *Pronto*!"

They both hurried to the pilothouse. Engine one was still running. It had enough power for them to leave by. Carlos twisted the key for engine two, on the off chance it would start. It cranked for a few seconds and it fired off.

"Ha," laughed Carlos as he slapped his brother on the back. "We now go to Tijuana, my brother. God has finally smiled on us." He slid the lever into the forward gear and then slowly left the scene, so as not to draw any attention.

Everyone was so busy with the whale and the rescue that no one seemed the notice the large yacht that was already there. It just blended in as a support and rescue boat; and as it left other boats arrived to take its place. Carlos and Miguel left totally unscathed.

Sandy and her daughter left Giovanni's and went to the Marina to wait for John's return. They found a small watering-hole called the *Bay Tavern;* it looked like a good place to visit and kill time. It had over twenty different beers on tap. Dani ordered an IPA and Sandy an Alaskan Amber. It was a sports bar, so it had several TVs. Since it wasn't quite football season, most were covering the whale hunt.

There were no cameras as yet on the scene, because no one was allowed within a mile of the whalers until after the kill. So, everyone was just listening to the talking-heads that were speculating what was happening out there on the water. One of the TV screens was covering a baseball game, but no one was watching it. The Mariners were losing.

As Dani and her mother sipped on a cold beer, a news flash came across the screen.

"This is KING 5 news. We have just been informed that the Makah whale hunt has been successful. Our man in the support boat says that a gray whale has been harpooned and that they are in pursuit. We should have some pictures shortly. Our traffic plane, the eye-in-the-sky, is on the way."

The Makah-filled tavern erupted in cheer. A chief bought rounds for everyone. Sandy and Dani touched glasses and drank heartily.

"I have just received this bulletin," announced a talking head on the TV screen. "There was a slight mishap with the whalers. It seems their great whaling canoe was swamped when the whale was shot with the high-powered rifle from the support boat. All the men are now being plucked from the water. There don't seem to be any causalities. Our plane should be there any minute now with an on-the-scene view. We will keep you informed."

The new news did cause concern. The tavern became quiet, as all eyes nervously stared at the wide-screen hanging over the bar. But on a lighter note, the Mariners scored a run.

"I sure hope John is all right."

"I'm sure he's fine," said Dani. "After all, he is a representative of God." Dani waved to the bartender and held up two fingers. He nodded and poured two more beers.

The beers arrived as the eye-in-the-sky began circling and broadcasting pictures. Now they could see the blood in the water, the whale, the broken canoe, and the rescue boats. It didn't look very good. Tensions were high as they watched rescuers pull men from the cold water, men that they personally knew, coworkers and neighbors. It was a dreadful scene, but at least the men were being saved.

"Dani, do you see John?"

Dani shook her head. "The camera is too far. I don't recognize anyone."

For the next thirty minutes they watched as rescuers pulled the men to safety. The newscaster was constantly speculating as to what had happened. He said it looked like the whale had attacked the whalers even before it was shot. He rattled on filling air time until more accurate information reached his desk.

"A small tug boat is now on the scene and it has tied up to the whale. It will tow the whale back to the reservation. The mighty hunters have been rescued and are all now in the coastguard cutter. Medics are treating for minor cuts and bruises and they all are being treated for hypothermia. And everyone is in good spirits. So far the only casualty is the beautifully carved whaling canoe."

The good chief bought another round at the tavern. The Mariners scored another run. It was the top of the ninth, but they were still behind. Although, no one seemed to care.

Sandy and Dani finished their beers and joined the crowd of people now anxiously headed to the crowded marina docks. Everyone was excited and concerned to greet the successful hunters, and especially to hug their surviving husbands and sons and lovers.

A sudden dark rumor drifted through the crowd creating an ominous hush. The cutter radioed to shore that one of the whalers was missing. They would not give a name until the next of kin was notified. The solemn onlookers watched and prayed as the coastguard boat slowed and then navigated through the breakwater. The cutter motored to the main dock and tied up.

Officer Hector Leaning Bear and Officer Mary White Owl worked their way to the cruiser. Mary took charge of keeping the crowd organized. Hector quickly climbed on board to find out about his son.

Sandy and Dani wormed their way down the ramp. They were the closest thing that John had, as next of kin. Soon, they caught up to Giovanni. He was frantic with the fear that it might be his son that was missing.

"Have you heard anything?" asked Giovanni. He was shaking like a leaf.

Sandy shook her head, "No."

Dani added. "Hector Leaning Bear is on board. We should find out something soon."

Before long, Hector came out of the pilothouse. He had a very somber look on his face. He was followed by his son, Henry, and Mateo, Giovanni's son.

Giovanni sighed and big happy tears formed in his eyes.

Sandy studied Hector's face. She could the anguish in it. He had found out who the missing man was. He now had the gut-wrenching job of informing who the unfortunate man was. He slowly walked to the cutter's rail and searched the crowd. When he saw Sandy's face, he stopped and looked into her eyes. And with a tear in his eye, he sadly shook his head. She then knew, and now she had tears in her eyes.

***

When the mighty gray whale decided to take matters into his own fins, John's heart was pounding with excitement. The sea's swell was gentle, while everyone waited for the whale to resurface. John peered over the side. He could see a dark shape in the water. It could be a whale or could be the shade of a small cloud. He looked up and the sky was clear. That was when the whale slammed into the canoe, sending it high into the air, along with its passengers.

John's trajectory took him in a high arch. He still had a hold of the steering paddle. He hit the water feet first and the surface tension ripped off his life jacket as he disappeared into the cold ocean. The paddle was ripped from his hands and the impact took his breath. Dazed and fighting for air, he swam for the surface.

His confused head bobbed up near the white hull of a support boat. He saw a small platform at its stern and swam for it. Cold and stiff he latched onto a stainless-steel boarding ladder and crawled onto the narrow shelf. He sat on the fiberglass ledge and caught his breath. He saw the whale come up again. He heard the killing shot. The noise was deafening and he saw blood start to flow out of a large hole from the whale's head. The Devil Fish rolled on its side and slowly worked his tail until he died.

John suddenly began shaking and his teeth chattered because of being wet from the frigid seawater. He forced himself to climb up and over the stern, and dropped to the deck. He curled up into a fetal position and began shivering uncontrollably. When he heard a second engine start underneath him, he passed out.

Chapter 20

Tucked into a small corner and laying in full sun, John soon warmed up. He could feel the smooth vibration of motors that were humming somewhere under the floorboards. He could also feel the slight roll of the boat, as it cruised through a mild sea. He opened his eyes and looked up into the vast blue sky. He saw a silver bird as it flew its passengers through the upper atmosphere. He began remembering what had just happened. Of being tossed high in the air and landing near this boat. On hearing a gunshot. Of watching the whale roll on its side and dying. Of the red-stained water. And of hearing the shouts of men in the water.

He realized that it was not just a horrible dream and sat up. "Where are the rescuers? Where are the rescued men? And why does this boat look vaguely familiar?"

He stood up to get a better look.

He was far out at sea. He could not see any land, not even the tall Olympic Mountains. A sickening feeling gripped his stomach. He then looked up at the pilothouse and saw two men sitting on captain's chairs and staring forward through the clear glass. John gasped when he recognized Miguel. He assumed that the other was Carlos. He quickly sat back down out of sight.

John glanced up at the sun. It was pretty high and no help in telling which direction they were going. He felt that they were heading south. He was guessing that they had not picked up their illegal cargo and that were headed to Mexico. Or even to Central America. He was also pretty sure it was a three-day trip or more, depending on their destination. And he was quite sure that he could not stay hidden that long. He now considered himself royally screwed and was sure he would be dumped at sea. He needed a prayer and a plan.

Carlos and Miguel were finally running south on a smooth ocean and making good time. The Cats were purring away in the engine room pushing the yacht at hull speed. The day was perfect and the brothers were happy.

Carlos was at the wheel. Miguel was beside him and a Yeti cooler, filled with Coronas, sat between them.

Miguel snatched one of the cold beers from the cooler. "Beer?" he asked Carlos as he handed it to him.

"*Gracious*," said Carlos as took the beer. "Check the weather fax. See if there are any storms out there that we should be skirting.

"*Si*, Carlos." Miguel turned on the Furuno's screen that talked to the satellite weather station that circled the earth with its magic pictures. While the instrument warmed up, he popped off the cap to a long-neck Corona and took a long satisfying drink. This was his and Carlos's truly happy time. They were alone on a comfortable yacht and in a calm sea.

But that was about to end.

"Knock, knock, knock," said the cabin door.

Miguel, very startled, dropped his beer. It shattered on the deck.

Carlos was in the middle of a hardy drink when he heard it. He was also startled and his beer, nose-sprayed all over the windshield. He did not drop his bottle, but his mess was disgustingly worse.

"The best defense is a good offense," said John to himself just before he knocked. He took a deep breath and opened the door. He looked up at the two surprised men and said, "*Muchas gracias, señors*, for saving my life. I would have drowned if you had not rescued me."

But, Carlos had a very good offense. He brought a gun to a knife-fight. He quickly put his beer into his left hand, and with the other, he reached under the chart table and pulled out the shiny gun. It was a stainless-steel Smith & Wesson .38 caliber revolver. And it was loaded; John could see the round lead bullets in the revolving chamber, looking right at him.

"Gringo, where did you... How did you..? Carlos coughed and he retrieved a handkerchief from his pocket and wiped the beer drool from his face. "What the fuck are you doing on my little ship?"

John ignored him and turned to Miguel and back to his offense. "Miguel, my friend, it is good to see you again."

Carlos pointed his beer bottle at John and asked his brother, "Do you know this gringo?"

Miguel studied John's face. It looked familiar, but he couldn't remember where he had seen him. "*Señor?*"...

"John," added John.

"*Si, Señor* John. How do I know you?"

"Oh Miguel, it was right here on this boat a week ago. You remember. We talked about our mother's *mole* sauce. I did try your recipe and you may have been right. It was very good. But in a different way. Have you tried my mother's recipe?"

Miguel shook his head. "No."

John looked up at Carlos. "You must be Miguel's brother. I am John Buckley." John reached for Carlos's hand, hoping that he would put the gun down and use it to shake his hand.

Carlos just spit at it, obviously quite annoyed and not wanting to put down his Smith & Wesson.

John forced a grin and looked back at Miguel. "I am hungry. Why don't you let me run down to your galley and make you some of my mother's famous sauce? I will make some bean burritos to slip under this sauce, *Si?*"

Carlos began swearing in Spanish at John and his brother. He was quite upset that this strange man was on board his yacht, and that his brother invited him there once before. He waved his gun back and forth and wanted to shoot both of them.

"Excuse me," interrupted John. "I see that you two are having an important discussion. Why don't I go start lunch? Whatever it is that you are planning, I am sure that it can be executed after a full stomach. No?"

Carlos stopped cursing and almost laughed at John's choice of words. "Fine," he said and then he motioned with his gun for John to leave. "Miguel, you keep a close eye on him. Next time I shoot you and keep the gringo." Carlos began pacing the deck. The longer he waited the harder it would be to dispose of the gringo.

He activated the autopilot and went out on deck. "**Wait**," he shouted. He quickly caught up to John and his brother. He needed to find out more about this strange man and exactly how much he knew.

He walked up to John and separated him from his brother. John was now against the rail that separated him from the sea, and a good push from Carlos would end this discussion. Now was the prayer time of his plan.

"Who are you and exactly how did you end up here?"

John scrambled for a good lie, or… Maybe the truth? What the heck. John remembered the silver cross under his white shirt that Dani had given him.

"I am Father John Buckley." John pulled out the silver cross and kissed it. "I was invited by the Makah tribe to go on the whale hunt when one of the crew had to take his very pregnant wife to the hospital. She went into early labor."

"*Dios mío*," gasped the brothers as they made the sign of the cross.

John blessed them to cement his case. But it didn't mean he was 'out-of-the-hot-water.' He added, "I am taking a sabbatical, and I am visiting churches all along the coast. I do not need to go back to Neah Bay. You could just drop me off anywhere along the way. Or I am fine with wherever you are going."

Carlos kept tapping his left palm with the gun in conflicted thought. His lips were very tight. Both Mexicans just stared at him incredulously.

John took a quick breath. "So, where are we going?"

"Tijuana," said Miguel.

Carlos turned to his brother and growled. He wasn't expecting what had just happened. He really wanted to kill this gringo, but killing a priest, was a little further than he wanted to go. Dumping young hookers was one thing, but a priest was just too big of a sin for him.

"I am hungry!" growled Carlos. "Stop wasting my time and go fucking cook something." He turned and stomped back to the pilothouse cursing under his breath at his misfortune of winding up with a gringo priest.

This yacht really **was** a little ship. The galley was bigger than most American kitchens and would have been the envy of Emeril Lagasse. John went through the latched cupboards like a child under a Christmas tree. The spices alone would have made Julia Child blush. The only thing missing was his mother's fantasy recipe for a *mole* sauce. His façade had worked so far, maybe he was one of Jesus' modern disciples.

John excused himself to wash his hands. He slipped a thick recipe book under his arm and covered it with a yellow apron, and then disappeared into the ship's head (bathroom), to do a little research. The *mole* recipe seemed simple enough. He memorized it. And with a little adlibbing of a few extra spices, 'what could go wrong?'

When he returned, Miguel was wearing a patterned apron. It was a cameo of oak trees. It was very masculine looking, unlike the yellow pattern of daises that John had on.

It looked like Miguel should be standing over his deer with a knife in one hand and a smoking gun in the other. He looked quite handsome in it. Father John was instantly jealous, which was not very Christian of him.

Miguel already had a pot of beans warming for the burrito part of lunch. John put a medium-size pan on the stove. Miguel started laying out the ingredients while Chief John started melting the chocolate; which was the *coup de gras*, the main attraction, in a good mole sauce. As he cooked, Miguel kept suggesting different spices. John would agree. And as he added them, he would watch Miguel's head for a slight nod when just the right amount had entered the pot.

The sauce was perfect. Miguel agreed that it was as good as his mother's, only different. Carlos enjoyed his lunch and calmed down a bit. John began to relax. He had fooled his captures and was going to live. He even had blessed their meal. He was saved.

"Father John," said Carlos. "You have surprised me. I want you to bless my little ship."

"Carlos, my friend, I would be happy to bless you and your fine ship, and its very, very, fine galley."

"Good," said Carlos. "Tomorrow right after you say Mass for me and Miguel, you can bless my boat."

Father John Buckley slept quite fitfully that night. Poor John slipped through Jesus' fingers and was now being tested. He prayed that he really was a real priest and that he would remember how to say a real Catholic Mass. He wished that he could remember more prayers.

Chapter 21

As the sun touched the ocean, two wine glasses touched in remembrance of a dear friend. And with wet eyes, the Kaminski women toasted to the short life of John Buckley. When their glasses were empty, they threw them into the surf as far as they could. They hugged and cried and cursed and sighed heavily. Then they slowly returned to Sandy's patio. It was going to take another bottle to ease a sorrow for a man they hardly knew.

"Should we have some kind of funeral for John?" Dani asked her mother as she uncorked a fresh bottle.

Sandy wiped her eyes, blew her nose, and shrugged her shoulders. "It would be nice. But, we are the only ones that really knew him. And without a body, it would be like a birthday party without the guest of honor."

"Maybe we should notify the parish in Toronto that their missing priest is dead," suggested Dani.

"We don't know for sure it was him. There is no body to identify; in fact, I never even took a picture of him.

"My God Dani! I can't believe I never took his picture."

"Really?" Dani quickly scrolled through her phone's album file. She had taken one. It was somewhere in it. As Dani searched her phone, the night sky turned blood-red. Sailor's delight.

The two grieving women leaned back on the cushioned patio chairs and sipped in sad silence. While Dani looked through her phone pictures, Sandy picked up her phone and went to the new app. The one that had a direct line to the drug-running boat. The little flashing light that showed where-in-the-world it was, made her feel closer to John. It was he that down-loaded it into her phone and the pulsing light was like a tiny heartbeat. It seemed to keep him alive in her heart.

Dani glanced up from her phone pictures, and when she saw what her mother was looking at, she asked, "Where are they at now?"

"Pardon?"

"The boat, the yacht that we put the tracker on, mom. Where is it?"

"Oh!" Sandy widened the image with her thumb and middle finger. She had just been concentrating only on the flashing light.

"Oh wow, they are on the move. It looks like they are off the coast of Oregon. They are moving fast. Where do you think they are headed?"

"John," Dani paused at the mention of the name. "John thinks they are picking up the drugs and the girls in Mexico. Somewhere just south of California; it would shorten their run."

Both women felt better talking about John, in a positive way. This was his mystery. He had solved it. And now it was up to them to bring these men to justice and finish John's efforts.

Dani raised her glass, "We will get these fuckers for John, right?"

Sandy nodded with a smile, and she raised her wine glass and touched her daughter's glass. They drank until the bottle was empty.

Sandy kept the flashing image on her cell phone under her pillow that night. It made her feel better and she dreamed about the poor man she took in.

***

Officer Mary White Owl turned on her cell phone as she made her way to the kitchen and her first cup of black coffee. She wore her red flannel pajamas year-round. Nights on the peninsula, even in summer, were chilly.

Mary still lived with her parents. Her father was a fisherman by summer and an active tribal member by winter. In the off-season, he also worked on his boat and his fishing gear, and he was one of the carvers on the whaling canoe. He liked working with his hands, and he was an excellent teacher of the Makah ways.

Mary's mother was also very industrious. In her spare time, she would weave traditional Makah blankets and sell them at a good price during the tourist season. They made a good living and were able to send their two children on to higher education. Mary went to the police academy and Mary's younger brother attended the University of Washington. This year, her brother was taking summer classes and stayed at the dorm in Seattle. Mary suspected that he had a girlfriend there.

When Mary walked into the kitchen, her father was sitting at the Formica table staring at his cup of coffee. It was almost empty.

"Good morning dad." Mary poured herself a cup and refilled her father's. She replaced the Mr. Coffee pot on its hot plate and she sat across from him. "Why the long face?"

He looked up and gave his daughter a warm smile. He loved these times alone with her. He knew they were limited. "Thanks," he said referring to the coffee. "I am fine," he said as he picked up his cup, gently blew on it, and took a sip.

But he wasn't. It took a minute and then the budding detective figured it out. "It's the canoe, isn't it?"

He nodded.

Mary laughed. "That old whale really put a hurt-en on it, didn't he dad?"

"That's not funny," he said and then he laughed. He couldn't help himself. Her laughs were contagious.

"Just think, dad, you get to do it again. It is a good thing that the other half of that red-cedar tree is still on the beach. You are already half done."

"Well, little girl, that was the easy half. Now we will spend hours and hours and hours carving and shaping that log into a proper Makah whaling-canoe, again."

"But dad, we both know that is the funest part, right?"

"Maybe." he smiled.

"And, don't forget the beer."

"That is true. The cold beer, after a long day's carve, does soothe the blisters on my hands."

He sighed. "Did you know that poor man that drowned? I understand he was not Indian."

"I did. I only met him a couple of times. But he was a good man."

"Will you go to his funeral?"

Mary thought about it for a second. "Yes, if there is one. I don't think he has any relatives. He was just a gardener and new in town. No one seems to know where he came from, and I can't find anything about him on the internet. And since his body was never found, I doubt there will be a funeral."

"No family." Mary's father bowed his head. "That is sad."

"Yes, that is very sad."

Mary sipped her coffee as she scrolled through her cell phone. She clicked on the app that was following Carlos and Miguel's Canadian yacht. The little flashing light said they were on the move and off the coast of northern California. It was time to talk to her partner, Hector Leaning Bear, and decide what they should do next. When she finished her coffee, she got dressed and left for the Makah Indian precinct.

***

When John finished his coffee, he got dressed and left for his makeshift altar in the galley. He spent the night going over and over the ritual of the Mass that he had attended in Forks as best as he could remember it. It was the one that had the pancake breakfast afterward. He wished he would have paid more attention to feeding his soul rather than his belly.

He draped the galley table with a white table cloth. He put two tall candlesticks on each side. He placed a large cookbook just right of center. It was the closest thing he could find that looked like a bible. Now he needed the wine and bread.

He put a white plate on the table and then put a slice of bread on it. It was Dave's Killer Bread. It kind of amused him. But, alas, there was no red wine anywhere onboard. "Maybe a Bloody-Mary will work. It is the color of wine, sort of." He said to himself. But the vodka was just as scarce as wine. All he could find was tequila.

"Tequila? That just might work." While he looked for the tomato juice he hummed one of the songs that he heard at mass. He couldn't remember the name of it, or for that matter, any of the words. But the tune was clear and simple and stuck in his head. He figured that could just make up the words.

Tomato juice, he discovered, was also missing from their galley. John found some paper and a pencil, and then began making a grocery list for his captors/parishioners.

"For God's sake, where in the hell is Jesus? I am surrounded by the largest body of water in the world. All I ask for is to turn a little of it into wine."

John continued his search. Back in the last cupboard and hidden in a far corner of it, he found an old can of beet juice. It was the right color and it was only a year past its expiration date. "What the hell!"

John carefully opened the can and gave it the sniff test. His nose detected nothing foul, other than the smell of beets. He poured some in a glass. The color test was close, it was a little dark. He added in a little tequila which thinned and lightened the color. Better. It was now time for the final test. The taste. He sipped a little into his mouth over the sink, just in case it failed the tongue test.

"Not bad," he said. "It needs more Tequila."

John smiled at his new mixed drink. This tastes as good as a Bloody-Mary. I shall call it a Bloody-Mexican."

The idea of serving it at mass with Dave's Killer Bread, made him laugh out loud. It somehow seemed fitting and right.

"In the name of the Father, and the Son, and the Holy Spirit, amen."

"Amen," repeated Carlos.

"Amen," Miguel made the sign of the cross.

The candles were lit; Mass had begun. John genuflected. He opened his bible, the former thick recipe book, and began mumbling made-up prayers from it. He would throw a saint's name in once in a while and a lot of Jesuses. Carlos and Miguel knelt through most of the service. John got to the communion part of the mass in record time. He had three tall water glasses filled with his consecrated wine. As John blessed his flock, he handed each a small piece of Killer Bread and a glass chalice. Each made the sign of the cross and drank until he emptied his glass. They got off their knees and sat through the rest of the service.

John decided now might be a good time to pass the offering plate. If he ever got out of here, he might need a little cash. He handed Carlos a pie tin. Carlos reached into his pocket and put in a Canadian five-dollar bill and then handed it to his brother. Miguel fished into his pocket and pulled out a hand full of loonies and toonies. He didn't bother to count them. He set the plate on the altar.

John quickly ended his mass. He blew out the candles, picked up the offering, genuflected, and left the Holy Galley. Once he got to his cabin, he counted the coins in his pocket. "Maybe tomorrow I will try a sermon."

***

Officer Hector Leaning Bear counted the coins in his pocket. He counted out enough for two doughnuts and a coffee.

He left the 7-Eleven and got into his police cruiser. He had gotten a call from Mary. She told him that the Yacht was moving south. By the time Hector had arrived at the precinct, Mary was already in his office.

Hector walked in and closed the door. He then handed her one of the doughnuts. The maple bar.

"Thanks," she said, as she stuffed one end of it into her mouth. After flushing it down with a little coffee, she slid her phone towards Hector. "See, they are making another drug run."

Hector studied the screen and sipped his coffee. "I see."

"Isn't there anything we can do?" asked Mary.

"You see that little wavy line that follows the coast?"

Mary nodded and took another bite of her maple bar.

"That is the continental shelf. They are traveling outside that line, which is in international waters. And when they come back, they will travel those same waters until they reach Canadian waters. We cannot legally search them for any reason in foreign waters. And Canada will not board them without solid evidence. Out there, beyond that line, they are beyond the laws of governments. They are now governed by Maritime Law, which is basically an unwritten code of the sea. And it is enforced by the captain of his ship."

"So, your saying, we are going to do nothing?"

Hector handed Mary a napkin. She wiped the sticky maple frosting from her lips and her hands.

Hector added. "I didn't say that. We watch. We wait. They will make a mistake. And, as people of the First Nations of this land, we have some wiggle room. Especially, when it comes to scouting for whales in a fast power boat between here and Canada." Hector slid the phone back to Mary and gave her a sly smile. He then asked, "Any more important questions?"

"As a matter in fact, I do." Mary looked into Hector's dark-brown eyes. "When are we going to meet your son's new girlfriend?"

Chapter 22

Casa de Mar cruised south for three days, and she was now entering her third night. It had been a pleasant run, at least weather-wise. Each day the sun would set a little earlier and the days were becoming a little hotter. John guessed that they were nearing the latitude of southern California.

John also noted a slight change of direction, south by southeast. They were entering American waters. John decided to spend the night on the deck. They were now in a warm latitude.

John made a cup of instant coffee and worked his way to the upper deck. He brought a wool poncho with him and spread it out on a chaise lounge. If it got cold he figured he could cover himself with it. He put the lounge in an upright position and snuggled in. He sipped the coffee as he watched the sun disappear into the far horizon.

Soon the stars began appearing across the infinite sky, just like popcorn popping in a black kettle. The moon's monthly cycle was moving towards its dark phase. The only thing to keep John company during the long night was a billion twinkling stars. It was enough. He felt content even though he was riding with drug runners that had no qualms about killing him.

An hour or so later, a haze of dim light polluted the ocean's eastern horizon. 'Probably LA,' he said to himself.

The west wind takes foul Asian air and filters it through rain clouds on its journey across the wide Pacific Ocean. The air arrives moist and clean and filled with oxygen. John took a deep breath of this air and sighed. He began wondering what was going to happen to him next. The night sky and the warm breeze were almost spiritual, almost heavenly. It was just too nice to worry about things that he had no control over. He looked up into the sky and was sure that a pair of the sparkling stars were the eyes of God watching over him.

He fell asleep fairly contented.

Somewhere between midnight and the wee hours of the morning, John's eyes popped open. Something felt different. He sat up. The engines' vibrations slowed to a slight hum. The yacht was slowing down. He jumped to his feet and saw a million lights that were flooding the sky not far ahead of them. They had reached their destination.

John went to the port rail and leaned over trying to get a better look at the town. It filled the western shore from as far as he could see in the north, to just as far in the south. This had to be Tijuana.

Carlos took his boat in a tight circle and then put it in neutral. John then heard the anchor chain as it rattled over the bow roller. When the anchor settled on the sandy bottom, Carlos eased the engines into reverse and slowly backed up until the thirty-ton Yacht stopped moving. The anchor was set. He killed his engines and turned on his anchor light.

John wasn't sure what was going to happen next. He was pretty sure he was still safe. If they were going to dump him at sea, it would have already happened. They now considered him harmless. So, he joined them on the upper deck.

The deck contained a crane, the one with the hidden tracking device, and two small fiberglass powerboats. They were the tenders for ferrying back and forth to land when anchored. And they could serve as lifeboats in an emergency. Carlos turned on the control box for the crane. He hoisted the boom and swung it over one of the tenders. Miguel took the cabled hook and fastened it to the hoisting straps on the small boat. Carlos lifted it out of its cradle and rotated the boom so that the tender was over the open water. He gently began lowering the boat into the water. Miguel quickly went to the lower deck and then over the side and into the small tender as it splashed down. He unstrapped it, fired off the Honda outboard, and left for the shore.

"Wow," said John. "He was in a hurry. Is he mad at us?"

Carlos shook his head and chuckled as he watched his brother motor to shore. "He has a lover in town. We won't see him until it is time to leave." He then looked at John. "You should get some sleep. In the morning I will take you to *San Pablo's*. I know the *Padre* there. I think you will like him and his beautiful church. He speaks good English."

Carlos yawned and went up to his bunk in the pilothouse. John went back to his chaise lounge. He put the poncho on and laid down. He closed his eyes and sighed happily knowing that he was not going to be killed, and within seconds, he was snoring.

***

Sandy woke up to the sound of raindrops as they fell and splattered on her rooftop. It had cooled a little, and the warm quilt that was snuggled over her begged her to stay in bed. But the coffee pot also wanted her attention.

She sat up. The coffee pot won. She climbed out of bed, threw on a robe, and went into the kitchen. She slipped her favorite mug under the coffee maker and pressed the start button. A few seconds later, it was done. With the cup in her right hand and her phone in her left, she went into the great room and eased into the light-green, cabriole-sofa that was in front of the fireplace. She set her phone on the end table and picked up the remote to the gas fireplace. She pushed the *on* button and put her feet up on the matching, cushioned stool in front of the soft couch.

She sat there quite content and stared at the fire on this rainy morning with a hot cup of coffee. She took a long sip and set her cup down and picked up the phone. She could feel her daughter.

Seconds later the phone rang. It was Dani.

"Hi mom; have you looked at your phone? The boat stopped moving. It is on the coast of Tijuana. John was right."

"Good morning, sweetie." I was just about to take a look."

"I'm sorry mom, did I wake you?"

"No, I have been up for hours. Since it's raining, I decided to work on my novel."

"How's that coming?"

"Slow," replied Sandy. It actually had stopped dead. "I am supposed to meet with my writing group at Giovanni's for lunch."

"That's good." Dani tried to sound positive. But she knew her mother was taking John's death pretty hard. It was good to hear that she was getting back into her old life. Even Dani missed the old fool more than she thought she would. He had touched both their hearts. But life moves on.

***

Hector stopped for doughnuts on the way to work. Mary White Owl was already in his office seated in front of his desk.

"Where are they now?" he asked as he sat in front of her.

"They are stopped in Tijuana. I am pretty sure this is where they will pick up their drugs and the slave girls."

Officer Leaning Bear took a bite of his bear-claw and studied Mary's phone. "Maybe they just stopped to fuel up. That was a long run for them. We need to watch and see what happens."

Mary took a bite of her maple bar. Hector could tell she was getting impatient. But there was still nothing they could do. He was thinking that a surprise visit when they hit the Straits of Juan de Fuca, might work. He just needed a way to justify it.

"You know what, Mary? I think that it's high time that we meet my son's secret girlfriend."

Mary choked on her doughnut. She quickly rinsed it down with coffee and smiled with excitement.

"Unless of course, if you don't want to go. I could find something for you to do here."

Mary ignored Hector's last statement. She quickly stood up and headed for the door. "Are you coming?"

***

Carlos carefully lowered the second tender into the water. John climbed in and unhooked the cable for him. He tied the small boat to the side of the yacht and waited for Carlos.

After Carlos climbed into the tender, he started the engine. He was wearing a light-colored silk-shirt and tan cargo pants and all of his pockets were full of something. He pointed to the tied rope and grunted. John unhitched it and shoved off.

Carlos clicked the lever into its forward gear and he throttled the engine up until it screamed in pain. A minute later he stopped the engine. They had arrived. The momentum slid the boat well onto the sandy shore. John retrieved the long rope that was tied to the bow and jumped out. Carlos climbed out and took the rope, and then he walked up to a small palm tree. He securely fastened the rope to it. Behind the tree, there was a run-down shack. It looked like a storage shed badly in need of a carpenter and a little paint.

Carlos whistled and then shouted, **"Guido, you in there?"**

From around back a small boy came running. He wore blue jeans and a faded HOGWARTS t-shirt. His thick black hair was cropped short and coverer the top half of his forehead. He had an innocent smile that exposed nice teeth. He seemed sweet.

"*Señor* Carlos, it is good to see you."

One of Carlos's stingy smiles appeared on his face. "Guido, my little friend, it is good to see you too." He reached into one of his pockets and pulled out a fist full of *pesos.* He handed the wad of cash to Guido. "You take good care of my boat."

"I will *amigo.*" He stuffed the cash into his left pocket and pulled a switchblade from his right one. He opened it and said with a stabbing motion, "I will kill anyone that touches your fine little ship."

Carlos fondly rubbed the sweet, little killer's head. "I know I can count on you." He turned to John and grunted something in Spanish, and then he turned and walked up the narrow path that led to the highway. John smiled at the nice, knife-wielding boy, shivered, and followed Carlos.

There was already a cab waiting for them. Carlos climbed in front and John crawled in the back. The cab was clean but smelled of tacos.

The cab driver accelerated down the narrow highway at an ungodly speed towards town. No one wore seatbelts. In fact, there were none in the backseat. And here John thought that he was out of harm's way, now that he was off the boat.

Somewhere near town and on a very narrow street, and what looked like pre-Columbian buildings on both sides of it, the cab stopped. The buildings were so close together that they seemed to be supporting each other.

John and Carlos got out. Carlos handed the driver a small wad of *pesos* while John just sweated. It was very hot. The cab driver left at an unsafe speed, especially considering all the pedestrians wandering the narrow sidewalks.

Carlos entered one of the buildings. It had large, dirty, plate-glass windows on both sides of the entrance door. One could not see inside. It looked like it had been a restaurant at one time. John followed Carlos inside.

"Wow!" It was a restaurant.

John had mixed emotions. But he was hungry enough to try it. The place was not up to John's standards of clean dining. In fact, on the 5-point dining-scale, Zagat would probably rate this place at negative 3. The flies alone were enough to make one run from the place. But John did notice that each table had a small Mexican girl that waved a palm-weaved paddle to discourage said flies. They actually made the place look kind of quaint, in a gothic sort of way. "What the hell?" said John to himself. The smell from the kitchen seemed fine.

John followed Carlos to an empty booth. When they slid-in, a pretty señorita came up to their table and began cleaning it. Carlos asked for a *cerveza, "Dos Coronas, Por favor."* She left immediately to fetch the beers. She would finish cleaning when she returned. She knew a man's priorities.

The dirty-gray walls were plastered and had many repair patches on them. A couple of light bulbs hung from the ceiling that gave out a dim light. A few large *Sombreros* hung on pegs between sticky-tubes of flytraps. Cigarette smoke clouded the ceiling. It was a little depressing.

The waitress returned with the beers and took the order. Except for Carlos, no one in the place spoke or understood English. So, Carlos ordered.

"Huevos motuleños. Y dos cervezas más."

The waitress nodded and then motioned to one of the young fly-chasers. A petite girl, around the age of, maybe twelve, forced a smile and came to the table. She raised her fly-chaser over the table and began swaying the palm paddle back and forth over the table. It also worked as a fan and the slight breeze felt good.

The girl wore a clean yellow dress that was a little large for her frail shoulders. Her skin was fair with flaxen brown hair, and she had dark blue eyes. She didn't look very much like the other Mexican children that John had seen along the streets. John then looked closer at the other children as they waved their long-handled fans. They also shared traits of different races.

Carlos saw the question on John's face. "They are children of prostitutes. American soldiers and navy men come to Tijuana for a little sex. Sometimes girls get pregnant. So their pimp, he brings children here. These nice people feed them and work them until they are old enough to work for the pimp. It is the only life that they know. Sad, no?"

John nodded, "It is a very sad cycle, Carlos. Very sad indeed."

Breakfast arrived.

As the waitress slid the hot plates in front of them, Carlos explained what he had ordered. "This is a Yucatan breakfast. Mi *madre* cook this for me when I was a small boy. This is the only place where you can find it this far north."

John sniffed his breakfast. There were two crispy tortillas topped with black beans, layered with perfectly fried eggs, and topped with a tomato-based sauce with peas, ham, and cheese that were lying on an oval plate. And it was accompanied by a fried plantain. It was a perfect mixture of sweet and savory. The Zagat scale just jumped into positive numbers. John dug in.

Carlos was in a hurry. He wolfed down his breakfast and chugged his beer, he then climbed to his feet. Which, John considered a mortal sin because the meal was heavenly good. And it should be savored and he wasn't quite finished eating.

Carlos put a handful of pesos on the tabled and started to leave. John thought that this might be a good time to ditch the crazy bastard, but, in a town that spoke a different language and a city John was totally unfamiliar with, he decided it best to stick with Carlos. He needed Carlos to drop him off at Saint Paul's Church, and from there, he had a good chance of finding his way back to America.

John stuffed his mouth and got up. The paddle-waving girl stopped and stepped back out of his way. John reached into his pocket and pulled out a Canadian coin. He wanted to tip the poor girl. He had no pesos. So, he put two loonies in her hand and chased after Carlos.

The little girl stared at the coins and her eyes brightened. This was not a peso; these were Canadian coins that were worth close to 40 pesos. She put the coins in her pocket and followed the man out the door.

No one saw her leave.

Chapter 23

Mary White Owl was on her second cup of coffee when Hector Leaning Bear arrived. Hector had suggested stopping for an early lunch at Giovanni's before going to his fishing cabin on the coast. He did not want to arrive too early. This was an unannounced visit to meet Henry's new girlfriend. He wanted to make sure they were up and dressed to minimize the surprise and keep it light and friendly. And then the hard part, he would have to break the news to his wife.

When Giovanni saw Hector walk into his fine dining establishment, he quickly retrieved the coffee pot and a clean mug. As Hector slid into the booth across from Mary, Giovanni set the cup in front of him. He filled the cup and then he added a little in Mary's.

"Breakfast?" asked Giovanni.

Mary nodded. "I would like a small stack of pancakes."

"Blueberries?"

"Please," and then she added, "And bacon."

Giovanni nodded and turned to Hector. "What does your belly desire this morning?"

"Just coffee for me, thanks."

Giovanni scoffed. "But you have criminals to catch and crime to halt. May I suggest Anna's hot biscuits and eggs that are swimming in white, buffalo-sausage, gravy? The buffalo gives you great power."

Mary gasped. "That's what I want…and a side of the pancakes."

Giovanni laughed. "I, so love a *giovane donna* that loves to eat." He turned to Hector and raised a shameful eyebrow.

Hector chuckled. "Fine, I will have the same."

"*Eccellente*!" chimed Giovanni just as a new customer entered his establishment. He picked up his coffee pot and vanished as quickly as he had appeared.

Hector finished breakfast with a heavy sigh. He stood up and loosened his belt one notch. Much better. He put enough cash on the table to cover both breakfasts and a good tip. Mary slid out of the booth and thanked Hector for breakfast, and then they left for their surprise visit.

Hector drove. It was a twenty-minute drive to his fishing cabin because he refused to drive over the speed limit.

"When was the last time you were there," asked Mary.

"It's been a while." He said with a little reservation.

Mary focused on her partner's anxious face and asked, "What's wrong?"

"I just realized that it has been over ten years since I took him fishing here. What has happened to the time, Mary? I still consider him a kid. After the whaling accident, and I thought I might have lost him, all I could think about was the years of not fishing with him. I was so happy that he was alive, and that it was John that died. And now I feel guilty about that."

Hector slowed down as a doe and a fawn crossed the road ahead of them. "I don't know what I am going to say to him. He is an adult now and living with a woman that I have never met."

He glanced at Mary "What if I don't like her?"

"Oh, Hector," she laughed. "You are going to love her. I have a good feeling about this."

"I sure hope so." Hector blankly stared out of the windshield with a tight lip for the next couple of miles without saying anything.

"What if Abey doesn't like her."

Mary sighed. "Mothers are bit more picky. My mom has scared off every boyfriend I used to bring around. But I am sure that if she treats Henry good, Abey will like her."

"I suppose you're right."

"Ain't I always?"

Hector shook his head and chuckled. Shortly, he began slowing down the vehicle and turned on to a narrow gravel driveway. It was barricaded by two large concrete blocks that had a chain fastened between them. They had arrived. This was the long driveway to Hector's beach cabin.

Hector put the vehicle in park and climbed out. The chain had a combination padlock connecting it to the blocks. He unlocked it and dropped the chain to the ground and got back into his police vehicle. He drove over the chain and wound his way around tall cedar trees towards the cabin. Mary noticed a little nervous sweat on his forehead, and that made her nervous.

Hector pulled up to the cabin and parked beside Henry's truck. He then shut off the engine. There was no sign of life inside. There was a little blue smoke gently flowing out the woodstove's rusted metal chimney. Mary got out first. She waited for Hector under the front porch roof. She tried the door, it was unlocked. Mary walked in, Hector followed.

"Hello…police. Is anyone home?"

The cabin was tidy and warm. It had the smell of recently cooked bacon and eggs. The curtains were clean and a vase of wildflowers, mostly fireweed, sat on the wood table that was covered with a checkered table cloth. The place definitely showed signs of a woman's touch.

"They must be on the beach," remarked Mary.

"Their fishing-poles are here, so they are not fishing. I wonder what they are doing."

"One way to find out," said Mary as she headed out the door. Hector nervously followed.

The beach consisted of silt, sand, and gravel spread among large boulders. And today, the beach was vast. It was a low tide. And out near the water's edge, they saw two people. One had a shovel and the other a bucket. They were busy digging clams and never noticed that they were not alone.

Mary watched intently as they slowly walked towards them. She saw a squirt of water shoot up from the soft silty mud. Henry's girlfriend pointed to it and then ran over and set her bucket down next to the tiny geyser. Henry quickly started shoveling and when he got close to the buried clam, he threw down his shovel. They both dropped to their knees and begin digging with their hands. When the girlfriend came up with a nice razor clam, she giggled and tossed it in her bucket.

Mary and Hector watched the distracted diggers for a long time and enjoyed every minute of it. The young couple seemed to enjoy each other's company. Hector started feeling better now. He saw that his son was happy.

When the girl happened to look their way, she panicked, and she jumped behind Henry.

Henry looked up with a very surprised look on his face. He wasn't expecting to see anyone on this wide, private beach, let alone his father. He began signing to his father. It was fast and with emotion.

"Henry, Henry, slow down. I am sorry if I startled you. I am not your mother. You are signing too fast." Hector understood a little sign. He was used to communicating with Henry through his wife who was very fluent in sign. This was going to be awkward.

Meanwhile, Mary wandered over to the bucket of clams. She was trying to get a better look at the girlfriend. "Nice clams," she said.

The girlfriend looked at Mary, so she obviously wasn't deaf. She was a petite Asian. She had blond hair with black roots, the hair was obviously dyed. Her skin was very pale and her brown eyes were wide with fear.

"Henry," Mary softly called. "What is your friend's name?"

Henry looked away from his father and signed something to Mary. She did not understand the signing.

"Can she speak?"

Henry nodded. He turned to the girl and signed something to her. She nodded slightly. He presented her to Mary and his father. She bowed and said, "Mei Ling."

"So, you can speak."

Mei Ling nodded. "Ah so, berry little English."

"Good," said Mary. "Where are you from?"

Mei Ling looked at Henry.

Henry signed to her what Mary had asked. She was very limited in her understanding of English. She understood Henry's sign.

Mei Ling then pointed towards the Pacific Ocean.

"Asia?" asked Mary.

Mei Ling shook her head.

"Well then do you mean China?" asked Mary.

Mei Ling was from China, but this was not what she wanted to communicate. Frustrated, she turned and signed to Henry.

Henry nodded and then picked up a small piece of driftwood and wrote the word BOAT in the sand.

Mary gasped at Henry, "I will be right back." She ran back to the police vehicle.

Hector was a little surprised as he watched Mary run back towards the cabin. "Where is she going?" he asked his son.

Henry just shrugged his shoulders.

Mary ran like a rabbit. She grabbed her briefcase from the vehicle and ran back even faster.

She rifled through her files and pulled out the pictures of Carlos's Boat.

When Mei Ling saw it, she froze.

Mary then showed her the pictures of Carlos and Miguel.

Mei Ling began shaking in fear.

Mary then showed her the picture of their Jane Doe. The dead girl that ended up on Sandy's beach.

Mei Ling began sobbing.

Mary looked at Hector. "Okay Hector, we now have our proof, our evidence, and a witness. We now can get a warrant and we can legally stop and search the yacht."

Hector understood and laughed. He hugged Mary. And then he jumped back. That was very unprofessional of him. Especially, in front of his son.

Hector now understood why the girl wanted to stay hidden. She was afraid of being sent back with the people that had bought and sold her. Her English was limited, but with a translator, she could be told that she was safe now. And now with her help, the men that had abducted her could be apprehended and sent to prison.

Hector turned to Mary, "Where is the yacht now?"

Mary turned on her phone. "They're still in Tijuana, Hector."

"Good." He said. Now we have time to get the Canadian Coast Guard to work with us and set up a trap. This will be their last run."

He then turned to his son. "I think it is time for your mother to meet your little friend."

Now Henry's brown eyes were terrified.

<h1 style="text-align: center;">Chapter 24</h1>

⸙

Carlos stopped to answer his cell phone in front of a hat store. Stetsons and sombreros covered the windows. John quickly caught up to him and as he looked at the many different styles and types of these western hats, he pretended not to listen to Carlos's phone conversation.

"*Sí…sí…sí.*" Carlos kept nodding his head. "*Sí…sí, rápidamente.*" Carlos ended the conversation and quickly redialed his phone.

John got nothing.

The second call was for a cab ride, apparently Uber. Carlos read the address from the street numbers written over the door of the hat shop into his cell phone and then he hit the end button.

John guessed that Carlos didn't feel like walking to San Pablo's Catholic Church.

"I am sorry. But I must leave you," said Carlos. "I just received a call, and my supplies," he paused to pick the right words, "the supplies for *mi restaurante* are now being trucked to my boat. I must supervise its loading." He pointed towards town and a short steeple. "That is San Pablo's. I already called Father Arturo. He is expecting you. He welcomes visiting priests from different countries. He said he is looking forward to saying mass with you tonight."

John looked where Carlos had pointed and it was not that far.

The Uber driver arrived in a small, Smart Car and tooted his little horn. The car was painted the colors of the Mexican flag. You couldn't miss it. Carlos waved and it stopped in front of the hat store.

162

Before Carlos crawled into the sardine-can of a car, John made the sign of the cross and pretended to bless Carlos. "You and Miguel have a safe journey home."

"Gracious," said Carlos as he climbed in next to the grinning driver. He barely got the door shut and off they went. The tiny car barely missed a donkey wearing a sombrero that was pulling a taco cart.

There was a small bench under the window of the hat shop. It had a canvas awning over the window that provided a little shade. It was already very hot. John sat on the weathered bench and tried to relax. He was relieved to be rid of his captors and happy that they suspected nothing. And especially happy that he did not have to say another fake mass. He was free and alive. Things were looking up.

Now all he had to do was to get back to America. And do it with very little money, and without being able to speak or understand the language of the country that he was marooned in, and without an ID or a passport in a foreign city that had notoriously horrible jails. John started to get a little overwhelmed. He was in quite a pickle.

"I need to call Sandy." He said to himself. "She probably thinks I'm dead. I need to call Officer Leaning Bear and warn him." John sighed and leaned forward and rested his chin on the palm of his hands. He had no idea of their phone numbers. He remembered the tracking device and knew that Sandy could track the yacht and that she would warn Officer Little-Bear, which made him feel a little better.

"I guess it's time that I just worry about myself. I just need to find a way to sneak across the Mexican border. Once in America, I will have more options. From there, I should have enough money for a bus fare part of the way back. I can hitch-hike the rest of the way." John started feeling a little better. At least now he had a plan. But if he spent any money on food, or anything, he would not have bus fare. His plan was a little weak but doable.

John suddenly felt very alone, a stranger in a strange land. He began thinking back about all of the people that came into his life. This didn't take long; because of his amnesia, he could only remember about a month of his life. But the few that came into his life, he felt very close to, especially Sandy. She took him in without knowing anything about him. Now he would give anything to be working on her garden.

Sandy was sweet. He began visualizing her on the beach sitting on a stool in front of her easel. Her hair was wind-blown. Splashes of paint were on her pretty face. He could see her determined look, as she dabbed oil paint on the canvas in front of her with the precision of a surgeon. The can of beer sitting between her small canisters of primary colors of paint, made him smile. He was missing her the most.

He remembered Sandy telling him how, on depressing days, she would go shopping for shoes, or sometimes even hats.

"Well, what the hell," John said. "I am going to go shopping for a hat, a wide sombrero that I can dance around." The thought of it made him laugh out loud. And when he did, a small girl's laugh joined his.

Quite startled, he looked to his left and there was a small girl sitting next to him. The stealthy little girl had dark blue eyes that were staring up at him. She was wearing a yellow dress that was a little large for her and she looked very familiar.

"Where did you come from?"

"She smiled shyly and pointed down the road."

"I remember you. You were the fan-girl at the cantina."

She nodded.

"So, you understand English?"

She added a proud smile to her nod.

"What is your name?"

"Regina." Her voice was soft and unsure and a little shaky. She was nervous.

"Why are you here, Regina?"

"Everyone calls me, Reggie." Her voice was firmer.

"Why are you not at the cantina fanning flies, Reggie?"

"I know a much better place to shop for hats," she said. "They have even bigger hats for dancing and small pretty ones for your head. You should have a head-hat."

John smiled at her. She was avoiding the subject. But he knew that he must take her back.

"You should go back to the cantina. You must never follow strange men. It is dangerous." John stood up and took her hand. "I will walk with you."

Reggie stood up reluctantly. She and John began walking back towards the cantina.

"Why did you pick me to follow, Reggie?"

"My mom told me to."

"I thought you were an orphan. And how does your mom know me?"

"I live behind the kitchen with other fan-girls. My mother comes by and visits me in the evenings on her way to work. She told me that I am almost old enough to go to work for her pimp. I don't have much time, she told me. She told me I must find a nice, rich, white man that will take me to America."

"The odds of finding that are pretty low, Reggie, pretty low."

Reggie sighed and quietly trudged along with a lowered head. After about a minute, she added, "Odds are worse with a pimp."

She had a point, but John wasn't even sure he could take care of himself. He also began dragging his feet.

Reggie stopped and pulled her hand free. "Are you not a nice man?" She looked him in the eye. "Are you not a rich American?"

"I don't know, Reggie. I really don't."

John really didn't know. He had no idea who he was before he had woken up in the hospital. And if he was a priest, he could be a Canadian citizen, or he could even be an American pimp from Chicago. But he doubted that he was ever rich.

"But I feel that I am a good man."

"And I feel that I am a good girl. I think you will be a good father. Can I call you *padre*?"

John sighed. Her being with him was probably the lesser of two evils for both of them. He began thinking about his short life. He was a vagrant, a gardener, a detective, a Father John, and now was going to be a father/*padre*; life so far had been interesting. "I wonder what I will be next month."

"What did you say?"

"Nothing daughter."

Reggie threw her arms around John and hugged him just like a father.

***

The first thing Sandy did when she got home was to call her daughter to tell her the exciting news.

When Sandy woke earlier that morning, she was feeling blue and melancholy. So, she decided to drive to Sequim for a little shoe-shopping therapy. It was the closest shoe store that sold more than just logging boots.

The nice, young handsome man in the shoe department made sure that Sandy got comfortable and then he wheeled in a small cart filled with women's shoes. When he knelt down and slipped on a pair of Christian Louboutin's blue, patent-leather, pumps, Sandy's sad heart smiled. Her feet begged her to keep them on. And her credit card crawled out of her purse and leaped into her hand. Even the young shoe salesman was impressed with how well they looked on her.

Sandy proudly walked out of the store wearing her new six-hundred-dollar shoes without even a hint of buyer's remorse. When she got into her car, she checked her phone for the time and then the tracking device. The yacht was on the move. She put the old Volvo into drive and sped towards Neah Bay. She had to tell Officer Leaning Bear that Carlos was running drugs their way.

After she parked in front of the Makah Police Department, she quickly went inside. The front desk sent her back to Hector Little-Bear's office. She stormed in with the news.

Officer Mary White Owl was sitting across from Hector. While Sandy caught her breath, Mary couldn't help but notice, "Nice shoes!"

Sandy smiled, "I know." She turned to Hector.

The first thing Sandy did when she got home, well, after finding a cigarette and pouring her wine, was to call her Daughter.

After three rings, "Hi mom, what's up?"

"Oh Dani, they got their evidence."

"Who got what evidence?"

Sandy took a quick draw on her cigarette to calm herself.

"Mom, are you smoking?"

"No," she lied. "Do you remember when John said that he found out that Henry had a girlfriend?"

"Who's Henry?"

"Henry is Hector's son." Sandy took a sip of wine.

"Are you drinking wine?"

"Maybe."

"Well hold on mom. I need a glass. I will be right back." Dani quickly went to her refrigerator and grabbed a bottle of cheap chardonnay. She twisted off the metal cap, tossed it in the sink, and took a drink right from the bottle.

"I'm back." She asked, "Who was Hector, again?"

"Officer Leaning Bear, Dani."

"Oh, right. And there was a female officer too. Officer …Officer White Owl."

"Right, Officer Mary White Owl." Sandy paused for a quick puff. "Well it turns out that Henry's girlfriend knows their Jane Doe."

"Who's Jane Doe, mom?"

"She was the dead girl, we found on our beach."

"Ah, right. Oh, well that's very sad. Were they close?"

"No…well… I don't know if they were close. I didn't ask." Sandy paused, "Oh, I guess that is sad."

"Ok, mom, are you going somewhere with this?"

"Right, yes. She was on the boat with the dead girl and she got tossed in the sea with her."

"Oh, wow. And she survived!"

"Well, apparently!" said Sandy as she rolled her eyes. "And she now can identify Carlos and Miguel. She witnessed the whole thing. Those killers will now get what's coming to them."

Dani began searching for a cigarette. "That's great! I am so happy…" she found her hidden pack "…that they will be caught. John deserves all the credit."

At the mention of John's name, the phone fell silent as they each shed a tear and smoked a cigarette in sad memory of a man that leaped into their life, literally.

Chapter 25

Hurricane Georgia was no peach. This tropical storm reached Category-5 somewhere in the middle of the Gulf of Mexico. It devastated a lot of islands on its western journey across the Gulf. It was predicted to swing north and into Texas.

But the fickle spinning-storm, instead, charged west across Mexico. Once on land, her counterclockwise whirl took her north and into Tijuana. But the mountains and the rugged land of northern Mexico tamed the beast; and by the time it reached the Pacific coast, it was just a thunderstorm. But it did carry a lot of water.

Rivers of rain-water ran down the rough, paved streets of Tijuana and then disappeared into storm-water ditches that eventually empty into the Pacific Ocean. An hour later, the storm was over. The hot sun came back out, the streets dried, and the ditches were empty. The smog and dust were washed out of the air, and the sky became a true blue.

John and Reggie ran for the shelter of the church, but not fast enough. By the time they reached the parish hall, they were soaked. The place was already filled with other wet Tijuanans. (Proper Spanish for these people is, Tijuanense, but most people use the slang, Tijuanero.) In case you cared.

The thunder became a distant rumble and the rain was short-lived. The storm-gathered people became an informal meeting of poor Tijuaneros. The church hall also sponsored a soup kitchen for the needy, so everyone stayed for a meal and a prayer.

So, John decided to check out the kitchen. Reggie closely followed. John immediately volunteered for the late afternoon's feeding of the poor. Reggie was his interpreter and she proudly introduced him as her American *papi*.

Buckets of beans were dumped into big, black pots alongside boiling kettles of rice. A couple of women were rolling corn and flour tortillas. John's clothes dried while working in front of the wide stove in no time. The shelf over the work table was filled with many, many, spices. John couldn't help himself. Some of them, he was sorry that he had tasted.

Pretty soon the parish priest began making his rounds. It was Father Arturo. It was the priest that Carlos spoke of. The one that John was supposed to meet…as a priest.

When Father Arturo saw the light-skinned man in the kitchen, he asked one of the women who he was. She told him she didn't know and that he didn't speak Spanish, but his daughter did. The curious priest immediately worked his way to the stranger.

"*Buenos días*, I am Father Arturo. I understand that you don't speak Spanish." He reached for John's right hand.

John quickly wiped his hands on his flowered apron and then shook the priest's hand. It was soft and warm, but firm. "My name is John. I am honored to meet you, Father Arturo." John recognized the name.

"I understand that you are here with your daughter. Are you a new member of my congregation or just visiting?"

"Just visiting. Your church became a very nice port in the storm. But I do admire your kitchen. I would like to help with the cooking for the unfortunate needy that have gathered here. If that is okay with you?"

"Gracias," said Father Arturo with a nod and then he blessed John and Reggie. He turned to Reggie and asked, "What is your name?"

"Regina, Father." Reggie answered shyly.

"*And where is your mother, Regina?*" Father Arturo asked in Spanish.

"*Sleeping*," answered Reggie back in Spanish. "*She works nights.*"

"*Oh, where does she work?*"

"*Not far from here. She is in the service industry.*"

John did not understand most of what they were saying, but he could tell Reggie was getting uncomfortable with the questions.

Father Arturo then asked, "*Why is it that your father cannot speak Spanish to his daughter? Where does he live?*"

John began to get the drift of what the priest was asking. "**Father**," John interrupted, "Will there be an evening Mass? I would like very much to attend it and see the inside of this beautiful church." John then turned to Reggie, "Reg, will you please fetch me a pan of water and put it on the stove to boil."

"*Sí papi.*" She put a relieved smile on her face and quickly disappeared into the back of the kitchen.

Father Arturo seemed annoyed. He turned to John. "*Sí*, yes John, there is an evening Mass. It starts at seven." He strained a smile and said, "I hope to see you there."

"I am looking forward to it, Father."

Father Arturo started to leave and then paused; he asked. "I am looking for a visiting priest from America. He speaks English. His name is Father John Buckley. Have you seen him?"

"I am sorry, Father. You are the only English-speaking priest that I have met today." John then turned and hollered, "Reggie, what's taking you so long?"

Father Arturo excused himself. "I will let you get back to your cooking and I hope to see you at Mass." He went back to making his rounds.

After John and Reggie finished working in the kitchen, they each filled a plate with beans and rice, and another one with corn tortillas. They found an empty spot in the large eating area. They sat on folding chairs at a long table across from each other. Meals were going to be precious, considering John's limited budget, which made this meal even more enjoyable.

Reggie put some rice and beans on a tortilla and rolled it into a burrito. She stuffed it into her mouth. John followed suit.

"When are we going to America, *papi?*"

"Soon, I hope. I just need to find a remote spot to sneak across the border."

"Why can't we just cross at the border crossing like everybody else? You just tell them that I am your daughter."

John leaned back on his chair, "They will need proof that you are my daughter, or that you were born in America. I have no passport. I can't even prove that I was born in America."

A middle-aged, round, Christian woman stopped at their table with a coffee pot in her hand. "*Café, señor?*"

"Sí," said Reggie, "Dos."

The woman filled two paper-cups with dark coffee and then she set them between Reggie and John.

"*Gracias.*"

She moved on.

Reggie sipped her coffee and made a quirky face, "And just where do you plan to slip across the border?"

John snickered, "First time drinking coffee?"

Reggie nodded, she took another sip and forced a smile. "You do know there is a very high fence on the border, right?"

"I suspected. Surely it's not all the way across Tijuana?"

Reggie shrugged her thin shoulders and started to take another sip.

"Wait." John got up and went to the kitchen and retrieved a small container of milk. He poured a generous amount in Reggie's cup and then added a little to his own. "Try that."

A genuine smile followed her next sip. "I think the wall is all the way across Tijuana," she said.

John sipped his coffee and pointed to an older man sitting near them. "Ask that old man how long the wall is."

"*Señor,*" Reggie slid down two chairs and asked the man if he knew how long the border fence was. He nodded and told her where it ended and what he knew about the wall. He spoke Spanish too fast for John to get any of it. From the look on Reggie's face, it didn't sound good.

"Gracias," Reggie said to him as she sat back in front of John. "Well?"

"He said that it runs a long way. He said there are breaks in it through the desert and it does stop in Texas. I have heard of Texas, but I don't know how far that is."

John whistled. "That is a long, long walk. But doable by bus, I guess."

Reggie added, "And, he said that it stops at a great river."

"Egad…the Rio Grande River!" John leaned back on his chair and laughed, hysterically.

Reggie thought it was a happy laugh and giggled. She sipped her coffee. It was quite good with milk in it.

John sighed and calmly asked, "Do you know how to swim?"

"No… why?"

"*Perdona!*"

They were interrupted by the old man that Reggie had just spoken to. He was standing next to Reggie and holding a cup of coffee. He was wearing old, faded blue jeans and a light-colored T-shirt. His hair was thin and gray and his round face was dark and clean-shaven. He wasn't much taller than Reggie and he looked harmless. "*¿Puedo sentarme?*" he asked.

Reggie nodded. "*Sí, por favor.*"

He sat down and turned his chair and faced Reggie. "*I may be of great service to you.*" He said in Spanish. He understood some English and could speak a little of it.

"*What kind of service?*"

"*I have a friend that has ways to get you on the other side of the border wall.*"

John couldn't understand and became nervous. "What is he saying?"

"He said that he has a friend." Reggie turned back to the old man. "*¿Cómo te llamas?*"

"Pedro," he said.

"*Sí, Pedro. I am Reggie.*

"So, Pedro, tell me about your friend."

"My friend has a friend that has a tunnel under the wall. And for not many pesos, he will let you use his tunnel."

"What did he say?" demanded John.

Reggie looked over at John and scoffed. "He says his friend has a friend."

"I heard the word, peso, Reggie!"

"Shush!" hissed Reggie.

"Don't you shush me; I am your *padre*!"

Reggie snickered and turned back to Pedro. *"¿Cuánto dinero?"*

Before he could answer, Father Arturo came back into the hall. It was time to close up the kitchen and get ready for evening services. Pedro lowered his head and stopped talking.

"Pedro," asked Reggie, *"do you live around here?"*

He nodded.

"Take us to you home and we can discuss this in private."

"Sí," said Pedro and then he got up and calmly walked out of the side door of the parish hall. Reggie followed. A very confused John quickly finished his coffee and followed them. He had no idea what his new daughter had gotten him into. He had only been a father for a few hours and already his twelve-year-old daughter was becoming quite a handful.

Chapter 26

Pedro rented a small shack not far from the church. It was once a tool shed behind the main house. Both buildings were unpainted, wood-framed, structures with small windows and tin roofs. Pedro shared his area with several chickens and a large rooster that had long, blue tail feathers and with red and gold chest feathers, and a few other exotic colors thrown in. He was a beautiful bird.

Inside the modest little hovel's kitchen area was a small sink that was installed on the wood workbench. It had an electric, two-burner, cook-top on one end, and at the other end was a small, noisy refrigerator. In the far corner was a commode that had a curtain on a rod in front of it for privacy. In another corner was the sleeping area with an army cot in it. An old La-Z-Boy recliner and an ancient couch, in front of a TV, sat in the middle of the room. It also had a small Formica table with a couple of folding chairs, just like the ones in the church hall. Several light bulbs hung from the ceiling that had pull chains to turn them on and off. The place was crude but surprisingly clean and tidy.

Pedro ushered John and Reggie into his house and sat them at his Formica table. He went to the narrow fridge and pulled out a can of Coca Cola and set it in front of Reggie. He found two clean glasses and set them on the table. He rummaged under his sleeping cot and pulled out a mason jar with some kind of clear liquid in it. He then set it on the table next to a shaker of salt. He was ready to do business.

An hour later, he realized that the rich American was not rich. He had hoped to collect enough money from him so that it would also pay for his own passage to America. But alas, it was not going to work with his new guests.

"Dios mío," he sadly exclaimed. And with a sigh, he poured a little tequila in his glass, shook a little salt on his wrist, poured the shot down his throat, he then licked the salt off his wrist. With a sad sigh, he got up and went to a paper sack near the door. He opened it, reached in, and filled his hands with dried rice and beans. He kicked the door open and walked out without saying a word. He called to the chickens and when they saw him coming, they quickly gathered around him. He fed and softly spoke to the little hens for a long time. When he was finally done, he went to the nesting box and gathered a few eggs. He came back inside with an unsure look on his face. He now realized that his guests needed more help than he did.

After he came back inside, he sat back down and gently picked up the mason jar of tequila. He poured it slowly and carefully so that the little worm in the bottle stayed in the bottle.

"Why is there a worm in that jar?" asked John.

Reggie shrugged her shoulders and then she asked Pedro.

Pedro laughed and shook his head, "Gringos!" He then explained it to her.

Reggie translated. "He said that the worm is a moth larva and that it makes the Tequila tastes much better."

"Wow, I am truly impressed," said John. "So, this stuff could actually taste worse." John shook a little salt on his wrist and said, "You tell Pedro I'm not eating the worm. He can have the whole thing."

Reggie slept on the couch and John snuggled into the La-Z-Boy and then he began his tequila-induced sleep. They all slept well that night. Tomorrow, the three of them would work on plan B. The America or Bust plan.

***

Hector Leaning Bear just got off the phone with the Canadian police when Mary White Owl walked into his office with their daily doughnuts. She set them on his desk and went for coffee. She came back with two cups and a question. "What did you find out?"

Hector picked up the apple fritter. "They seemed a little hesitant at first. But when I told them that the yacht was Canadian registered and that there were drugs and trafficked girls ending up in their country, they decided to help with the sting."

"Oh, gooud," mumbled Mary with a mouthful of doughnut. She clicked on the phone's tracking device as she sipped her coffee. "They are running off the coast of northern California now. Another day or so and they should be here."

Hector leaned back in his chair. "I talked to a couple of our tribe's fishermen. The ones with larger boats; and they volunteered to help with the blockade. Since they're fishing boats, Carlos should not suspect anything, and they should be able to get quite close in case Carlos decides to dump his cargo. My fisherman will be armed deputies."

Mary leaned back in her chair. "What did you find out about that Chinese girl, Mei Ling. Will she be sent back to China after she identifies Carlos and Miguel?"

"Mei Ling comes from a poor family. Her father thought that he was sending her to America for a better life. He paid a man to arrange her passage but once he got the money, she was thrown into a container and shipped to Mexico with forty other young girls. She says she is in love with my son and wants to stay in this country. Henry says he wants to marry her."

Mary choked on her doughnut. "Wow, does your wife know?"

"Only that he has a girlfriend." Hector leaned forward. "With all the questions and with finding an interpreter, they have been stuck here in town. I rented a motel for her and Henry while in town. But tonight, I am planning on bringing them home for dinner and a formal introduction, and hopefully, the good news."

Mary leaned forward. "Can I come?" She then stood up, "Please, can I come?" She leaned over the desk. "Does Abey drink wine?"

Hector leaned back. Mary was uncomfortably close. "She prefers beer."

"Good, I will bring a case."

***

Sandy didn't feel like painting and was bored, so she decided on a late lunch at *Giovanni's*.

By the time she got there, she had lost her appetite, so she just ordered the house wine. When Giovanni brought the wine he also brought a small basket of sliced Italian bread that was buttered adequately and dusted with a little garlic power. She pretty much had the place to herself. The wine was good and the warm bread was excellent. She was already feeling less melancholy.

Giovanni was his chatty self and he kept up on all of the Neah Bay's small-town gossip. His feminine side was greatly appreciated by all the old bitties in town.

"Have you heard the news?" Giovanni didn't wait for an answer. "Hector's son, Henry, is marring that Chinese girl."

"That's nice," said Sandy. And then she realized what Giovanni was saying, "Oh, the Chinese girl. Well good for them. I should take them a bottle of wine." Sandy then pulled out a pen and an old envelope from her purse. She flipped it over and asked, "Where does Hector live?"

Giovanni took the pen from her and drew a detailed map to the Leaning Bear residence. He recommended beer just as another customer walked in. He scurried to the door.

Sandy stopped at the Mini Mart and picked up a six-pack of IPA beer, it was a favorite of Dani's. She threw in a pack of cigarettes at the last minute. She promised herself that this pack would be the last one… again.

Giovanni's directions were good and it didn't take long to find the long gravel-drive that wound its way to Leaning Bear's humble home. She parked close to the front porch and decided to wait inside her car, because she was greeted by a bunch of barking beasts.

Soon an old lady came out onto the front porch. She waved her cane and cursed at the noisy hounds. The dogs lowered their tails and went to the shady side of the house and plopped down. They had done their duty. With panting-tongues, they just watched. It was a hot day.

By now, they seemed harmless enough, so Sandy opened her door and slowly got out. She put the cigarettes in her purse, hung its long strap over her left shoulder, grabbed the brown bag of beer, and with a deep breath, walked to the porch. She had met Hector's wife once, and the old woman on the porch was definitely not her.

Sandy stopped at the first step and smiled at the old woman. "Hi, I am Sandy. Is Abey around?"

The old woman turned towards the screen door and shouted something in an odd language. Sandy assumed the Makah dialect. She was surprised that anyone still spoke it. She had noticed that the younger generation never bothered to learn it and only spoke in English.

A tall woman came to the door. Sandy could see it was Abey through the screen.

"Hello, are you lost?" she asked.

"Hi Abey, it's me Sandy, John's landlady."

"Ah, right." Abey came out onto the porch. The old woman went to a metal patio table and sat down. She lit a cigarette and quietly watched.

"Well, Sandy, this is a pleasant surprise." Abey turned to the old woman, "This is my mother. We just call her Grandma Leaf."

"I am pleased to meet you, Grandma Leaf."

The old woman nodded and then pointed to the brown paper-bag that Sandy held under her right arm and said something in the old language.

Sandy looked up at Abey. "She can't speak English?"

"Oh, she can; she just won't. She asked what's in the bag that you're carrying."

"Beer." Sandy pulled out the six-pack."

"Well come up on the porch and have a seat, Sandy. Would you like a clean glass?"

Sandy grinned. "Oh, I can drink out of the can, just fine." She put the beer on the round patio table and popped open three cans. Abey put the unopened cans in a cooler under the table that was already filled with ice and Olympia Beer. She faced her guest. "So, what brings you here, Sandy?"

"I just heard the news. And I wanted to congratulate you on the upcoming wedding."

Abey leaned back on her chair and raised her thick eyebrows. "What upcoming wedding?"

"The wedding of your son to that poor the Chinese girl that…" Sandy stopped talking when the look on Abey's face went from confused to an angry red.

"Oh, I'm sorry," said Sandy. "You didn't know they were getting married, did you?"

Abey took a deep breath and calmed. "Who told you?"

"Giovanni."

Abey squeezed her beer can so hard that it erupted into an IPA foam.

Grandma Leaf snickered and handed her daughter another beer.

Abey sighed opened the fresh can and chugged it. "I just found out that he had a girlfriend." She crushed the empty can. "How does that Italian man know everything about everyone? What is he, Mafia?" Abey looked a Grandma Leaf. "What you smiling at?"

The old woman handed Abey another can and said something in Makah.

Abey shook her head. "I know he needs a woman, mom. But I don't know this woman. She's a foreigner. She is not tribe."

Sandy pretended not to listen and began to read the fine print on her beer can.

Abey tightened her lips as her mother talked seriously, and then the old woman laughed at her indignant daughter.

Abey threw her hands into the air. "I don't want to hear about exotic Chinese sex." She popped open the beer can and took a drink. "Where did you…and how do you know about all this sex stuff, mom?"

"The Discovery channel," she said in English.

Abey shook her head and continued in English, "Discovery…Ha, I think you have been watching porn. And here I have been blaming Hector for that…that, smut on my computer."

Grandma Leaf sighed heavily, "I miss your father."

Sandy finished what was left of her beer. Too much information. She was definitely going to need another one. She was now wishing that she would have purchased a whole case. As she started in on her second IPA, a blue Honda came up the driveway. It parked beside Sandy's Green Volvo. It was Officer Mary White Owl.

When Mary climbed out of her car, she grinned and waved at everyone on the porch.

Grandma Leaf waved back.

The horde of crying canines ran down and greeted her. She petted them enthusiastically, and after they were properly greeted, they moseyed back to the shade. Mary retrieved a case of Rainier Beer from the back seat and brought it up on the porch. She set the case on the wood deck and then she began transferring the beer to the large white cooler. What didn't fit, she placed on the table as their next round of beer. She pulled up a chair, popped open a beer, and sat down.

"What?" she said as she looked at the odd expressions of the females staring back at her. "Ohhh, you already know! Who told you?"

"Giovanni," said Sandy.

"That damn fascist! What is he, Mafia?" exclaimed Mary White Owl while keeping a straight face. She then added, "Hector is on his way here with Henry and Mei Ling with the good news. It was supposed to be a surprise." Mary looked at Abey. "Mei Ling seems nice. I think you will like her."

During the awkward silence, Sandy reached into her purse and pulled out the pack of cigarettes. "Would anyone else like a smoke?" They all nodded.

Hector's police SUV was the next to arrive. He parked beside Mary's Honda. He was warmly greeted by his four-legged friends. He got out of his vehicle and petted each one vigorously. They were happy to see him. When he looked up at the smoking women on the porch, he saw cold stares, and they sure didn't seem to be near as friendly as his pets. He took a deep breath and walked up to his house. As a cop, he was used to forcing himself into walking towards danger.

Hector could see that someone had spilled the beans. "Good afternoon ladies. It seems that my news has traveled a bit faster than me. I am glad that you all are here. Henry will be pleased."

"And just where is Henry?" asked Abey.

"He is right behind me. I wanted to come ahead to prepare you for the exciting news. Just how much do you know?"

"Oh, she knows everything, Hector, everything," said Mary. The rest of the beer-drinking women confirmed it with a quick nod.

Grandma Leaf chuckled at her poor son-in-law, and then she handed him a beer and just shook her old gray head. Hector sat on the porch swing. He felt a little safer at the far end of the porch.

Chapter 27

enry was running late. But before he presented his girlfriend
to his mother, he knew that he had to take Mei Ling shopping.
The first item on their list was hair dye, black hair dye. It was
her natural color. Next was a pretty new dress. Dresses were limited in
the small reservation town of Neah Bay. But they did find a secondhand
store and it had an acceptable dress. It was light-blue with short sleeves,
and the soft fabric draped to the top of her knees. The nice lady there
found a pair of matching, high-heeled shoes. The picking and buying
took a little longer than they anticipated because Mei Ling could not
speak English and Henry just could not speak. But the people in the
store were patient and very helpful. The dress looked especially nice on
her.

Even though he was late, Henry drove his old Ford pickup at the speed
limit. He was quite nervous and very much wanted Mei Ling to make
a good impression on his mom. This would be the first girl that he ever
brought home. He drove with one hand on the wheel so he could sign
with the other one. Mei Ling sat quietly and nodded to his comforting
words. But she was terrified. Almost as scared as she was, when Carlos
shoved her off the Yacht that horrible stormy night, only about a month
ago.

Henry stopped signing and turned on his left turn signal. He slowed
down as he pulled onto the long gravel drive that led to his home. As he
drove up the dirt road, he reached over and took Mei Ling's hand. She
squeezed back hard and forced a smile.

Henry parked beside his father's tan SUV. The dogs immediately ran to greet him. Mei Ling cried in panic at the dogs that were charging her way and threw her arms around Henry. He pulled her hands free and signed that it was alright. "*The dogs are friendly, they are pets.*"

Henry got out of the truck and the dogs surrounded him, each one was excited and wanted to be petted first. Between the licking, the panting, and the patting, the dogs calmed and Henry coached his girlfriend out of the truck. At first, she was afraid to touch the big dogs but after a while, she found them quite affectionate.

While Mei Ling was befriending the dogs, Henry noticed that besides his dad and mom, and his Grandma Leaf, two other women were waiting for him on the porch. He recognized Mary White Owl but not the other woman sitting there. He also noticed a lot of empty beer cans on the patio table. '*Well at least, they should be a little relaxed,*' he thought to himself. He waved and they all waved back. '*Well, that's a plus.*'

He took Mei Ling by the hand. It was time. With sweaty palms and forced smiles, they approached the porch.

Hector quickly got up from the porch swing and met them halfway. This was his show. He gave his son a hug and said, "Congratulations, and don't worry, I still wear the pants around here." Henry stepped back and signed, "But I worry that mom's balls are bigger. Sorry, dad."

Hector understood and chucked. He cuffed Henry on the shoulder. He turned to Mei Ling. She gave him an honorable bow. He had never seen her in a dress or with black hair. She was beautiful. He returned her bow, even though he really wanted to give her a hug, but thought it might be inappropriate. He put his arm around his son's shoulder. "I think it's time for Mei Ling to meet the rest of the family."

***

Carlos leaned back on his captain's chair and put his feet on the console. The yacht was on autopilot, the sun was setting, and he had a glass of Patron on ice in his right hand. He was happy. He loved being on the water.

He had thought about retiring from these illegal runs. The restaurant was making good money, but he would miss the raw excitement and these special times at sea.

Miguel interrupted his moment when he came in with two plates of fish tacos. He set one on the console in front of his brother and the other in front of the empty chair. He then retrieved a cold beer from the cooler for himself.

"How are the girls doing, Miguel?"

"Good, Carlos. Their drugs are wearing off and they seem to like my cooking. They were quite hungry." Miguel picked up one of his tacos and filled his mouth.

Carlos did likewise. He glanced at his GPS. "We are close to Oregon. We will be home in two days."

Little did he know, he wasn't the only one that knew of his position, and of where and of when he would be home.

***

After Hector introduced his future daughter-in-law to her new family and friends, he fired off his Webber barbeque. Since Henry had not been fishing for salmon for a few days, Hector had to forage in his freezer for meat. He found several packages of elk steak. He laid them on the kitchen counter to thaw. Abey began cooking some red beans. She remained quiet and ignored her inconsiderate husband. Hector could tell that she was mad at him, but he could tell she wasn't displeased with Mei Ling. He began humming.

As Hector prepared the meat, and as Abey added spices and fried bacon to her beans, she seemed to relax. The beer was definitely helping his cause. He caught her snickering. She always made fun of his gravelly voice when he hummed or sang. Hector smiled and continued humming. He now knew that he wouldn't be sleeping alone tonight.

Mary White Owl and Sandy sat on the porch swing and each agreed that they liked the girl. She seemed very loving of Henry and he seemed protective of her. They talked of many things as the evening wore on, but neither mentioned her gardener, John. Neither of them wanted to ruin the happy feeling they had for the young couple.

Sandy and Mary were sitting on the porch swing. The young couple spent most of their time talking to Grandma Leaf while sitting around the patio table. Their conversations were slow, to say the least. Grandma Leaf only spoke Makah and understood a little sign. Mei Ling only spoke Mandarin and understood a little English. And poor Henry couldn't speak at all and didn't understand women. He was kept busy signing.

Henry signed a question to his grandmother.

She snickered and told him in her language that, "*Of course Abey won't like her. She's your mother. I didn't like your father the first time she brought him around.*"

"*You like him now, don't you?*" signed Henry.

Grandma Leaf nodded, slightly. "*Maybe.*"

"*Do you like Mei Ling?*"

Grandma Leaf shrugged her thin shoulders and asked, "*Does she understand your sign?*"

"A little," signed Henry.

"*Ask her if she is Christian.*"

Henry asked.

Mei Ling was confused as to what he was asking. They had never discussed religion and so, the sign for the word *Christian* was never learned or explained to her. Henry made the sign of the cross in front of her.

"Ah," she nodded in understanding of the word, and then she shook her head and said, "Confucianism."

"What the hell is Confucianism?" asked Grandma Leaf in English.

Henry turned to Mei Ling and silently asked her what Confucianism was.

She hesitated in thought. She raised her hands to sign and paused, trying to think of the simplest way to explain her concept of her God.

"Confucianism," she signed, "is a form of Chinese-Christian-ism, only it is a lot older and it is more earthy, like your old Indian customs."

Grandma Leaf liked her answer. She signed her next question directly to her, and Mei Ling understood and started signing her answer, but she was rudely interrupted by Henry clasping her arms. He also understood Grandma Leaf's question.

"*Grandma, you cannot ask her that!*" signed Henry.

"*Shush, little man.*" She was back in the old tongue. "*Is she good in bed, Henry?*" She explained, "*It is very important for two people to have good sex. Your grandfather and me, well…*"

Henry covered his eyes. This was too much information. When he heard Mei Ling laugh, he opened them again. They were smiling at each other. He just shook his silent head.

Grandma Leaf signed to Mei Ling. "*My ears are bad. I could not understand your name. Please say your name to me.*"

"Mei Ling." She said and then she respectably bowed to the old woman.

"Ah, May Leaf," repeated Grandma Leaf.

Mei Ling nodded. "Yes, Mei Ling."

Grandma Leaf nodded. "Yes, May Leaf. I like it very much."

Henry threw his hands in the air. His ears were working just fine, it was his voice that didn't work. Then it amused him and he laughed silently. Perhaps his mother will like her new Indian name.

Mei Ling asked honorable grandmother if she would let her braid her long, beautiful, gray hair.

Grandma Leaf nodded but added, "*Must be in two braids. That is squaw way. Only men have single braid.*"

Henry became pleased, as he watched Mei Ling brush his grandmother's long thin hair. The two women were bonding. He grabbed a beer and decided to join his father at the barbeque; he was just throwing the elk steaks on the hot iron grill.

Later that night, after Henry and Mei Ling, and after Mary White Owl had left, Sandy shared a cigarette with Abey. Hector and Grandma Leaf were down for the count and were happily snoring away inside on the couch in front of the TV. The sun was long down and a quarter of a moon smiled down on Mother Earth.

Abey inhaled and savored the cigarette smoke and then she slowly exhaled. She had also quit smoking a few years ago.

"I miss smoking." She said as she handed the cigarette back to Sandy.

Sandy nodded and took a slow drag. "It's like dieting. You really crave what you shouldn't have."

"Ain't that the truth. The good thing about it is that I now smoke less and enjoy it more. Hector is happy and I am happy." Abey then reached into the cooler for a beer. "You want one?"

"Sure."

Abey retrieved two Olys, popped them both open and then handed one to Sandy. She took a sip and said, "I kind of liked John. It was too bad about the accident. He would have made a good friend." Abey took another sip and noticed that Sandy's eyes were watering. "Oh, I am sorry. I didn't realize you were so close to him."

Sandy wiped her eyes and smiled. "He was quite likable, wasn't he?"

"So, where was he from?"

Sandy shrugged her shoulders. "I don't know. He didn't know. He had amnesia."

"So, he just showed up at your door looking for work?"

Sandy paused to take the last puff of the cigarette and decided not to tell her that she had kidnapped him from the hospital after he tried to commit suicide.

"So, was he looking for his past life?"

"Not really. He says he liked this one."

Abey was now intrigued. She leaned forward. "Do you think he was running away from something?" Do you think he is wanted by the police?"

Abey shook her head. "A leopard does not change his spots. He was a good man."

"So, how about you? Were you looking into his past? You know there are a lot of discrete resources on the internet."

"Actually, my daughter has been doing some research and she may have found something."

Abey was on the edge of her seat.

Sandy lit another cigarette and handed it to Abey. "She found that there is this missing priest from Toronto that looks a lot like him. My daughter and I took John to mass after we found this out, and he seemed right at home there."

Abey was chewing the end of her cigarette. "Wow, do you suppose he's that missing priest?" She paused, leaned back, and drank from her beer can, and suddenly gasped. "Oh, you poor thing. I guess this means you are not sleeping with him." She took a quick drag on her cigarette and raised her eyebrows, "Or were you?"

Abey had decided that Sandy had too much to drink to drive home. So she put her on the porch swing, gave her a pillow, and lots of blankets. It was a warm night and the stars were out. Abey would have spent the night out there with her, but she suddenly got an erg to snuggle up to her husband who definitely wasn't a priest.

Sandy was happily lying out there with just her beer buzz. She began looking at all the different constellations in the night sky. She felt small but quite safe with all the dogs that were curled under, and around the porch swing.

Suddenly one of the dogs got up and started wagging its tail. And then she saw someone come up to the porch. It was dark but with the small moon, she could tell he was tall and wide. He was wearing what looked like a fury long sleeve sweater and maybe black sweat pants. She was now afraid to move and take a closer look. She lay perfectly still and prayed not to be seen. He crept up on the porch and helped himself to a beer. Now all she could see was the back of him. She couldn't help but notice that his head almost touch the ceiling. He was huge. He stooped down and petted the dog that went to greet him. He made a purring noise as he stroked the dog's ears. When he stood back up, he chugged his beer and then belched. His breath was disgusting.

As he reached for a second beer, he looked at the porch swing and cocked his huge head. He stopped purring and quietly went to investigate.

Sandy almost wet herself and was too scared to scream. He gently tucked the blanket under her chin, and then he smiled. His stained teeth were as wide as Wyoming.

And then as quickly as he appeared, he was gone. Sandy began breathing again. She remembered John telling her about his same experience on this very same porch the night that he wrecked the borrowed bicycle. She began feeling sorry that she disbelieved him.

"I think he said that they called him, Gary." She said out loud. "Or maybe I'm just dreaming."

Chapter 28

Yesterday, John and Reggie took a short bus tour of the wall. It ran from the Pacific, and all across Tijuana, and…beyond. It was tall and formidable and heavily guarded. It looked nigh on to hopeless. They sadly rode the bus back to Pedro's to work on a plan C.

By day, Pedro was the church's gardener. He would show up early with a large plastic garbage bag and slowly go through the grounds and pick up last night's litter. Cigarette butts, bottles, broken glass, and an occasional condom were scattered just off the sidewalk. But mostly it was the beer cans that filled his bag. As far as his actual gardening duties were concerned, it was the occasional watering of the cacti and palms that was needed maybe once, every couple of months. Unless, of course, it happened to rain.

Today Pedro finished early. He gathered the rice and bean scraps from the kitchen for his chickens and then went to the pastor for his meager pay as their church groundskeeper.

"Gracious, Padre, gracious," said Pedro when he received his pesos. He reverently bowed as the pastor blessed him, and then Pedro left. His first stop was at a friend's house for more homemade tequila and important information. His friend was an entrepreneur, and quite a shady one, I might add. Pedro asked him if he knew of a way to cross the border into America. Sadly, it was out of his price range. Pedro's acquaintance added that there was another way.

"The cartel is looking for mules. If you or anyone that wanted to come along would swallow a couple of plastic bags, it would be free."

Pedro, back at his humble hovel, thought that that might be doable. Reggie agreed. John swore, **"Oh, hell no!"**

They sat around the rickety Formica table that evening drinking tequila and scheming. John finally came up with a plan.

"Well, if we can't climb over the wall, then we will just go under it."

Reggie translated to Pedro and he just laughed. He then went on to explain that there was a lot of concrete under the wall to keep it from blowing over and to slow down pesky diggers.

"*And,*" Pedro added, "*that is what most people try first and the policía are constantly watching for human gophers. And they shoot them. I can't swim, but would much prefer crossing the Rio Grande.*"

With a sad sigh, Pedro poured more tequila in his and John's glass. He added a little to Reggie's coke to help ease the sober moment.

It was time to work on plan D.

***

"You saw Bigfoot? **No way!**" exclaimed Dani as she fumbled with her phone. Her mother had caught her off guard. She had called to tell her that the yacht was entering the Straits of Juan de Fuca.

"Jumpin Jesus, where did you see Bigfoot?"

"The same place that John saw him. It was on Leaning Bear's front porch…at night…from their porch swing."

"Okay mom, what were you doing on Leaning Bear's porch and how much wine did you drink?"

"I stopped to congratulate Abey on the engagement of her son, Henry, to Mei Ling. Her Indian name is May Leaf. And I didn't touch a drop of wine."

"Let me get this straight, Henry is marrying a Chinese girl with an Indian name, and they invited a Bigfoot to the wedding.

"Mom, are you sure you weren't dreaming?"

"I don't think so… No, he seemed so real. And John said that they called him, Gary."

"So, he has a name." Dani then asked, "And who is, they?"

"I don't know. John said that was what Abey Leaning Bear said that they called him." Sandy needed to change the subject. "So, why did you call?"

"Oh…right; my phone says the yacht is getting close. Is Officer Hector ready? Is he going to catch him?"

Sandy paused to light a cigarette. It helped to settle her nerves. "Hector says yes, he is ready and that the Canadian Coast Guard and the Victoria police are also monitoring their waters. He is positive that they will have Carlos and his brother in custody by tonight."

"I hope they hang the bastards, mom."

"Me too."

"Are you smoking?"

"…Maybe."

***

Hector Leaning Bear and Mary White Owl rode in an aluminum fishing boat that belonged to Jim Bird. It was a bow picker. This means that it had a large wheel for rolling in salmon nets on its bow. I don't know why they preferred the bow over the stern. It's a fishing thing. Anyway, it was one of the largest of the fishing boats that Hector had deputized in his pursuit of Carlos, and it was the fastest. Hector was in constant communication with the fishing boats and the Canadian boats, via cell phone. Mary kept track of the yacht's position on her phone, which was listening to the tracking device on the yacht. She would relay the position to Hector and he would pass it on to the other boats. Soon it would be in radar range, and then all the boats could see the image on their radar screens. The plan was to slowly surround the yacht.

It was late in the afternoon. The fishing boats were spread across the straits and milling around like they were actually fishing.

Mary looked up from her cell phone and said, "The yacht is turning east and coming up the straits, Hector."

Hector called the Canadian Coast Guard first.

Mary glanced up from her phone and looked west across the blue ocean. They were still too far to see. She glanced at their radar. It made a blipping noise and a small dot lit up on the edge of the screen.

She pointed to it, "Hector, we have radar contact."

Hector smiled and gave her a thumbs-up sign and then he passed it on.

Meanwhile

Carlos slowed down both engines and pulled back the forward gear lever to the neutral position. He sat back on his captain's chair and studied his radar.

Miguel looked at his brother. "Why are we slowing down?"

"There are a lot of boats in front of us, Miguel."

"This is a main waterway. It's always full of boats," pointed out Miguel as he studied the radar screen.

"I know. But it seems more than usual. It doesn't feel right."

Miguel looked back at his brother. "What do you want to do?"

"I think we should wait until dark and then slip in without our running lights."

Miguel nodded in agreement. "I will make some burritos and bring up some cold beers. It looks like it is going to be a fine sunset tonight."

"That would be good, my brother."

Meanwhile

"Hector," Mary looked up from her phone. "It looks like they stopped. Do you think something is wrong? Do you think they have engine problems? Do you think they suspect?"

Hector shook his head. "I don't think they suspect anything. I think they are being cautious. I am pretty sure they are planning to come in after dark." Hector made his calls and everyone stayed on standby.

Shortly Mary bored. She looked at their fishing-boat captain and asked, "Jim, do you have anything to eat on this vessel?"

Jim leaned back on his chair, "When I'm out fish-in, the wife usually is with me. It's her kitchen down there. I know there's some bread, and peanut butter down there. I'm sure there's more if you look. Help yourself, girl."

"Thanks," said Mary. She went down to the lower level and inspected the tiny galley. The fridge contained mostly beer and a few slices of bologna. She found the bread and decided that the sandwiches would be the fastest and simplest. She made two bologna and two peanut butter and strawberry jam sandwiches. She sliced them in half and then brought them and three beers up top.

They ate and drank and watched as the sun's fiery lips touched the endless cold sea. The boat drifted with the tide.

Meanwhile

Carlos and Miguel put their feet up on the consul and also ate, and drank, and watched as the sun as it peacefully slipped into the western ocean. But they ate better, I might add.

Thirty minutes later, Carlos throttled up and set a GPS course for Victoria's harbor. He was running dark. His radar showed that the fishing boats were still out there and on the American side of the line. There were some commercial ships and a couple cargo ships and a crude-oil tanker that was being escorted with tugs. As Carlos cruised down the center channel, he slipped in between two of the large commercial vessels.

Before long, his marine radio started receiving emergency calls. They could see his yacht on their radar and informed him it was illegal to navigate these waters without running lights. Carlos cursed and apologized to the ships. He turned his lights on. He had now drawn attention to himself.

Miguel studied the radar screen as he carefully watched for any unusual activity with the small boats on the American side of the straits. These small fishing vessels should have gone to port by now, that is if they were actual fishing boats. He had a foul taste in his mouth.

Meanwhile

"There he is, Hector. I just saw his running lights come on."

Hector and Mary were listening to channel 16 on the marine radio and heard a cargo ship's radio reprimand for running without lights. They now had a visual of Carlos. And they knew that he was listening to his marine radio.

Hector called the other boats on his cell phone. He told them that he needed normal radio chatter. He had them call each other and talk about their pretend catch. He had the furthest boat out, to radio engine problems as an excuse to be out so late. He wanted Carlos to relax.

Hector called the Canadian Coast Guard. He told them to wait about twenty minutes and then to approach the Yacht. By then, Hector figured, he and his deputies would be close to Carlos. If he ran, Hector would be in a position to surround the drug-running boat and stop him before he had a chance to dump his cargo.

The trap was set.

Meanwhile

"Carlos," Miguel looked up from the radar screen and pointed to a set of red and green lights on the Canadian side of the water, "I think that is a coast guard ship. And it is coming our way."

All boats have running lights. The port side, the left, is red and the starboard side is green. If you see a boat's green light at night, the vessel is moving the right of you. If you can see both lights, it is on a collision course with you, which is bad. And if it is a coast guard boat and you have contraband on board, it is worse.

Carlos throttled up and started passing the cargo ship in front of him. He needed to get the huge hull between him and the other boat. That would block his radar.

And it did.

Meanwhile

"What's he doing, Hector," asked Mary.

"Hiding."

Dusk was done and the stars flooded the sky. Carlos was indeed hiding. He slowly gained on the huge ship that was running beside him. If the coast guard ship crossed behind the container ship, he planned to cross in front of the ship. Once the coast guard was on this side, Carlos would make a run for the Canadian coastline. It was a game of cat and mouse. Once there, he could hug the shore and safely run without lights; he would be invisible. He would even be unseen on the radar, because of all the obstructions onshore. He was a crafty mouse.

Hector gasped when he figured out what he was doing. He quickly called the coast guard boat and told them not to cross behind the container ship. "Captain, you must stay beside the container ship. We need to keep Carlos between you and us." The captain understood and adjusted his course. Hector sighed nervously and ended his call. He called his fleet and told them that it was now time to make their move.

"Watch him close." Hector instructed his men. "He will try and dump his cargo. Some of it may be human. Rescuing them will be our first priority."

Meanwhile

Carlos got in front of the container ship and peeked left. He and Miguel strained their eyes, hoping for open water to the far shore. It looked good. Carlos steered slightly to port.

"**Carlos**," screamed Miguel, as he pointed to the bow of the coast guard cutter. It was coming towards them from the Canadian side of the ship.

Carlos spun his wheel to starboard and into American waters. He was busy watching his tail because the Canadian Coast Guard did not have authority in American waters, as was Miguel. But Miguel's ears alerted him that something was amiss. The radio chatter from the fishing fleet had stopped. It was too quiet. He studied the boats in front of him. They were closing in on him.

"Carloooos!" called Miguel.

Carlos looked at his brother and saw what he was looking at. "*Dios mío*! Quickly Miguel, we must get rid of…"

"Please, my brother, not again. Please not again." He pleaded. But Miguel knew he had no choice. He took in a sad breath and bowed his head and started for the cabin door.

Meanwhile

Hector unhooked the microphone from the marine radio. It was on channel 16, the emergency channel. He keyed the microphone. "Motor vessel *Casa de Mar*, this is the Makah Police Water-Patrol. You are in Reservation waters."

Mary looked at Hector and mouthed, "Is that true?"

Hector shook his head and put his finger to his smiling lips, and continued. "This is a routine safety check. I ask that you put your boat in neutral and put out some fenders. We need to board you, over."

The radio silence was deafening.

And then.

"He's turning, Hector. And he's speeding up. He's running."

Hector turned to the fishing captain. "Catch him, Jim."

Jim smiled, "No problem." He shoved the throttle forward and the old bow picker's engines roared to life. The stern sank into the water and the bow raised as the boat shot forward. The fishing boat had a planning hull. Its speed was not limited like the displacement hull was on the yacht they were chasing. He was a lot faster.

Hector crawled out on the deck and up to the bow. He put his left hand on the large wheel for pulling the nets and steadied himself. He slowly pulled out his stainless-steel Ruger. It was a 44-magnum capable of penetrating an engine block. He was not hunting rabbits today.

As they pulled up alongside the half-million-dollar yacht, Mary turned on the floodlights and then she keyed the microphone. "Carlos, stop your craft or we will be forced to shoot."

She repeated it. But Carlos ignored the warning. So, Hector decided to put a round through the pilothouse door.

Meanwhile

Chapter 29

Pedro kicked open the door of his humble abode swearing up a storm…a Spanish storm. John turned to Reggie, "What is he saying?" Reggie held up her pointing finger towards John without looking at him. It meant 'shush' I am listening to Pedro!

While Pedro finished spewing Spanish, John retrieved the mason jar of tequila. He also had a long day of inspecting the wall. John poured a generous portion in a glass and then he handed the jar to Pedro. He stopped talking and sat down. He was done venting and started drinking.

"Reggie, what happened?"

Reggie went to the fridge and found a can of coke. She popped it open and sat down at the wobbly table across from John. She took a sip and laughed.

Pedro shook his head and sighed.

"Well, *papi,* it seems that the patrons at the soup kitchen are complaining about the food."

"But, it's free."

"But it's mucho bland," said Reggie. "They remember when we showed up and you went into the kitchen and cooked. They want you back. They said even if Father Arturo paid them, they would still not eat there."

"So, why is Pedro so upset?"

"They made him go to Father Arturo with their list of demands."

"They had demands!" gasped John as he took a quick drink of tequila and leaned forward.

"Sadly, yes. They want him to fire Adelita, the old cook."

"Oh, that is sad for the poor woman."

"And for Pedro," Reggie added.

"Why for Pedro?"

"Because Adelita used to give Pedro extra beans and rice for his chickens."

John smiled at Reggie. "Well, we can do the same thing for Pedro. And maybe, we add a little more rice. I see no problem."

Reggie glanced at Pedro. He was busy staring at the worm in the bottom of the Mason jar. "Well, it seems," Reggie paused to think about the right words. "It seems that Adelita also took him behind the church, while everyone was eating, and lifted her skirt for him."

John gasped at the mental image. "Behind the church? That's sacrilegious! We are not doing that."

Reggie laughed.

John looked over at Pedro and started to feel sorry for the poor old groundskeeper. He began thinking about Sandy and started to miss her. He began wondering if she would lift her skirt for him. He looked over at Reggie and dropped his head. "I am surely going to hell."

***

Miguel froze when he heard Officer Mary White Owl's voice on the radio. He looked at his brother and shook his head. "I cannot send those girls to their death, Carlos. I just cannot."

Carlos engaged the autopilot and growled at Miguel. "You take the controls. I will do it myself." Carlos stomped to the cabin door.

Hector steadied himself on the large, hydraulic wheel as he aimed at the yacht. The boat was jumping waves and pounding hard on the surf as he tried to steady his aim. The cabin door was a lot bigger than a rabbit, but it wasn't holding still and he was used to solid dirt under his feet. "It is just a warning shot." He said to himself. "I only need to get close."

He squeezed the trigger and the revolver roared.

The bullet shattered the door's tempered glass window without slowing down or losing any energy. It continued on with full force as it went through Carlos's chest. It then traveled through a fiberglass wall and finally, it harmlessly made a tiny splash in the Straits of Juan De Fuca.

Carlos was thrown back against the wall that had the bullet hole in it, and he slowly slid down into a sitting position. He looked up at his brother with a confused look on his face, and then he slumped forward, quite dead.

"**Nooo**," screamed Miguel, as he watched his brother's head drop to his chest. He shut down both engines and quickly went to him. He knelt down and put his arms around him and began sobbing as he cradled and rocked Carlos in his arms.

After Miguel had cut the engines, the yacht slowly drifted to a stop.

"I think he's surrendering," said Mary to Jim Bird. Jim slowed his fishing vessel as he matched the speed of the drifting yacht. He eased alongside. Carlos holstered his gun and began attaching the fenders to the side of Jim's boat.

Meanwhile, the rest of the Makah fishing fleet began circling the yacht; not unlike their former brothers in the Wild West that used to circle the covered wagons.

When Jim's starboard side gently eased into the yacht's port side, he quickly ran out on the deck and helped Hector raft up the two boats. Mary followed. She unholstered her Glock and kept it pointed at the yacht's pilothouse. She could see the shattered glass on its door but no sign of life.

When the two boats were securely fastened together, Jim fetched his shotgun. He kept careful aim and covered Carlos and Mary as they climbed aboard the Yacht. Mary followed Carlos up the companionway ladder to the pilothouse.

Mary was the first to hear Miguel's soft wails. She pointed to her ear and Hector nodded that he heard it too. Hector peeked in the door and gasped.

"**Oh shit!**" he yelled and quickly he went inside. Mary followed.

Hector stood over Carlos shaking his head, quite stunned. He had never shot a man before. He was in shock and just stood there. Mary quickly checked Carlos for any sign of life. There was no pulse. She looked at Hector and shook her head.

She saw Hector's distressed face and knew that she had to take charge. She put her Glock back in its holster and looked at Miguel. He was staring at his brother and still quite dazed.

"Miguel, look at me."

He focused on her and asked, "Is he dead?"

Mary nodded. "Now I need you to stand up." When he did, she checked him for weapons and then cuffed him. "Miguel, do you have girls onboard?"

He looked at his brother and then back at Mary and nodded.

"I need you to show Hector where they are at."

Miguel seemed relieved that it was over. "They are down in the forward cabin." But he didn't want to leave his brother.

"I need you to show Hector where they are." She turned to her partner. "Hector," she calmly called. He was still in shock.

Again, she called, "Hector, please look at me." She took his hand and softly turned him away from the man he had just shot. She gently took the gun he was still holding, uncocked it, and put it in his holster.

"Hector, Miguel here is going to lead you the girls. I need you to make sure they are safe." She gave him a comforting smile, "Do you understand?" He nodded and tried to smile.

"Go," she said as she pushed Miguel out in front of Hector. She had to get both men out of the cabin. She watched them for a few seconds and made sure that they were following her orders.

After they left, she called the Canadian Coast Guard and informed them that she had everything in control and that she didn't need them anymore. They volunteered to tow the boat back to Victoria. She told them that they were in American waters and that her people could tow the boat into Neah Bay without any problem. She thanked them and they congratulated her on the capture.

"Illegal drug runners are enemies to both our countries," commended the Coast Guard Captain over the marine radio. He again offered to tow the Yacht into Victoria. Mary politely turned him down. "Good luck," said the captain and he signed off.

"Thanks." She signed off.

"Ah," Mary said to herself after a moment's thought. "Drug running boats are impounded and eventually auctioned off, and with the proceeds going to the local law enforcement. They wanted that half-million-dollar yacht." She chuckled at the idea of the Makah Indian Reservation Police now owning such a fine yacht.

She called the Makah fishing boat that had their crime scene investigators on it. The chase was over and now it was time for them to do what they were hired for.

She had them tie up to the other side of the yacht. After she got her investigators busy with the crime scene, she sent the rest of the fleet home. The two fishing vessels, which were tied to the yacht, began carefully motoring towards Neah Bay Marina with the yacht being towed between them.

Mary took a lot of pictures of the cabin with her cell phone. When she finished, she went below and to take more pictures of the contraband. She also needed to check on Hector. She could tell he had taken the death of Carlos pretty hard.

Miguel was now resigned and accepted his situation. He was sorry for what he had done and was ready to take his punishment. When he got to the V-birth cabin, he unlocked it and opened the door, and walked in. Hector followed.

Hector was still in shock over the idea that a man died because of him. It weighed heavy on his pounding heart.

He had been trained at the police academy for such an event. They told him it would affect him deeply and that he would need therapy. But he told them that he was sure that he could handle it. But then who is actually ready, when it comes to taking another life?

When Hector walked through the door, the room looked empty. And then he saw three girls cowering on the floor between the bed and the curved wall of the boat's hull. They were holding each other and crying. They were small and looked, so young. They did not deserve this. Hector became enraged as he looked at the poor helpless children in front of him. He was now able to do his job.

Hector turned to Miguel. "Do these girls speak English?" They looked Mexican to Hector, with their dark complexion and black hair.

Miguel nodded and added, "They are from Indonesia." He then sat on the edge of the bed and laid his cuffed hands on his lap. He just sat quietly there with a sad, bowed head.

Hector knelt down in front of the girls. "You are safe now. I am a police officer. I will protect you." They stared at him with wide, brown, fearful eyes. "Do you understand me?"

They each nodded and then slowly stood up and faced him.

As Hector looked at each young girl, Miguel looked over at Hector. He could see the guilt in Hector's eyes, over the killing of his brother. He had to say something.

"Officer," Miguel took a deep breath, "you were just doing your job. If you had not killed my brother, these girls would now be dead. You did the right thing."

Mary got to the cabin door in time to hear Miguel's words. She suddenly felt a little sorry for him. She just stood silently in the doorway as she watched Hector sit each girl on the bed.

Hector was now able to smile. He looked closely at the middle girl; she seemed to be the oldest and most relaxed. "What's your name?"

She looked over at Mary White Owl and saw the badge hanging around her neck. She looked back at Hector. There was still a little panic in her eyes.

"I am Lily," she said. "I am from Manila. Manila is in the Philippines." She then pointed to the girl on her left. "This is Mia."

Mia nodded.

Lily pointed to the girl on her right. "And this is Citra. They are from a small village in Indonesia. They can speak some English."

Hector politely shook each of the girl's hands and very professionally introduced himself. He asked them, "Would you girls like to go home?"

They gasped, they grinned, they stood up, and they said, "Yes," as each hugged Hector; and in that order.

Hector was still kneeling, which made all the hugs at a proper height.

Mary smiled and wanted to hug Hector.

Even Miguel smiled.

Chapter 30

"Padre," humbly said John to Father Arturo. "I am honored that your parishioners requested me to cook for them. I do pride myself in the art of kitchen spices."

"Yes John, it seems you made quite an impression on them." Father Arturo pointed to a cafeteria bench and said, "Please have a seat." He sat across from John.

"I am curious, Padre, how much does this important position pay?"

"There will be many rewards for you in heaven and all you can eat while you are here on this earth."

John rubbed his chin. His goatee was coming in nicely. "Father, my belly is very happy with this plan, but my pocket, not so much."

"We are a very poor church here," said Father Arturo. "But, now and then, we have important visiting clergy that comes to our parish. And at these times, I could arrange for you to work in the rectory's kitchen. I could then pay you handsomely in pesos."

John smiled at Father Arturo. "That would be nice. I can do that. But I do have one favor to ask."

"A favor? What kind of a favor?"

"Oh, it will cost you nothing. I am concerned for the widow, Adelita. I feel sorry for her. I would like to teach her to cook. She has many good qualities." John would have mentioned them but, other than skirt-lifting, he really didn't know her.

"That is very Christian of you, John. It would be good for her to learn this. When can you start?"

John grinned, "Immediately. I have brought my own apron." John shook the padre's hand. He was now gainfully employed. He figured if he saved his money for a couple of years, he would have enough to buy his way back to America. He was a the-glass-is-half-full, kind of a guy.

***

Officer Mary White Owl showed up at Sandy's front door with a Glock on her right hip and a bottle of merlot in her left hand. She rang the doorbell.

Sandy was on the back patio when she heard the chiming of her doorbell. She was sitting on her chaise lounge watching the evening sun, as it shined in a blue sky over a sparkling sea. She was busy trying to decide on whether or not she felt like a beer or a wine to end the day.

"Now who could that be?" She was wearing old blue jeans and her stained T-shirt. She had planned on painting this nice sunny day but lost the desire and decided to work in the yard instead. She was really not expecting anyone.

She stopped to put on a bra and prune her hair on the way to the front door. She glanced out the window at the car. It looked familiar but she couldn't place as to who it belonged to. She quickly went to the tall, entry double-doors and opened the active side.

"Oh, hi Mary," said Sandy as she analyzed Mary White Owl. The gun and the wine gave her mixed emotions. But she was glad to have the company. "Is anything wrong?"

"No, I just got off work and I found something that might be of interest to you." She handed Sandy the bottle of wine. "May I come in?"

"Oh, the wine, yes, that always interests me. Please come in."

Sandy took the bottle and went into the kitchen.

Mary followed. "Well, actually there is something else I wanted to pass on."

While Sandy looked for the corkscrew, Mary crawled up on one of the counter stools. Sandy uncorked the wine and filled two glasses. She slid one in front of Mary. "What's your interesting news?"

Mary took a sip. "It's about the drug-running boat that we captured yesterday."

"Yes," said Sandy. "I heard that you caught those two criminals and that one was shot." Sandy raised her glass. "Here's to the Makah police force." They touched glasses and drank heartily. Sandy then asked, "I heard that you rescued three girls, what is going to happen to them?"

"They will be sent home. I contacted their home authorities and told them that we would put them on the next available plane going their way. The poor girls were thrilled and could not thank us enough." Mary drank the remaining wine in her glass. She seemed excited.

Sandy smiled and stared refilling Mary's glass, "That is so sweet. It is too bad that John could not have been here. He would have loved to see them go to jail."

Mary's eyes brightened and her lips exploded into a wide grin. "This is why I am here. **John is still alive!**"

Sandy gasped and dropped the wine bottle. It hit the tile floor and shattered blood-red onto her floor. She ignored it. "How... Where... Who told you?"

Mary got off her stool and went around the counter to help Sandy clean up the mess. "When I was interrogating Miguel yesterday, he told me that a priest, he called him Father John Buckley, had somehow ended up on their boat. He said that it happened after some kind of whaling incident. He didn't elaborate. He just said that when they got to Tijuana, Carlos just dumped him at a Catholic Church where he could continue his priestly duties." Mary then asked, "Where is your mop?"

Sandy was still speechless. She went to the pantry and found the mop and a bucket.

Mary began filling the bucket with hot water. She looked at Sandy. "I didn't know John was a priest."

After they cleaned the mess on the kitchen floor, Sandy invited Mary out onto the back patio for another drink. They switched to beer. Sandy went on to explain to Mary what she knew about John and about his short stay on this side of his amnesia.

They drank well after the sun had gone down, at which time, Sandy insisted that Mary sleep in the guest room. But Mary insisted that she was just fine and could drive. She passed out on the chaise lounge. Sandy covered her up right there, and then she staggered to her own bed. She figured Mary would be fine outside. After all, she was well-armed.

***

On the following day, Sandy fretted over the thought of John being stuck in Tijuana without any money and without anyone to take care of him. She smoked a whole pack of cigarettes and drank two pots of coffee by noon. Finally, she called her daughter.

Dani was on lunch break and was just about to call her mother when the caller ID on her phone lit up and said, 'MOM.'

"Hi, mom. I heard about the big drug and trafficking bust in Neah Bay. It was on the news last night. I wish I could have been there."

"Oh my God, Dani, you didn't hear the best part. Are you sitting down?"

"Yes," lied Dani. "What do you know?"

Sandy paused to sip her wine. She was trying to dilute some of the caffeine and nicotine in her excited blood. "It's John." She finally blurted out. "He is alive and stuck somewhere in Tijuana."

There was a pause followed by a thudding sound. "Hello… Are you still there?"

"Sorry, mom. I dropped the phone. I thought I heard you say that John is still alive."

"I did. He is."

"How is that even possible?" Dani was now sitting down.

"Well apparently, he ended up on Carlos's yacht after the whale dumped everyone in the water."

"Carlos was at the whale hunt and rescuing men?"

"No," said Sandy. "I mean yes he was there. Well, apparently his boat was dead in the water and he was down below working on his engine when the accident happened. He had no idea what was going on just outside his hull until he came up top. When he saw all the other boats, he quickly got the hell out of there. He had no idea that John crawled onboard."

"So, mom, the whale just happened to be going by, stopped by Carlos's boat, charged and wreaked havoc on the whalers, and their canoe, and nobody noticed the half-million-dollar yacht floating there?"

"Yes, ain't that crazy?"

"That's fucking crazy, mom, really fucking crazy. So, when is he coming back?"

"That's the rub, Dani. He was not kidnapped. He entered Mexico illegally. He has no passport or ID of any kind. He has no way to prove who he is, even if he, himself, knew who he really was. The poor man is in a pickle, Dani, a fucking pickle."

"So, what are we going to do, mom?"

"I don't know. I am worried about him. I have been thinking about driving to Tijuana and looking for him."

"Have you ever been to Tijuana, mom? I have been there. It's huge."

"When did you go to Tijuana?"

"When I was in college," answered Dani. "It was during spring break."

Sandy paused and changed direction. "And why did you pick Tijuana?"

"Oh, it was just a bunch of us girls. We decided we wanted to check out the beaches there, and to get a tan." Dani neglected to mention anything about the cheap beer, the bars, and the handsome Latinos on the beach, which were also there.

"Oh, mom!" exclaimed Dani, in order to get her mother back on track, "You can't go to Tijuana by yourself. It is dangerous down there. I refuse to let you go."

"Are you forgetting who's the mother here?"

"No, you can't go by yourself. Period."

"But I have to."

"**Mother**…" Dani was exasperated. "Okay mom. Wait till this weekend and I will go with you."

"Okay, fine."

"Promise?"

Sandy took a deep breath, "I promise."

"Do you have any idea where we should start looking?"

"Officer White Owl told me that Carlos and Miguel found out that John was a priest. That was why they didn't dump him at sea. They just dropped him off at a Catholic Church when they got to Tijuana. So he should be fine. Surely there can't be that many Catholic Churches in the Tijuana district."

But unfortunately, her Google map would differ with her.

Chapter 31

When Sandy got off the phone with her daughter, she packed a few things and loaded them in her car. She decided that she had enough caffeine in her to keep her awake all night anyway. She climbed into her Volvo, adjusted the radio, and headed south. She was hoping to be back before Dani found out she had gone. She felt like an errant child. It felt good.

*****

When Pedro found out that John insisted that Adelita continue to work at the soup kitchen, he gave John a big hug. He poured two glasses of tequila to celebrate. He was so happy that he offered John the fat worm resting at the bottom of the Mason jar.

"*Gracious, Pedro.*" John smiled and then he shook his head. "*pero, no gracias,* no thanks.*"*

Chef John Buckley thrived in San Paulo's soup kitchen. And Reggie blossomed. She quickly learned the different spices and a plethora of different ways to cook rice and beans. Even Adelita began to enjoy cooking and the wide world of taste. And she was becoming impressed with her archenemy.

By the time John had tasted each pot of beans and each kettle of rice, he had eaten his fill. He pulled up a stool and sat near the serving window and watched his customers eat. He saw Pedro sitting by himself, quietly eating his lunch with a sad look on his face. He felt sorry for the old gardener and so, he told Adelita to eat her meal with Pedro.

"*Gracious*," she said, and she joined Pedro.

Reggie poured two cups of coffee and got on the stool beside John. She handed him the cup without the added milk.

"Thank you, Reg." John took a sip. He smiled at Reggie. He was becoming quite fond of her. "I don't suppose you have a birth certificate?"

"Why?"

"Well, Reg, if we ever get back to America, I would like to adopt you, properly."

Reggie chuckled. "You sure are a sweet old gringo."

"Old!" Is that any way to talk to your father?"

"Sorry, *papi*" she laughed. "I was born in my grandmother's house. So, I am pretty sure there is no birth certificate. But I do know a man that can make us one. He would even list you as the father. And that way, *papi*, you won't have to adopt me."

John just stared with open mouth at his new daughter in awe. "Wow! You sure are quite handy to have around. Does he do passports?"

"He can, but they are very expensive." Reggie sighed and changed the subject. "I would be a lot smarter if I could go to school."

"You have never gone to school?"

Reggie shook her head.

"Can you read?"

"A little, mostly, just signs. I recognize the symbols."

John was incredulous. He slowly sipped on his coffee while he thought about this. He really wanted to take Reggie back with him to America and give her a proper education. As he sipped, he looked over at Pedro.

"**Where's Pedro?**"

"Oh, he left a few minutes ago with Adelita. They should be back shortly. Pedro is very fast."

John opened his mouth to say something but nothing came out. He just stared at to ceiling and shook his head.

***

Sandy stopped in Portland Oregon for gas and a cup of coffee, and to pee. The nice station attendants in this state would not let her fill her own tank. It was their law. It had something to do with job security for the lesser-income class. She was fine with this.

When she came back to her car the attendants were done and gone, and her windows and headlights were nice and clean. When she opened her car door a young person came up to her and said, "Excuse me."

Sandy turned towards the perky voice. "Yes?"

The perky voice stood, maybe at five and a half feet tall and had short, cropped hair. The voice was wearing tattered blue jeans and a thin jacket over a T-shirt. Sandy could not tell what sex this person was and the voice was no help either.

The voice smiled pleasantly at Sandy and asked, "Are you going south?"

Sandy slowly nodded as she studied the person's face. She guessed on the sex and that he was going to ask for a ride.

He asked, "Would it be okay for me and my boyfriend to hitch a ride with you?"

"Sure," said Sandy. She was glad that she figured out her sex before she embarrassed herself. But then she thought, 'What if she is gay? And she really is a he.'

"My name is Sandy. What's your name?"

"Ryan."

No help. That name would work for either sex. Sandy sighed and shook her hand; it felt soft and smooth. Sandy guessed, girl.

"I will go get Tobin," said Ryan as she disappeared around the side of the gas station.

Sandy unlocked her back doors. She was not sure what she had just gotten herself into. But she was now very curious, and she decided that the company might help pass the time.

Pretty soon Ryan came around the corner wearing a large backpack, and she was followed by Tobin, who was also wearing a large backpack, and a big cheesy smile. He was also carrying an old guitar case. He had long, blond hair and a pretty face. Other than being taller and wider than Ryan, he could easily pass for her girlfriend. Interesting.

After the two backpacks and the string instrument and the boyfriend were stuffed into the back, Ryan crawled upfront. A few minutes later, Sandy was back on I-5 and cruising south.

"I need to charge my battery. Is it okay to plug my phone into your charger?"

"Sure," said Sandy. "Where are you guys headed?"

"California."

"California? That's a big state. Do you have a town in mind; do you have friends there?"

"We were thinking of maybe, Hollywood. Have you heard of it?"

Sandy quickly glanced at Ryan's face to see if she was kidding. She was dead serious. Apparently, she assumed that everyone from the state of Washington must be an apple farmer. But she was curious. "What do you plan to do in Hollywood?"

"I write songs." She was still deadly serious.

"Wow, that's nice." Sandy tried to sound impressed. "So, how old are you and Tobin?"

Ryan ignored the question. "Everyone calls him, Toby." Ryan then asked, "Do you want to hear one of my songs?"

"Sure," sadly said Sandy. He could hear Toby fumble with the guitar case. She heard him check each string for its proper tune. Once satisfied, he slowly strummed and hummed away.

Ryan began slapping her leg to create a beat as she sang softly. Her voice wasn't bad, and her lyrics weren't good.

Sandy guessed that they were still in high school and that they would be hitchhiking back penniless before school started. The good thing was, they would at least keep her awake for the rest of the night's drive.

Before long, Sandy caught herself humming along. Toby was pretty good with his instrument. Sandy glanced at Ryan, "You two are sounding a little like Sonny and Cher."

"Who's Sonny and Cher?"

By sunup, Sandy's two passengers were sound asleep. The brightening sky perked her up and Sandy was feeling pretty good and now wide awake, and very hungry. She was getting near Sacramento and decided to stop there for breakfast. One of the exit signs listed a Denny's Restaurant ahead. The food was cheap and not that bad. She assumed her passengers were on a tight budget and pretty sure one of the backpacks was full of junk food.

As she pulled into the parking lot of Denny's, the hum of the road noise faded and her hitchhikers woke up.

"Well good morning. Are you guy's hungry for a Grand Slam? I know I am."

Ryan yawned and politely said, "No Thanks. We packed a few things. We will be fine."

Sandy looked in her rearview mirror and saw Toby's mouth sag. "Oh, but I insist."

They didn't turn her down the second time.

The next hour of driving south on I-5 was a quiet one, as Ryan and Toby gaped out the car's side windows. They had slept through northern California.

"Where are all the trees?" Toby asked. Now all he saw was low rolling hills that were covered in a sparse yellow grass. It didn't look anything like Oregon. "How far did we drive last night?" he asked.

Sandy chuckled. "California gets a lot less rain than Oregon. And they have hotter temperatures. Your northern trees don't do as well here. But they do have orchards. Soon we will be going through hundreds of acres of olive trees, walnut trees, grapefruit trees, and orange trees. And there are the vineyards towards the coast and there is the great valley, which lies between the coastal mountains and the Rockies, which grow all kinds of vegetables."

By late afternoon, Sandy was their geography teacher, and her two students were happy to quietly sit, listen, and learn. It was a pleasant drive for all.

By day's end, Sandy hopped on I-405 and headed west and towards Hollywood. She was exhausted and found a cheap motel. They had arrived.

"Well, we are near Hollywood," said Sandy as she put her car in park. "It is time for you two to make your fame and fortune. When you are rich, please remember me."

"Oh, we will." They both said at the same time. And then they began unloading their gear. Sandy went into the motel office to rent a room. She slipped the manager her credit card and gazed out at her car. The two hitchhikers looked like a deer-in-a-headlight. She turned to the manager, "Put two rooms on that card."

"Yes, Mam."

Sandy was exhausted and slept until noon the next day. She had been up two days and one night. She was stiff and sore. Time is not on your friend after fifty.

She got up and showered. Put on some clean clothes and decided to check in on Ryan and Toby. She was feeling responsible for them.

Their room was next to hers.

Their door was open and when she looked in, she saw two Mexican cleaning ladies. Her traveling buddies had already left. She decided to walk to the restaurant on the other side of the parking lot for coffee and breakfast. She stopped at her parked car to put her suitcase in it and found a note under her windshield wiper. It was from Ryan. She put it in her purse and decided to read it at breakfast.

"Good morning," said the waiter. "Coffee?"

"Thank you," said Sandy.

"Menu?" asked the waiter as he poured the coffee.

Sandy nodded. "I am hungry enough to eat a horse."

"Oh, sorry, mam. Our horse is out of season. But I could recommend the pig and, of course, the chickens are always in season. I find the eggs benedict here to be excellent, mam?"

Sandy chuckled at his attempt at humor. "Eggs benedict, that sounds good."

"Yes, mam." He gave her a slight bow and then left.

Sandy carefully unfolded the note from Ryan.

Hey Sandy.

Thanks for the ride. Toby and me are grateful to you. I am now writing a travel song about a great lady. You. I will dedicate it to you and I will give you half of all the royalties it earns.

I will never forget you, Ryan & Toby

Chapter 32

❦

Sandy found that her phone was good company. It was perched on her dashboard in its own special cradle. As she traveled down the road, its cheery female voice would tell Sandy when and where to turn and it would give her plenty of warning. It did everything but compliment her on her hair. And if Sandy missed her exit, the voice would calmly tell her that she fucked up and how to get back on track. The phone was like a husband that was a woman.

Sandy was cruising south somewhere between LA and San Diego on a multilane highway. She tried to count the lanes on her side of the divided highway but kept losing count because of rude California drivers cutting her off. They all seemed to be in a hurry, or late for…something.

The phone's miniature TV screen went off its MapQuest app and Dani's name flashed across it. Sandy touched the 'answer' button. "Hi Dani, what's up?"

"I'm on lunch break. So, what are you up to?"

"Oh, I'm just doing my laundry," lied Sandy.

"That's nice," mumbled Dani and she went on to why she really called. "I have done some research on Catholic Churches in Tijuana. And boy, there are a lot of them. There are almost as many churches as bars. Jesus, the town is crawling with Catholics.

"Anyway, my guess is that Carlos was in a hurry and probably dropped him off somewhere at a church on the west end of town."

"That makes sense, Dani. Have you made a list of these churches?"

"Yes, mom; I will bring them with me this weekend. I already told my boss that I had an emergency and need next week off."

"That's great," said Sandy reluctantly. "Can you email your list to me, so that I can go over them before we leave?"

"*Your next exit is in five miles*," said MapQuest.

"Who is that with you, mom?"

"Oh, it's just the TV, Dani," lied Sandy, again.

"Oh, what are you watching?"

"Um, just the news," said Sandy just as an impatient driver passed her and hammered his horn. "And they're doing a traffic report." She quickly added.

Dani stopped talking and just listened. She knew something was amiss.

Sandy suspected she suspected something. "I have to go. I have to put my clothes in the dryer. I will call you later. Don't forget to send me that list of churches. Bye now."

"But mom…" the phone disconnected, now leaving Dani very suspicious.

Sandy found a cheap motel near the border. She felt safer sleeping in America. She had dinner at one of the Mexican restaurants in this border town. The one she chose included a serenade at her table with a trio of men wearing sombreros and silver-studded, leather vests and tall cowboy boots complete with spurs. They strummed fancy guitars and they had dark weathered faces and bright teeth. They were damn good. She had a taco and drank three *grande* Margaritas. She tipped them handsomely.

She left the place feeling quite happy, as she wobbled her way back to her motel room. Once safely inside, she passed out. Sandy slept fitfully that night. The night was hot and her noisy little air conditioner was not conditioning. She woke up early and lay on her bed with a splitting headache. She stayed like that until long after the sun was up. Her mouth was dry enough to grow a cactus.

"I am never drinking again…ever," she mumbled as she staggered to the bathroom. She turned on the cold faucet and put her hand under the running water waiting for it to get cold.

Five minutes later and with no change in temperature, she filled a plastic cup and drank it anyway. She then took two aspirin and crawled into the shower. The hot water worked fine and she came out a new woman. "But," she told herself, "I am still not drinking anything today."

After coffee at the motel's continental breakfast, she headed to the border.

The line was not very long and moved steadily. When she got to the window, a uniformed border-policewoman was behind it. She was young and her pretty face had a no-nonsense look on it. She asked to see Sandy's passport.

Sandy handed it to her through the window.

The officer studied it for a second and then scanned it. She asked if Sandy had anything to declare, and, "What is the purpose of your visit and how long will you be staying?"

"I am meeting a friend and I will only be here for a couple of days," replied Sandy.

The border policewoman raised an eyebrow and handed Sandy back her passport.

Sandy realized that it did sound like she was having an affair, so she added. "He's a priest, Father John Buckley. Do you know him?"

The border patrol officer smirked and shook her head. She waved Sandy on through.

Tijuana was a sprawling concrete and ghetto jungle. The signs were in Spanish and the streets were narrow and seemed to wind in endless circles, and it had low hills that were filled with hovels and rickety shacks that surrounded the city.

Sandy's phone was the first to complain. Its little screen flashed a message. Sandy pulled into a parking lot to read it. It politely informed her that she was in a foreign country and that it needed more money if it was to continue to be her friend here. Sandy clicked okay and agreed to the extra daily rate. She was becoming a little overwhelmed and began wishing that she had waited for Dani.

They phone chirped and an emoji of a smiling face wearing a sombrero appeared. It was ready.

Sandy took a deep breath and said, "Well, it's a good thing that I put on my big-girl-panties this morning." She entered the first name of Dani's church-list onto the phone's map. The female voice calculated the distance and the route, and then they were off on a wild church chase.

***

John was busy at the electric cook-top when Pedro entered their humble hovel. He was carrying a fresh jar of tequila, a fist full of dandelions, and a wide smile. He put the jar on their little table and went to the sink and filled an empty mason jar with water for his 'flowers.' John immediately became suspicious.

Reggie was studying an old first-grade reading book that John had found for her at San Pablo's grade school. So, she missed it. Although, when Pedro set the yellow blossoms on the table, she became very suspicious. John was making tortilla soup with chicken. Pedro had killed one earlier that morning and requested the soup. John thought it was a nice change.

John laid down his stirring spoon and turned to Reggie. "What's going on with Pedro?"

Reggie shrugged her shoulders. "Pedro," she called out, "*¿Qué pasa?*"

Pedro gave Reggie a shy smile and explained to her that he had invited Adelita to dinner. And he told her that he was cooking it just for her, and it was his famous tortilla soup, which was her favorite. He poured himself a shot of tequila. He seemed quite nervous.

"What did he say?" asked John.

"He said that he invited Adelita to dinner."

"Why does he seem so nervous? They seem to be old buddies behind the church."

Reggie asked Pedro why he needed dinner with her since he already had lunch with her.

Pedro blushed as red as enchilada sauce. He told Reggie that this was different and that he wants to ask her to move in with him. "*La quiero*," he exclaimed as he pounded a fist against his heart.

John chuckled. He understood and went back to stirring Pedro's tortilla soup. "What the hell. After all, it is his home."

Adelita showed up wearing a long purple dress trimmed in lace. Her blouse was white with short puffy sleeves and a neckline that swooped quite low, revealing nice ample breasts. She looked quite fetching this evening.

After cocktails and a candlelit meal, John and Reggie excused themselves; and then they went for a walk to give Pedro some alone time.

***

After two full days of churches, burritos, and bottled water, Sandy was getting a little overwhelmed. Her phone calls to Dani were shorter than she would have liked, but she could not tell her that she was already in Mexico. She had to continue her lie.

She was on her way back to her motel room when she passed San Pablo's church. She glanced at the time and decided to try it. At most of the churches where she had stopped, she had found the priests in charge could not speak a lick of English. It had been a long and frustrating day.

She parked her car in the church parking lot and then she went to the rectory and knocked on the door. She could hear two men talking in Spanish. Then one of them answered the door.

"*Hola, ¿en qué puedo ayudarle?*"

Sandy smiled at him. "Do you speak English?"

The man was young. He was wearing a white T-shirt and dark slacks. Sandy guessed that he was a priest, but without a collar, she wasn't sure.

He turned and called to the other man. He was older and also collarless.

"Good evening Señora," he said when he arrived at the door. "I am Father Arturo."

"Good, you speak English."

Father Arturo nodded. "How may I help you?"

"I am looking for a visiting priest. His name is Father John Buckley. Have you seen him?"

Father Arturo rubbed his chin in thought. The name was familiar. "Ah, yes. I remember the name. He is a friend of Carlos."

Sandy's heart almost leaped out of her chest.

"But he never showed up at my church and I haven't heard anything back from Carlos.

"How do you know this Father Buckley?"

Sandy's heart sagged. "Oh, he was just a friend. If he shows up will you please have him give me a call?" Sandy pulled out a piece of paper from her purse and wrote her phone number on it."

"Si, Señora." Father Arturo took the paper and gave Sandy a quick blessing. "I will pray that he is okay and shows up soon."

"Thank you very much, Father." Sandy sadly turned and walked back to her car. "So close, and yet…" she couldn't say it. She became very concerned and now at a loss as to what to do next. She decided to go for a walk and clear her head.

The dim, quarter-moon seemed to be sad and wailing. Sandy looked up at it and said, "I know just how you feel." She found a rickety bench under a short, neglected, palm tree and sat down. She pulled out a pack of cigarettes and fumbled for a lighter. She really needed the smoke, but the lighter eluded her. "I know you are in here," she said to her purse. "And I really need to organize this thing."

Frustrated and angry, she frantically searched for the little blue Bic lighter. "Fuck," she cursed as she dumped the purse upside-down on the bench, and then she cried.

She slowly calmed and put everything back in her purse. The lighter was gone. "Oh, well. I guess God is telling me it's time to quit." She looked up at the stars and sighed. "Please God; I don't know what to do. If he is one of your servants help me find him. I don't know who else to turn to." Sandy took the cigarette that she was going to smoke and threw it across the sidewalk.

"And God, if you help me find him, I promise to quit smoking… forever." She added, "Amen." And that was when her phone rang. It was Dani. She just stared at the name until it stopped ringing.

Chapter 33

Why does the moon do that?" asked Reggie. She was pointing towards the eastern sky at the quarter-moon. "Why does it fade away and then come back again?"

"Oh, Reggie," replied John, "The whole moon is always there. We just can't see the other half." The earth gets between the sun and the moon, so it doesn't get any light. It becomes nighttime in that part of the moon." John found a stick and began drawing in the dirt, parking area between the road and the concrete fence on someone's small front yard. He drew three circles, the sun, the earth, and the little circle that hid behind circle-earth. With a series of straight lines, he showed how the light rays only reached part of the moon. The drawing was rough and a rather ambiguous.

John and his new daughter had been walking for a long time. They wanted to give Pedro plenty of courting time.

The day was a scorcher; and the evening's westerly winds, coming from the ocean, were cool and refreshing. John was settling into his new life. His cup was still half full, and with Reggie, it was a little better than half.

After he was done confusing Reggie with his crude drawing, he sat against the concrete wall and gazed up at the waning moon, and sighed. "I will ask Father Arturo for a book on astronomy tomorrow." John leaned back and drifted off somewhere deep into his mind.

Reggie bored and walked up the street towards San Pablo's Church. She kept staring up at the moon trying to see the dark half and she still had questions.

"If the earth is round, why does the half-moon have such a straight line?" She was beginning to think her new father was mistaken. Some of his stories seemed pretty farfetched.

Her deep thoughts were suddenly interrupted by the ringing of a phone up ahead. There was a woman sitting on a bench just staring at her phone without answering it. She looked American.

"Are you going to answer that?" asked Reggie.

Her sudden voice startled the woman. She gasped and looked towards Reggie. She was older. Reggie guessed fifty. She considered anyone older than thirty as being old. She was pretty and well dressed and seemed to be crying.

The woman glanced back at her phone, and it stopped ringing. She wiped her eyes and turned to Reggie. "Oh, you speak English. I was just sitting here and enjoying the night. The moon is quite lovely tonight, isn't it?"

Reggie glanced up at the moon and then back at the woman. She decided to get a second opinion. "How does the moon do that? I mean, how does it get smaller and then get bigger again?"

The woman smiled at Reggie. "Hi, my name is Sandy. What is your name?"

"Regina," said Reggie as she sat down on the bench next to Sandy.

"Regina. That is a very pretty name. I am very happy to meet you." Sandy shook Reggie's small hand. "What was it that you asked? Oh right, it was about the moon.

"It has something to do with the earth blocking the sun's light. I really don't understand it all that well."

"That's what my father said. I thought that he might have made it up."

"No, he didn't, Regina. So, what does your father do?"

"My friends call me Reggie. And my father is a cook."

"That's nice," said Sandy sweetly.

Reggie noticed the pack of cigarettes in Sandy's hand. She hesitated and then asked, "May I have a cigarette?"

"Sure." Without thinking, Sandy handed Reggie the pack. "Here, take the whole thing, I just quit smoking."

"Thanks." Reggie reached for the book of matches that she had in her purse.

"Wait," said Sandy. "Just how old are you?"

Reggie put a cigarette between her lips. "I am twelve." And then she quickly added, "It is legal for twelve-year-olds to smoke in Mexico."

"Does your father know that you smoke?"

Reggie lit a match and casually said, "Yes." She put the match to the cigarette and inhaled. That was followed by a quick exhale and a small cough.

Sandy suspected that Reggie was lying. She also remembered catching her daughter smoking a cigarette when she was in her early teens. This was not her child so, she said nothing.

Sandy's phone rang again. She knew that she had to answer it this time. She didn't want to worry her daughter. She had already decided to go back home in the morning. She would then tell her the truth. She took a deep breath, turned to Reggie, "Don't talk," and touched the 'answer' button.

"Hi, honey, what's up?"

"Mom, why didn't you answer your phone? I have been calling and calling you. I thought something might have happened to you. Where were you?"

"I am sorry, Dani. I was doing the dishes and left my phone out on the patio. I promise to keep it closer next time." The lying was getting taller and the hole was getting deeper.

Reggie could hear both conversations. She sat quietly and listened, trying to understand what Sandy was hiding.

"Okay mom." Dani sounded excited. "We need to bring bottled water. You don't want to drink the local water. I am going to exchange some money for pesos. We should bring sweaters. It usually gets cold at night. I am packing a bathing suit. Are you going to bring one? They have nice beaches there." Dani babbled on and on without waiting for a response from her mother. She sounded very thrilled to be making this trip with her mother.

Sandy felt lower than pond scum by the time she got off the phone with Dani. She just blankly stared up at the moon as tears filled her eyes.

Reggie handed Sandy her lit cigarette.

"Thanks," said Sandy. She took a long drag and slowly exhaled. "I needed that."

"You're welcome. I take it that was your daughter that you were talking to."

Sandy nodded.

"Does she know that you smoke?"

Sandy nodded and chuckled.

"Why are you here without your daughter?" asked Reggie.

Before she answered, Sandy looked up past the moon and into the blue, infinite eyes of God and said. "I will quit smoking tomorrow, I promise." She turned to Reggie and decided to tell her all about the man she was looking for.

But before she started her confession, a call from the dark interrupted her. "Hey, Reg, where are you at?"

Reggie looked at Sandy and shrugged her shoulders, she then hollered, "I am coming, *papi*." She stomped out her cigarette, hid the remaining pack in her purse, and disappeared into the dark.

Sandy picked up her purse and walked back to her car. She stopped and bought another pack of cigarettes on the way to her motel. She would smoke them all before midnight.

When John and Reggie returned to Pedro's little shack in the back, the place was empty. There was still a half jar of tequila left. John retrieved two glasses and a can of coke. He poured a little coke into his glass and the rest into Reggie's. He added a little tequila into Reggie's coke-filled glass and a generous portion into his own.

"Have a seat Reggie and tell me who you were talking to." Reggie sat on the chair across from John. She took a sip and smiled at the taste. "Oh, it was some old lady looking for someone. I can't remember her name. She was a gringo."

"I don't like you talking to strangers. You never know what they want. They could be bad. They could kidnap you and demand a ransom, or worse, sell you as a slave. They come on to you as being nice. They might even offer you a cigarette. And then, **WAM**! They got you."

Reggie gasped and looked over at her purse which concealed the cigarettes. "But she seemed so nice and really sad."

John took a sip of his coke-flavored tequila. "That's how they operate. Promise me that you will never talk to strangers, ever again."

"I promise."

They toasted and finished their drinks. John was tired, so eased into his barcalounger, tipped it all the way back, and was soon snoring. Reggie slid her sleeping couch next to the tattered recliner and curled up on it. John made her feel safe and she had grown quite fond of him this past week.

John was up early. He filled the old percolator with water and ground coffee. He put it on the electric cook-top and then went out and looked for eggs. He missed reading the morning paper…in English. He had no idea what was going on in the world.

When he returned, Pedro was sitting at the table bright-eyed and bushy-tailed. "Reggie, wake up. I think Pedro has something important to tell us."

Reggie yawned, stretched, and sat up. "What?" she sniffed and asked, "Is the coffee done?"

"Almost," said John. "Pedro seems to have some news. I am guessing he proposed last night." John then went to check on the coffee.

Reggie quickly scrambled to the table. *"¿Qué está pasando, Pedro?"*

Pedro went on and explained his important news. His Spanish was rapid with excitement, and his hand gestures could hardly keep up with his mouth. By the time he was done, so was the coffee. John poured three cups and set them on the table.

"Well, what did he say?"

"He said, he said… I don't know where to start."

"Calm down, Reggie. Just start at the beginning."

Reggie took a sip of her coffee and then a deep breath. "He said Adelita wants to move in with him. But this place is too small and that we must leave."

John sat up in his chair, "**What**?"

"No, it's fine," said Reggie calmly. "Adelita has a brother."

John gasped, "And she wants us to move in with him?"

"Stop talking!" scolded Reggie. "No, he doesn't want us living with him."

John started to say something and Reggie quickly held up a finger and shushed him. "Adelita's brother works a little farm east of here. And his farm is very poor, so for extra money to support his family, he smuggles people across the border. He is a coyote at night and a poor farmer during the day, and he has agreed to take us across the border."

John looked over at Pedro and said, "I could kiss you." He looked back at Reggie who had a startled look on her face. "He can't understand English."

Reggie nodded with relief. "But, it will cost us 30,000 Pesos."

John dropped his jaw and moaned.

Reggie did the quick math. "That's only about a fifteen-hundred American dollars. And he said you could pay him after you were in America."

John perked up. "That is doable. When can we meet her brother?"

"He is staying at a motel near here. He leaves today for his home. He said we should go now."

"Well get dressed little girl, we have an important Coyote to meet."

While Pedro drew a detailed map to the motel, John gathered their meager possessions and stuffed them in a gunnysack. The motel was only a couple of miles away and Adelita's brother, Julio, was a late sleeper because he worked nights, coyote-ing. So, they had plenty of time to walk the short distance to the motel.

Once in America and everything went back to English, John figured he could borrow the money from Sandy and send it to Julio. He could work off his debt to her in gardening services. Of course with a daughter, his thinking might have been a little bit overly ambitious.

This might be the last time he would see Pedro, so John shook Pedro's hand and gave the stout little Mexican a hug. "Pedro, thank you so much for giving us a place to stay. And tell Adelita *muchas gracias* and I hope you find happiness with her. And I hope I never have see you again, in Mexico."

John turned to Reggie, "Don't translate that last part."

Reggie nodded.

The morning sun was smiling its warm face down upon the early birds of this bustling, Spanish-speaking city. Reggie was tightly holding her nervous little hand onto John's warm firm hand as they worked their way to the motel. Reggie was moving out of her comfort zone and into a whole new world. Her heart started beating frantically in apprehension, but she knew she was doing the right thing. She trusted this man.

As they walked up the motel parking lot, she took a couple of deep breaths and calmed down.

"What room is he in, Reg?"

Reggie let go of John's hand and looked at Pedro's map. "It's room 107."

John found the room and saw an old, red, crew-cab pickup parked in front of the door. He headed straight for it. Reggie followed closely.

In his hurry, John walked past a green Volvo with Washington plates on it. Only Reggie noticed the plates, but she didn't think anything of it.

John pounded on the door and nervously listened.

Nothing.

He pounded again. And this time he heard a coarse voice mumbling something in Spanish. From the tone, he knew they were swear words. Finally, the door opened a crack and John could see a brown eye staring back.

"*Buenos días, señor,*" said John in a friendly voice and then he put his little translator in front of him.

Reggie froze.

Julio opened the door. "¿Qué?"

He was wearing bright-red, boxer-shorts and a confused look on his face. Unlike his sister, he was tall and lean. His head was covered in thick, silver hair and he had a gray-stubble on his cheeks. And his bare chest was covered with a rug of gray, curly hair. It was startling, to say the least!

Reggie remained speechless.

So, Julio spoke. "Are you the gringo that my sister recommended?"

John nodded. "Oh good, you speak English."

Julio took a quick survey of the parking lot and motioned them on in.

"I will wait out here," mumbled Reggie. The man frightened her. "I will sit there." She pointed to a bench under room 108.

John nodded and disappeared into room 107.

Reggie took a deep breath and walked over to the bench. It was the one that the green Volvo was parked in front of.

She took one of her cigarettes and lit up. And just as she exhaled a lung full of smoke, a familiar face came out of room 108.

Chapter 34

❧

While Julio got dressed, John made two cups of coffee. There was an electric pot that was full of hot water; so, all he had to do was add the instant coffee into the paper cups. After he filled the cups, he looked out the window and checked on Reggie. She had just sat down on the bench next door.

When Julio finished dressing, he poured a little dried creamer into one of the cups and sat on the end of the bed. With his free hand, he reached for the remote and turned on the TV. He went straight to the weather channel. It was in Spanish and it annoyed John.

John took his cup of coffee and pulled up a chair. He needed Julio, so he politely waited.

Julio turned the volume down and casually said, "You know my sister really hates you." He kept staring at the TV. "I am only doing this to get rid of you for her sake."

"Why does she hate me?" asked John.

"She told me you took her important job as the cook at San Pablo's, and she said that you are sleeping with her boyfriend, Pedro."

John gasped and jumped to his feet. "I am not sleeping with Pedro. I am sleeping **at, not with, at Pedro's**. John calmed and sat back down and explained, "And I did get her job back."

Julio scoffed. "As an assistant cook. We are a proud family."

"Well, Julio, with me gone, she will become the head chef again. Win, win."

Julio smiled at John and then at the TV. "*Excelente*, it looks like the weather will be good. I can make the run across the border tonight with you." Julio looked back at John and asked, "Adelita discussed my fee with you?"

"*Si*," John nodded. "One thousand five-hundred American dollars."

Julio nodded and added, "With half now and the other half when I get you there."

"**Half…?**" hollered John.

Meanwhile

Sandy had her suitcase packed and was headed to her car. She was going home. She decided to sit down with her daughter and confess. Maybe she should have waited. When she closed the door to her hotel room, she didn't notice Reggie sitting on the bench under the window in front of her car, but she smelled the cigarette smoke. She got a sudden craving. She looked at the person smoking and recognized her.

"Oh, hi! What are you doing here?" Sandy was thinking, stalker, and becoming a bit paranoid.

Reggie froze and shrugged her shoulders. She was thinking, kidnapper, and becoming quite paranoid.

"It's Reggie, right?"

Reggie nodded nervously.

"I am Sandy; you remember me from last night?"

Reggie took a quick puff of her cigarette.

"Where is your father, now?"

Reggie pointed to the room next door.

That was when they both heard John yell, "**What…? That was not the arrangement your sister made with me.**"

They saw the door burst open and an irate John came storming out.

"Come on Reg, we are leaving." When he saw Reggie, he stopped and threw his hands in the air. "**Are you smoking?**" John was fit to be tied.

Reggie jumped to her feet and quickly handed Sandy her cigarette. She shook her head and pleaded, "Oh, no *papi*." Then she began crying.

Sandy did not recognize John at first. He now had a goatee, a dark tan, and his hair was longer. But she did recognize his voice. She gasped and gaped at him, speechlessly. She threw the cigarette to the pavement.

John never really looked at the strange woman. He just dropped his head after his fit of anger and sadly said, "Sorry, I am so sorry Reg." He regretted yelling at the poor girl and was very angry now at not being able to leave this god-forsaken country with her.

Then, a familiar voice softly entered John's ears.

"John?"

John looked at the woman and he recognized her beautiful smile. Big tears filled his eyes as he slowly staggered her way. He was afraid that if he blinked, she would disappear. When he reached her, he threw his arms around her to make sure she would not get away, and then he hugged her until it hurt.

He wiped his eyes and let go a hardy laugh. "Oh my God, there is a God." And he hugged her again.

Sandy exhaled a relieved sigh. She looked up at him and said, "So, you missed me."

"Well maybe, a little." He said. "How did you find me? Why are you here?"

"You still owe me some work on my garden. I just decided that it was too much work to break in a new gardener."

John grinned. "Speaking of which, I may need another advance on my wages."

"I see," said Sandy trying to sound very business-like. "And just how much of an advance are we talking here?"

"Just seven-hundred and fifty for now."

"Now?" asked Sandy.

"And maybe another seven-fifty when we get to America. That's what it's going to cost to get us across the border."

"Well why can't you just ride with me across the border? And, who is *us?*"

"I have no passport. I have no identification to show the border patrol. Your people are not going to let me cross the border on my good looks."

"My people? And you still haven't answered who the *us* is."
"Yes, your people. Without papers, I am just an illegal alien."

Sandy thought about it for a minute. She realized that she could get into trouble if she tried to take him across the border without any ID and that they both could end up in jail. She looked over at Reggie. "I am guessing this is *us*." Sandy pointed at Reggie. "She claims that she is your daughter. I didn't know that you had a daughter."

John had some explaining to do. "Reg, please come here. You need to meet Sandy."

Reggie had become quite curious by this time and joined the two adults. She looked up at Sandy.

"Sandy, this is my daughter, Regina."

"Yes, we have already met," said Sandy.

"Oh, I now remember *papi* talking about you; you are his old landlady in America." She turned to John, "She was the woman that tried to kidnap me yesterday."

"Oh, I see," said John. He turned his attention to Sandy and asked, "Did you give Reggie one of your cigarettes?"

Sandy countered, "Did you call me an old landlady?"

"No," said John with a tight lip.

"Well then no, I did not give her a cigarette." Sandy snickered, it was actually a pack.

"And yes, Regina is my legal daughter."

"And I have proof he is my *papi*," proudly said Reggie. She pulled out the forged birth certificate from her purse and handed it to Sandy.

Sandy carefully took the certificate out of its envelope and inspected it. When she got to '*the father's name,*' she read it out loud, "John J. Buckley."

Sandy laughed. It did look very authentic. She handed the document back to Reggie. "What's the J stand for?"

"Jay," said Reggie as she put the envelope back into her purse.

"Yes, the J?" asked Sandy again.

"Jay," Reggie repeated and then she began wondering if Sandy was hard of hearing.

Meanwhile, Julio, besides being a dirt farmer and a coyote, was also a good businessman. He had followed John out the door for further negotiations. He really didn't want to lose a paying customer. But he was interrupted by the chance meeting next door. As he watched the soap opera unfold in front of him, he knew that he was back in business.

"*Mi amigo*," called Julio to John. "I think now our problem is of no concern. Bring your friend inside. I have some Jack Daniel's to sweeten this bitter motel coffee. I know you Americans love your whisky."

Once inside Julio's motel room, the shrewd Mexican sat John and Sandy at the small table. He handed Reggie the TV remote. She took the remote, studied it, and then sat on the edge of the bed. She got her first glimpse of watching anything she wanted and all by herself.

Julio dumped a packet of instant coffee into three cups. He poured hot water into each cup and put them on the table. He retrieved his bottle of whisky and joined his clients.

Both Sandy and John declined the whisky.

"Suit yourself," said Julio as he poured a liberal amount into his cup. He took a sip and laughed. It was time for business. He rubbed his hands together and looked at Sandy. "My guess is that you have come to rescue your friend. My name is, Julio. And we need to discuss my services and how I am to be paid."

John started to speak but Julio cut him off. "Quiet, my friend, you are just my cargo. This is only between me and the man with the money. In this case, a very pretty Señora with the money.

Sandy looked at John with a confident smile and then back at Julio. "My name is Sandy. I understand your fee is one-thousand five-hundred

American dollars. I do not carry that much cash with me. I will need an international bank to transfer funds. Would you prefer cash or a cashier's check"

"Cash is good. And there is such a bank near here," said a smiling Julio as he sat back and sipped his spiked coffee.

"Good," said Sandy. "Now, when you take them across the border, exactly where do I pick them up at?"

"I live in Bandero Mexicana. We will leave from there and you will pick them up in Jacumba Hot Springs. It is a small American town about three kilometers north of me. There is a small cemetery plot north of town. You will pick them up there. *No problemo*."

"Good," said Sandy. "When do we leave?"

Julio leaned forward. "We have not discussed the young *muchacha*. Do you wish me to smuggler her across also?"

John jumped to his feet. "Yes, she was part of the deal that I made with your sister. **She goes**!"

"*Mi amigo*," Julio calmly said. "That was between you and Adelita. This is between me and the Señora. I suggest that you remain quiet or I will go find other cargo for tonight's run."

Sandy took John's hand and made him sit back down. "Please John, I got this." She turned to Julio. "How much?"

"Same as anyone else, fifteen hundred American dollars."

"But she is small. I think five hundred American dollars is plenty."

Julio leaned back in his chair and scoffed, "One thousand two-hundred."

Sandy knew that most Mexicans lived to barter. It was more important than the actual price. "Seven hundred dollars," she countered.

Julio shook his head. "You gringos have so much money and yet are so cheap to us poor Mexicans. I will not go any lower."

"Fine," said Sandy. She stood up and turned to John. "Let's go. We will find someone else to take you across the border." She turned to Julio, "I am sorry that I could not do any business with you." She grabbed John by his right hand and physically forced him out of the room.

"Sandy! But…but…Sandy…" John was beside himself in this sudden turn of events. She shoved him into her Volvo and then climbed into the driver's side.

Julio stood stubbornly at the motel room door and watched. It was a Mexican standoff.

Reggie happily missed the whole thing as she just flipped through all the channels. She was in awe. She stopped at a rerun of Gilligan's Island that was dubbed in Spanish. It made her laugh.

Sandy started the car.

Julio balled up his fists.

Sandy put it in gear.

Julio gritted his teeth.

Sandy left.

Chapter 35

Sandy, you have to go back."

"I know. I just want to let him stew for a little bit. He will cave; they always do."

"But Sandy, my daughter is still back there!"

Sandy lowered her head, "Oh fuck!" She turned right at the next intersection.

"She is not your real daughter. I know the birth certificate is fake. John J. Buckley is not your birth name. So, how did you end up with her, and why?"

"She followed me home when Carlos dropped me off at San Pablo's. She spoke English and I was a stranger in a strange land. She actually adopted me."

Sandy made another right at the next intersection. "Okay John J. Buckley. By the way, what does the letter 'J' really stands for?"

"Jay. Why?"

"Just 'J'?"

"Yep, Jay."

Sandy drove around the block and then back into the Motel's parking lot. Julio was still standing at the door. He now had a big smile on his face. Sandy parked beside his dusty old truck. She turned to John. "Tell Julio, I will drive him to the bank now."

"Thank you, Sandy." John went up to Julio and told him to get into the car.

Julio climbed into the passenger side and closed the door; Sandy countered with, "Eight hundred American dollars."

Julio chuckled and began rubbing the soft leather seats with his hand, "Nice car."

Sandy put the car in gear and drove to the motel's parking lot entrance. "Which way?"

Julio pointed. "I like you *Señora*. You bargain well. You must have a little Mexican blood in you."

"My mother," Sandy said with a slight smirk on her face. "My father met her in an orchard along the Columbia River. It was late summer and she was picking ripe apples with her family. My mother's people were migrant workers.

"My father had pulled his car to the side of the road to steal an apple. When my mother confronted him about stealing, he just laughed at her."

"Really, then what did she do?" asked Julio.

"The laugh really pissed her off so she threw the apple that she had just picked at him."

"Did she hit him?"

"Beamed him in the head. He went down like a sack of potatoes. She thought she had killed him."

Julio laughed and so did Sandy. He had a good laugh.

Julio leaned back and crossed his fingers. "I will do it for an even thousand for the little *niña*." He asked for Sandy's phone. "I am putting in the address of the cemetery where you should wait for us and my phone number. We should be there around midnight, depending on the wind. And you need to watch for us very carefully."

"What do you mean the wind?"

Julio pointed, "Turn there." He leaned forward and looked up at the sky. He had a smile on his lips and a twinkle in his eye. "We will be coming to you as silently as a cloud. We will float over the wall in my big balloon that will be filled with hot Mexican air.

"We will soar like an eagle on the evening's hot desert winds that flow north towards the high mountains at sundown. And then around midnight, the cool mountain winds will flow south and take me home. These winds keep a better schedule than most Mexican busses."

Julio turned and looked at Sandy. "My balloon takes me up and away from my poor dirt farm, and high enough to touch the stars. And I get paid handsomely to do this. As John said earlier, for me, it's a 'Win, win.'"

"Aren't you worried that they will see you?" asked Sandy.

Julio leaned forward. "There," Julio pointed to a tall brick building. "The bank is just up ahead on you right."

He laughed and answered her question. "I am invisible. My balloon is as dark as the night. Your border patrol is so busy watching the wall that they never bother to look up. With the glare of the lights of the town and along the wall, they are blinded anyway. Yet from above I can see them so well. It is like a game, as I watch them scurry around like rats chasing Mexican cheese. It is a game that I find thrilling, and one that I have never lost."

Sandy pulled into the bank's parking lot and parked near the door. She and Julio then went inside. She transferred half the money into an account for Julio and got the other half in cash. She put the envelope full of money in her purse.

She took Julio back to the motel. The die was cast, it was time to leave. They each had an important job to do and the day was already on a downhill run.

John and Reggie climbed into Julio's old truck. John noticed all the propane bottles in the back. Other than making him nervous, he didn't give it a second thought.

Sandy watched as John left with the crazy Mexican. They were headed east. She was already missing him, but she had no choice. Sandy drove north towards the border. Once she crossed it, her phone would take her to a little graveyard north of the small American town of Jacumba Hot Springs.

Four hearts beat faster than normal; each for a little different reason.

Reggie sat between John and Julio. The old truck's air conditioning unit had quit working years ago, so both side windows were rolled down. Julio drove at the speed limit and beyond. The wind whistling through the cab was loud and hot, making speech hard at best.

After about an hour of terrifying speeds, the road narrowed to one lane in each direction and began climbing, forcing Julio to the speed limit. The country became dryer and rugged. The palm trees disappeared and were replaced by cacti. Tall, spiky cacti with arms held high as if warning people that you're traveling in dangerous territory.

The paved road became narrower and Julio slowed down even more. The wind noise lessened. It became possible to hear spoken words.

"Julio, I am curious. How do you plan to smuggle us across the border? Will I need a bathing suit?"

Julio chuckled. "No; you will stay dry."

"Good; will I be crawling through a dark, dirty tunnel?"

"Oh no, gringo, you will stay clean, and the view will be out of this world."

"Will I need my wall-climbing shoes or my sprinting across-the-border shoes?"

Julio glanced at John to see how serious he was. "You will need no shoes. You will ride in style all the way from my *casa* to your waiting *Señora*."

John was now becoming quite suspicious. "Riding in style, in what kind of a vehicle?"

Julio suddenly swerved to avoid hitting a jackrabbit. The bottles of propane bounced and rattled in back. But they didn't explode. "Thank you, Jesus," whispered John.

Julio chuckled and shook his head. "You will be riding the clouds in my balloon."

"In a basket that will carry one of those bottles that you have rolling around the back of your truck and which have a very flammable fuel in them?"

"*Si*, two actually; I always take a spare."

"Cool," said Reggie.

"I, I, I, am afraid of heights…and baskets…and things that can explode," wined John.

Julio laughed and Reggie joined him.

For the next hour John just stopped asking questions. He had heard enough nervous news. Shortly the pavement ended, and the gravel and dust began. Every time they passed a vehicle they had to quickly wind up the windows. The sun would turn the old truck's cab into an oven. It was like they really were riding to hell…in a hand-basket.

Julio's little ranch was nestled in a small valley. It had a small stream that ran through it when it rained. It was now dryer than the road that came in on. There were a few trees, each was old and tough enough to live in this high desert region. Julio's house was larger than most. Its walls were plastered adobe with a low-pitch red-tiled roof. And it had a large covered porch across the front of the dwelling for a little shade. There was a large wood-planked barn behind his house. It was not for animals, it was his shop. It was where he kept his precious hot-air balloon hidden.

When they arrived, Julio had John and Reggie sit at a table under the shade of the porch. He made them some sandwiches and served them with a pitcher of ice tea. He joined them for a quick meal before setting up his balloon.

"Julio, you live here by yourself?" asked John.

Julio shook his head. "My wife takes the kids to her sister's when I make these runs. She is afraid of my balloon and refuses to ride in it. She says, 'God would have given me wings if he wanted me to fly.' She can't bear to watch me leave in my balloon. She is sure I am never coming back."

"She sounds half-bright to me," remarked John. "What kind of meat is this in my sandwich? It is very tasty." John took another bite.

"Rattlesnake."

John stopped chewing, paused, shrugged his shoulders, and decided it was okay, and continued chewing.

By sundown, they had drug the large balloon to its launching pad and inflated it. The dark balloon was huge and impressive up close. It was now anchored and waiting for the hot desert wind to come charging north. John studied the basket. It seemed sturdy enough. But he still didn't trust it.

"Julio, is this basket bulletproof?"

Julio knew the right answer, "Yes."

John knew he was lying, but still, it made him feel a little better.

Julio looked at his watch. "It is time to get into my carriage. We shall soon begin our journey into the heavens."

"In a basket," added John.

And right on schedule, the winds came, a thin slice of the moon rose, and Julio cut the rope that once held them to the earth. Reggie giggled, Julio laughed, and John prayed.

They were off and up, up, and away.

Chapter 36

Gently, ever so gently, the balloon rose up towards a blanket of a billion stars. John forgot about his fear of heights as he gazed at the heavens. The moon was just coming up with its sideways smile. John smiled back. He was going home.

He looked down at Reggie and caught her staring up at him. When she saw his face, she smiled and hugged him. "I knew you were my real *papi*."

Julio had installed a metal shield around the torch that shot hot air up into the balloon so that the light from the flame could not be seen from the ground. He also instructed his passengers not to speak because their voices could be heard a long way off.

John watched the dark desert beneath him. He could see small ranches and homes with their porch lights. As they gained altitude, they appear everywhere. From the ground, they were lost in the dry hills of this country, but up here, their little lights, covered the earth, and they twinkled like the stars in the sky.

Soon John felt the warm south wind as it pushed the balloon north. It was like sailing in an endless sky. As they approached the border, the horizon brightened with the lights of the small towns that were on both sides of this tall metal line between countries. Small vehicles, with their headlights, could be seen as they hurried home after a long day at work. Life continued on totally unaware that they were being watched from above.

Julio fired the propane jets forcing more hot air into the balloon. The jets were noisy and he wanted a little extra altitude as they floated silently into the foreign country. He was confident and was enjoying the ride. It was another perfect night.

Or so he thought.

Five minutes later, the winds died and the balloon slowed to a stop. It was now hovering directly over the wall.

John looked over at Julio. Julio just shrugged his shoulders.

An agonizing fifteen minutes passed and nothing happened. The balloon was cooling and slowly losing altitude. Julio was about to fire off the jets when John stopped him. He was pointing at the ground. They were over a green, border-patrol Pickup that was driving along the American side of the wall.

The wall was flooded with lights to deter foreigners from sneaking across, although it did aid the climbers, in that, they could see what they were climbing on.

The four-wheel-drive truck stopped and the passenger side door opened. A man quickly got out with his gun drawn and ran towards the wall. The movement startled a deer on the other side and it bounded off.

The driver got out laughing. "Good eye Wade. I think that alien deer was about to climb the fence." He laughed again. He was carrying a thermos of, probably coffee. He went to the rear of their vehicle and dropped the tailgate. He unscrewed the cup from the thermos top and helped himself to a cup of dark liquid. He sat on the tailgate.

Wade holstered his gun and walked back to the truck.

Three faces, six eyes, cautiously peered over the basket's sides. It was uncanny how well they could hear the men that were several hundred feet below them.

Wade retrieved his cup from the cab and then joined his partner. He filled his cup and also hopped up on the tailgate.

Wade took a sip and looked up at the balloon. "Sure is a nice night."

The partner glanced up. "Yep, it sure is."

Neither man noticed the missing space between the stars. Julio was right, they were invisible. But if they didn't fire off the propane jet soon, they would end up sitting in their laps. It was too noisy to chance it. Especially, with a trigger-happy Wade sipping coffee, just below them. So, they just listened and prayed that this would be a short coffee break.

The two talked about sports, football mostly. They argued about who was going to the Super Bowl and which quarterbacks were their favorites. The balloon slowly sank their way as if to listen. It also drifted towards Mexico, and its home.

Finally, after two cups of coffee, they both hopped off the tailgate. Their break was finally over. Each went to his side of the truck and promptly relieved themselves on the big knobby truck tires. As Wade reached for the passenger door handle, Sandy called Julio to check on them. Julio forgot to turn off the ring tone on his cell phone.

Wade pulled his gun. "Did you hear that?"

"Yes," said his partner as he zipped up his fly.

Julio quickly fumbled for his phone and muted it. He looked up at John and shrugged his shoulder and mouthed, "Sorry."

Both John and Reggie just shook their heads. They cautiously peered over the side to see the damage. Julio texted Sandy, "We are on the border. All is good. We should be there shortly. Please text only."

Wade and his partner pulled out their flashlights and walked to the wall. This section was built with tall, smooth, metal poles with pointed tops to discourage climbers. Each pole was spaced about six inches apart. They shined their lights through the spaces looking for the illegal on the other side. They had recognized the sound as a cell phone. One walked east, the other went west, and the balloon quietly floated lower.

Julio's phone lit up. He quickly covered it. It was Sandy's response. "Okay. Do you have an ETA?"

"Do you see anything?" Wade called to his Partner.

"Nothing yet." He flashed his light through the poles. Although, he did see an armadillo scurry behind a cactus.

Again, Julio's phone lit up impatiently. "Hello! Did you get my last text?"

"Yes," typed Julio.

The balloon was now sinking close to the floodlights that were strung all along this portion of the wall. They would soon reflect their light on the basket.

"Well?" It was Sandy again."

"I'm going to kill her," whispered Julio to himself. "Midnight."

"Thanks ☺"

An old Peterbilt truck down-shifted one of his eighteen gears as it drove up the dusty access road along the Mexican side of the wall. It was hauling cattle to a market near Tijuana. As it approached the engine noise grew very loud and there was a cloud of dust following it. Wade and his partner decided to give it up and got back into their pickup.

Julio gave a short blast of hot air. The balloon responded and its round canopy swelled. Julio looked back down and saw the green pickup truck slowly moving back down the road. They had heard nothing. He gave a long blast of flame and the balloon began rising safely into the heavens. They had skated. But they were still missing the wind from the southern desert. They continued on up.

John's fear of heights turned into fear of being too close to the ground. He became happier and happier as everything below him slowly shrunk in size.

Sandy no sooner finished texting Julio, when her cell phone lit up announcing a call from her daughter.

"Oh shit!" Sandy was hoping to be back before she called. It was now Thursday evening, and if everything went according to plan, and if she drove all night, she should be back by late Friday. She touched the answer button. "Hi, Dani, What's up?"

"Jesus mom, I have been trying to call you for the last two hours and your phone just kept going straight to voice mail. Where have you been?"

Sandy remembered losing cell service shortly after leaving Tijuana and not getting much of a signal until she reached Jacumba Hot Springs. She needed a quick lie. "Oh, I forgot to plug my phone in last night and my phone went dead. It's charged now."

"You forgot to plug it in! Are you getting senile? I was very worried about you."

Senile? Sandy gritted her teeth. "I'm fine, honey. What was it you needed to talk about?"

"I think we should take my car to Mexico. It gets better gas mileage."

"But mine is bigger. We might need the extra room, in case John brings a friend." Sandy just shook her head at the, 'brings a friend' comment. 'Maybe I am a little senile.'

"A friend? Why would he be bringing a friend?"

Quick, another lie. "I don't know. Maybe another priest that needs a ride north."

"Okay mom, we will take your car in case John brings a friend."

Sandy could hear her sarcasm but ignored it.

"I will come to your house Friday night, that way, we can get an early start on Saturday. I have a good feeling about this trip. I know we are going to find John."

"Yes, in my heart, I know I will find him." Finally, a truth.

Julio looked at his altimeter. They were over a mile above sea level and still no wind. Julio was now praying for a north wind to push him back into Mexico. It was starting to get cold and if they kept rising, it was going to get much colder.

John felt the drop in temperature and put his arm around Reggie. "Julio, my friend, I hope you have a plan. A good plan before we run out of fuel. I don't want to fall out of the sky." John's fear of heights was back.

Julio forced a chuckle. "Have no fear *señor*. I have many plans. I haven't decided on which one."

John suspected he was lying. "Please hurry and choose one. Or I am going to have to insist that you put me back on the ground."

Julio faced west and took a deep breath and then he felt it. The prevailing winds, the westerly's, gently started pushing the balloon east. "See," Julio proudly pointed out, "we are now moving."

John felt the breeze and checked the compass he had mounted on the basket. "But we are moving east and following the Mexican border and headed to the Gulf of Mexico. I don't like your plan."

"Ah, *señor* Doubting Tomas, the Mexican border will soon run to the southeast. We will then be in America. I should charge extra for this added part of your travels in my fine balloon."

Sandy's phone buzzed twice. "I got to go Dani. I am getting another call." She ended the connection with Dani without saying goodbye. It was Julio's phone calling.

"Hello," she whispered.

"Sandy, it's me, John. Why are you whispering?"

"I don't want to give away your position. Are you close?"

"You don't have to whisper. And yes, I can see the lights of town."

"Oh, good. I'm at the rendezvous point. But I still can't see you."

"About that, we are currently hovering over the border and Captain Balloon has taken us uncomfortably high in the sky. The good news is, we are now moving again. The problem is, we are moving east and we are not going to make it to Jacumba."

"Oh, well that sucks. What happens now?"

"We need you to follow us."

"But I can't see you."

"That's okay. You now need to get on Old Highway 80 and go east. Put on your flashers and drive slowly and we will be able to see you. When we do, we will begin our descent. We will tell you when and where to stop.

"You got that?"

Sandy was quiet for a minute. "That just might work. You are not only pretty; you are also smart."

"Will you settle for just pretty? It was actually Julio's idea."

"Oh, okay fine. I am on my way."

The wind was light and steady, so Julio stopped the balloon's climb. He could now see several miles ahead and saw where the lights of the wall quit. It was there that Old Highway 80 turned north and the unlit wall continued on and up into the high rugged country. Only small, four-wheel-drive RVs patrolled this part of the wall. He knew that if he went past that point, it would be a long way before he was close to a main highway again. This would be the last chance for miles.

Julio increased his descent as they anxiously searched the ground for Sandy's emergency, flashing lights.

"There she is," said Reggie as she pointed to the small flashing light running up the road behind them. They were still very high.

Julio released some more hot air to speed up their descent. Their westerly winds slowed and died. If this was going to happen, it was going to be here.

John called Sandy.

"Hello," said Sandy. "Do you see me?"

"Yes. You need to speed up a little. We are several miles ahead of you." John felt hope.

Sandy accelerated to forty miles per hour.

Julio's balloon was dropping rapidly and they were still straddling the wall. They leaned over the basket on the American side of the wall in the false hope that it would somehow steer it that way.

Sandy began catching up. She was on the paved road that paralleled the boundary's dusty service road. Julio pointed to a pull-off not far ahead of her. "Have her park there."

John called Sandy and told her to get ready to park.

Julio slowed his decent.

"*Oh mierda,*" cried Reggie as she pointed to a green, four-wheel-drive truck coming their way. It looked like Wade, and his partner, we're on the prowl again, and they were slowly patrolling their way.

Julio stopped his decent.

Sandy stopped at her designated spot.
Reggie cursed again under her breath.
John cursed out loud.

Chapter 37

Again the invisible fugitives peered over the side of the basket. Breathlessly they watched as the border patrol truck searched the wall. It had a floodlight mounted on the top of the truck's cab. Wade operated its control handle as he shined the bright spotlight towards the wall looking for any kind of movement. His partner drove slowly with occasional stops.

The balloon and the pickup were on a collision course. If Wade shined his light upward for even just a second, he would be able to see the Balloon. If the driver didn't soon speed up, the basket was going to land on the truck's hood ornament. But on a high note, this also meant they were now in America.

John looked at Julio. He had his hand on the burner. He looked back at John and shrugged his shoulders. John shook his head and whispered, "Wait."

Julio waited.

Wade switched off the spotlight and leaned back on his seat. "I guess it was nothing."

His partner eased down on the accelerator and said, "I'm out of coffee. Let's hit a Quick Stop."

Wade nodded. "Yep, and a doughnut sounds good to me too."

If either of them had looked in their rearview mirror, they would have seen a large basket almost land in the bed of their truck. The

Balloon's basket barely missed the cab and would have hit the tailgate if wade's partner had not sped up because of a doughnut craving.

"Go," cried Julio when the basket touched the gravel road and stopped moving.

He handed John a small hand compass. "She is about a quarter of a mile due north of here."

The area between roads was mostly boulder-filled desert and cacti. "And don't step on any rattlers," Julio added.

"Good safety tip," said John as he handed Julio the enveloped with the cash in it that Sandy had given him.

Julio smiled and stuffed the envelope in his pocket.

John helped Reggie out of the basket and then he hopped out. Without the extra weight, the balloon immediately started rising.

John suddenly felt like he was losing a friend. He looked up at Julio and shouted, "*Hasta la vista, baby.*" And then Julio and his wonder balloon disappeared, as he ascended high into the heavens.

"Are you crying, papa?"

"No, Reg, it's the dust. It's happy dust." John pointed north. "We must go that way." As they crossed the road and into the cover of darkness, John turned to Reggie and asked, "Are there really rattlesnakes here?"

Reggie laughed, "You're kidding, right?"

Sandy turned off her car's engine but left the flashers on. She placed her phone on the consul beside her and waited in nervous anticipation.

"Please God, I know we haven't spoken since 1 promised to quit smoking, and I know before that, it was when I cursed you when my husband died. But now I am very sorry for the curse. I was emotional and didn't really mean it.

"I have another favor to ask. If I promise to quit drinking…" Sandy was startled by a double-tap on her side window. After regaining control of her wits, she lowered her window.

"Excuse me mam, my name is Officer Wade of the border patrol. Do you have car trouble? I can call a tow truck for you."

"No, I'm fine, thanks."

"I see you are from out of state. Are you lost?"

"No, I just pulled over to check my map."

"Where are you going? Maybe I can help you."

Sandy became a little flustered. "I'm looking for Highway 80."

"Well mam, you are on Old Highway 80. If you keep going, this will connect you to New Highway 80."

"Oh, thank you, officer. Yep, that's the one I was looking for."

"You are very welcome, mam. But, I am going to have to ask you to move. You are in a no-parking area. It's for security reasons this close to the border."

"Oh, I am sorry officer. I will leave right now. Thank you for your help."

"You have a nice day now."

Sandy started her Volvo, turned off her flashers, put in gear, and slowly eased out on Old Highway 80. She kept watching her rearview mirror as she drove. She saw Wade get into the passenger side of an official truck. The truck never moved as Sandy drove on until she lost sight of it.

Sandy's phone suddenly lit up indicating a new message. She pulled over again and parked. She went to messages. It was from Julio.

"They are on the ground and heading your way. Do not move!!!"

Sandy nervously glanced back into her mirror. "Oh, shit!"

John glanced down at the compass and he got behind the little arrow pointing north and looked up. He was searching for a landmark to walk towards. All he saw was night. He looked up higher and saw the stars. He searched the heavens for one particular star and there it was. Like a sparkling diamond calling to him, it was the North Star.

"Reg, follow me and stay close," whispered John, and he disappeared into the darkness. Reggie tightly latched on to his shirttail. She was taking no chances.

The going was slow and rough and the covering of a quarter of a mile seemed a lot longer than John anticipated. It felt like they were stumbling around in circles. John religiously followed his star and prayed. Finally, he could hear a vehicle's road noise. He was getting close to the meeting point. His heart raced.

The next car that traveled the lonely highway showed its headlights through the tall cacti between him and the road. Cautiously John and Reggie finally made it to the pavement. The star led them right where the pullover was that Sandy was supposed to be at. It looked right but it also looked different on the ground. Maybe he was at a different one? John knew that Sandy was around here someplace, but which direction? Rather than walk the wrong way, he decided that he would wait for her to drive by.

John pointed to a large cactus just off the road. "We will hide behind that one, Sandy should be along anytime now."

They no sooner got hidden, when the next vehicle to come speeding down the road, appeared. It was a green, border-patrol pickup just like they had seen from the air. They quickly laid flat on the ground just barely out of sight.

Again, John's heart raced.

Sandy watched as the headlights came speeding her way. She needed to get back on the road. She put her left turn signal on and then pulled back out on Old Highway 80.

Just as the headlights got close, Sandy's phone rang. She glanced at the screen. "Fuck, it's Dani."

Sandy kept driving. She was afraid to answer it, in case that it was the border-patrol police. They could stop her, for talking on her phone, if they saw her put it to her ear.

Soon they were right on her bumper.

Suddenly, they blared their horn and wildly passed her, and then the pickup shot on down the road. It was just an impatient local. Sandy's phone was also becoming impatient. But Sandy didn't answer. She was busy making a U-turn. After she safely made her turn, she finally answered her phone.

"Hi, Dani. What do you need now?" Sandy tried not to sound too annoyed.

"What took you so long to answer your phone?"

"I was in the bathroom."

"Well, you know that you can take the phone with you, mom."

Sandy really didn't have time to talk now. "I'm sorry, but I can't pee and talk at the same time."

Dani paused and thought about that for a minute. Her mother had a good point.

"Oh shit," cursed Sandy, "My phone is about to die. I have to plug it in. We can talk tomorrow. Bye."

"Mom, but…but…" Dani's phone disconnected.

Sandy shut her phone down, so that if Dani tried to call back, it would go straight to voice mail.

Sandy found the pull-off where she was supposed to wait at and eased into it. She did not turn on her flashers this time. She didn't want to get any stranger's attention. She just sat there in the dark and decided to finish her prayer.

"Okay God, I am sorry for the interruption. I am begging You to help me find John. And if You do, I promise to stop drin…"

She was again interrupted by a double tap at her side window. She wound down her window expecting to see an officer of the law but was pleasantly surprised to see the faces of two fugitives smiling back at her.

Sandy cried all the way to New Highway 80.

As she headed north, she felt that everything was right with the world again. She thought about the pact with God. Yes, she vowed to quit smoking. And since John showed up before she actually finished making the other vow, she figured there was a little wiggle room there. She looked up into the star-studded heavens and said, "Thank you, God."

Chapter 38

Dani was frantic. All-day Friday at work, she kept trying to call her mother but her phone went straight to voice mail. Dani gave her mother the benefit of the doubt and just assumed her phone was broken. "It better be!"

Dani had a lot to get done at work before she could leave, if she was going to take the following week off and help he mother look for John. She was excited with the anticipation of going with her mother to Tijuana. But mostly, she couldn't wait to tell her of the new information she had found out about John. She tried to share it with her mother the night before, but that was when her mother's phone went on the fritz.

Dani had her car packed and ready to go straight from work. She had told her boss that she had to go out of town for a funeral and needed the week off. When the clock finally worked its way to quitting time, she quickly made her way to her car and joined the endless traffic heading home for the weekend.

She sped towards the Kingston ferry in heavy traffic. She was trying to make the 5:25 ferry. It was going to be close.

She made the ferry.

When Dani zipped into her mother's driveway, she couldn't help but notice that her mother's shiny, green Volvo was now a dirty gray. It was filthy with road dust. She was at a loss as to how it got that way unless she was driving on a logging road. And that didn't make much sense either.

She parked beside the dirty Volvo and climbed out of her car with two bottles of wine. They had a lot of planning to do before their early morning departure time and it also included a little drinking.

The door was unlocked. As Dani made her way to the kitchen, she saw her mother through the great room windows sitting on a chaise lounge enjoying the sunset, she yelled, "Mom, I'm home." She never noticed John or the young girl sitting beside her. Dani uncorked one of the bottles and poured two full glasses of wine. As she walked through the opened sliding glass doors carrying the wine, she asked, "Mom, how in the hell did you get your car so dirty?"

But before her mother could answer her question, John stood up and faced her. Dani stopped in mid-step. She opened her mouth to say something but nothing came out. Speechlessly, she looked at her mother with a very surprised look on her face.

Sandy stood up with a devious grin on hers.

John took the wine glasses from Dani and handed them to Sandy. He smiled at the astonished young woman. "Do I get a hug little girl?"

"Oh, John. You bastard!"

John laughed and gave her a tight squeeze. "I missed you."

Reggie indignantly climbed to her feet and stepped between John and Dani. She looked up into this strange girl's tear-filled eyes and asked, "Who are you?"

Dani looked over at her mother, "Who's this?"

Sandy had a slight smirk on her face. "That's John's daughter."

Dani looked at John. He shrugged his shoulders and nodded. "Yep, it's true."

Sandy stooped to Reggie's eye level. "Reg, this is my daughter, Daniela."

Sandy straightened back up. "Dani, honey, this is Regina. She is John's long-lost daughter from Tijuana."

Dani looked at her mother, and then looked at John, and then she looked at Reggie. She shook her head and looked incredulously back at her mother. "I don't believe it."

"I am so!" proudly replied Reggie. And as she rummaged through her little purse, she said "I can prove it." Reggie pulled out her precious birth certificate and handed it to Dani.

Dani quietly read through the official-looking document. When she got to the father's name, she smiled. She looked at her mother. "What does the 'J' stand for?"

"Don't ask."

Dani neatly put the certificate back into its envelope and handed it back to Reggie. "Well, Miss Regina, I am very happy to meet you and pleased to welcome you to our home.

Regina nodded with acceptance and a shy smile. "Do I get a hug?"

Dani wiped the tears from her eyes, "Sure." And that was followed by a warm hug.

As the evening sun slowly slipped into the wide Pacific, Sandy told her daughter her part of their great adventure. John went on and explained how he lived through the whale hunt and how he had survived on the yacht. He told of how he kept from being thrown overboard, by saying daily mass and of how he even collected money from his captors by passing the plate during the Offering at his Mass. And of course, the exciting balloon ride they had had.

Soon, the stars filled the infinite sky and everyone became contented and quiet. They were talked out. Day was done and the adventure was finally over. They all could sleep in peace tonight.

John reached into the cooler and found another cold beer. As he opened it a movement caught his eye. It was dark, so John dismissed it as a deer. But he sensed it was still there and might not be a deer.

"Is that you, Gary?"

"Who's Gary?" asked Dani.

"He's the Bigfoot I told you about," whispered Sandy.

"Oh, pshaw, mom. Bigfoot is just a legend."

"**Gary**!" again called John. "It's okay."

The shy, huge legend slowly walked into the light and smiled.

"Here, have a beer," said John as he handed him his freshly opened bottle.

Gary grunted something. It sounded like a thank you. He took the beer and shyly glanced at everyone. "Gerranks," he said as he squatted down to human level and then he chugged his beer.

Reggie, wide eyed, jumped on John's lap, and hung on to him tightly.

Dani wet herself.

Gary wistfully looked at the cooler.

John opened him another beer and handed it to him.

Gary smiled and slowly sipped it this time.

When it got uncomfortably quiet, John asked, "So, Gary, what brings you to our neck of the woods?"

Gary smiled and tried to articulate some words. He was trying to mimic the human language.

John got the gist of what he was saying. "So you were catching salmon?"

Gary nodded and kept glancing up at his hosts as he sipped his beer. He wasn't much of a conversationalist around strangers. When he finished his brew, he stood back up and patted John on his head, and then he winked at Sandy.

"Bye, Gary," she said with a friendly smile.

Gary disappeared into the dark in about three strides.

Dani excused herself; something about changing her shorts.

Reggie jumped to her feet and begged, "Can we keep him, *papi*? *Por favor!*"

A small sliver of the moon appeared in the east and joined the stars in the diamond-studded sky. The moon was on its last leg and would soon disappear. And in a couple of nights, a brand new one would be born.

Reggie had fallen asleep on John's lap. He carefully picked her up and took her to his bedroom. After he tucked her in, he took a blanket and a pillow from the linen closet and then went to the great room. He placed them on the couch for himself. When he joined the women, he found Dani covering her mother with a quilt. Sandy was peacefully sleeping on the chaise lounge.

Dani yawned and looked over at John. "Are you going to be out here for a while?"

"Yes. I am still unwinding. It is great to be back."

Dani yawned again.

"Go to bed Dani. When your mother awakes, I will bring her inside."

"You sure?"

John nodded, "We're fine. Go."

After Dani left, John leaned back on his chaise lounge and contently gazed up into the vast sky. When he found the northern constellation that pointed to the North Star, his chest warmed and he felt at home. He smiled and whispered, "Thank you, God."

"It sure is pretty. Isn't it, John?" Sandy was also gazing at the stars.

John sat up and faced her. "I'm sorry. I didn't mean to wake you."

Sandy sat up and faced John, "What were you thinking about?"

"Oh, nothing really.

"Well maybe I was thinking about life and about who I am now. And maybe, who I once was."

Sandy looked into John's eyes and grinned. "I know who you are not."

John studied Sandy face. "What do you know?"

"While you were gone, Dani informed me about an interesting piece of news that she came across."

"About me?"

"In a roundabout way, yes."

"Okay Sandy, you are scaring me. Is it good news?"

Sandy nodded. "I now know that you are not a priest."

"How?" asked John.

"Well, it seems that the missing priest from Toronto, one-day last week, just showed up back at his parish. And Dani informed me that there are no other missing priests."

"So, I'm not a priest?" said John.

Sandy nodded. "Sorry, I guess you're not."

John thought about this piece of personal news for a minute and suddenly he gasped. "Well then, I guess that means that I never took the vow of chastity."

Sandy nodded and with a coy smile, she said, "And by coincidence, neither did I."

John did not sleep on the couch that night.